THE LORD

THE LORD

SORAYA ANTONIUS

Henry Holt and Company
New York

First published in the United States in 1988 by
Henry Holt and Company, Inc., 521 Fifth Avenue,
New York, New York 10175
Originally published in Great Britain.

Library of Congress Cataloging-in-Publication Data
Antonius, Soraya.
The lord.
1. Palestine—History—Arab rebellion, 1936–1939—
Fiction.   I. Title.
PR9570.L43A58   1987   823   87-12097
ISBN 0-8050-0477-7

First American Edition

Printed in the United States of America
1   3   5   7   9   10   8   6   4   2

ISBN 0-8050-0477-7

To Q

'Le monde d'avant la guerre est mort, mais le monde d'après la guerre n'est pas encore né; si nous nous trompons aujourd'hui, nos petits-enfants supporteront le châtiment de nos fautes . . .'

– from a speech given by Sir Mark Sykes
in Paris on 23 December 1917

The brilliant yellow of the rounded fold of skin, like a rubber flange sealing an expensive clunky beak, showed how young the bird was. Its body was firmly trussed with string and it lay on its back in the grubby hands of the child, rearing its head to glare at me with yellow-rimmed eyes. 'Buy it, buy my pigeon,' roared the child. I had made the mistake of saying, 'O poor little thing, why tie it so tightly?' It was more than trussed, swaddled – exactly as its captor had been after his mother first dropped him on a pile of dirty cloths, drenched in blood, water and the screams of life.

'Ten lira, ten lira,' he yelled, now out of swaddling clothes for a good four years. 'A fine pigeon, buy it, buy it.'

All the little boys began shouting.

'Don't sell it to her.'

'Ten lira Syrian, he means, not Lebanese.'

'Leave her alone.'

'Six lira.'

And suddenly, in the starling screams, the voice of the serpent, all of seven years old and knowledgeable in the ways of the Levant, in the chinks left gaping in armour: 'Buy it and you can untie the string and let it go free.' The cunning was too crude and killed the thought of liberating the wretched thing. It would anyway be caught again as soon as we left, its wings paralysed by numbed blood.

I opened the Guide Bleu. We were standing in a village square, surrounded by ramshackle huts that, unusually for this level of the mountain range, showed little sign of architectural imagination or fantasy. It was a small village, poor and unattractive, not picturesque. Small and cramped, hostile in its outlook on the greater world, and the sweep of the mountain to the sea was almost ignored in its siting. A dark aura, perhaps for lack of trees – no wide grey trunk of the carob sheltering the old men at backgammon, no gathering-point, no apparent centre. It seemed to be nothing but a huddle *against*, rather than an organic growth from the heart.

We were not standing, in reality, in a village square at all; but in the centre of a Crusader castle. A very minor one, its only importance as a link in the chain of beacons that had once had to sweep uninterrupted down to the furthermost point of conquest, across the Syrian coast, all of Lebanon and Palestine, and gutter out in the desert of Kerak, on the outskirts of Asia, utterly divorced from the soft corruptions of the Levant coast. The castle, really a fortress, had never been of much architectural interest and it was only the desperate hunt for a picnic site that had forced me through the small print to find that once, by the road we were driving on, it had existed. The Guide did not mention that it was now inhabited by almost as many persons as in the eleventh century, only said ambiguously that it was 'abandoned'. We spent several minutes in the village, asking hopelessly for a road to the castle – *al-qasr wehn?* – before we realised that we were standing within its perimeter and that the stones of these charmless houses were all that remained of its one-time strength and the terror that it had imposed on the villagers' ancestors.

Their descendants were returning hostility with interest. Surrounded by a circle ten children deep, all screaming, not an adult in sight, there was no question of tracing the fortress's enceinte, let alone of eating wine and sausage in the cool embrasure of a ruined window. Nicholas was furious. This was by no means the first time that I had refused to stop at a more convenient hour to eat, the reason always being the same: that on a coast so full of beauty, of views, of ruins, Nicholas invariably chose the only dull place for kilometres around, and often the only place without a tree or boulder behind which one could pee without an interested audience commenting on one's clothing, state of bladder, scent of produce of same, shoes, way of walking before and after, religion, probable nationality – 'don't trouble yourself, they can't be Arabs, they'll understand nothing of what you say' — and probable role in the spy networks of the world.

Leaving our city lives for a moment of release, a flight from routine, we usually ended the long day worn out by driving, by climbing loose screes to find I had misread yet another map, by squabbling over the acquisitive spirit. At this moment the car held a large, unhappy Syrian tortoise and several unwrapped bulbs, cuttings, and thistles, so the inheritors of the Crusaders were quite justified in huskily whispering to each other, in a throaty yell that could be heard as far as Safita, but which was intended to be a confidence: 'They can't possibly be from Beirut, they're too poor and their car is too dirty.'

I gave up tourism and got into the car, seating myself in the back, in the prudent and sensible expectation of evading some unacceptable situation in front. Nicholas ground gears and teeth and slowly nudged the children out of the car's path. The little pigeon-fancier ran beside my closed window, unbelieving. Dreams of easy wealth were vanishing as easily as they came. A substantial future, a release, for at least two or three days, from the midden of his castle. His voice rose in hectoring rage. A *woman* was doing this: it was true then that in Lebanon the women were – held – power.

'Two lira,' he shrieked. '*Syrian.*' The trussed bird was flattened against the window pane, still glaring. It seemed almost dead. I opened the window and handed out two lira, grabbing the body as the boy tried to remove it from me and as Nicholas accelerated. There was a melodramatic silence for several seconds, then he said: 'Now we have a bird too.' The tortoise slid across the rear sill with a metallic thump. We drove on and ate by the side of the main road to the north without talking.

There was only one domestic animal that Nicholas wanted at home: a well-buttocked admirer/slave who cooked well and abased herself. On none of these counts, except possibly one, could I qualify.

In the car I untrussed the bird, which lay numb, still on its back, still giving me its un-dovelike, yellow-rimmed, unblinking stare. Equally unattracted, I scratched it under its chin, cooing. We reached the hotel where Nicholas, in one of his manic flights of generosity mixed with moral caution, had reserved a suite. In those days the consumer society was still only the name of a painting that had bewildered the critics of Beirut, consisting of several tatty brassières superimposed on a Volkswagen. And the Latakia Palace's idea of a suite was two monastic cells, linked by a tiny wedge-shaped place containing a WC, a water-tap and a bucket. Yes, but the window gave on to a deep blue-green sea lashing against the rocks on which the Palace was built. As reservers of this magnificence,

7

the manager as well as a waiter showed us up, opened the cupboard, which gave a deep wail, patted the thin khaki blanket covering the single bed in one of the two cells, and offered to supply a chair once the restaurant had closed. The waiter, more down to earth, asked me whether I wanted some raw meat for the bird.

'No, a little milk, perhaps some bread, it's very young.'

'Raw meat,' he said again, 'perhaps it's still young enough for hard-boiled egg, but I think raw meat is what it really wants.'

Ignorant about birds though I was, this didn't really sound like the daily bread of fat pigeons, strutting around Egyptian dovecotes, and I paid no attention.

We dined out, eating grilled meat and onions and tomatoes wrapped in bread, and a sweet coffee afterwards, and I brought back some bread and left it in a saucer in the slice of bathroom. In the night a scream woke me. Nicholas burst out of the bathroom. 'It attacked me. It went for my eyes.' The next day we crossed the frontier to Turkey, and never before or since have I been through a Syrian frontier post with such speed. I walked in with the pigeon sitting on my wrist. The customs officer leapt to his feet crying a word I didn't then know. I replied soothingly, 'It's just a baby pigeon I picked up on the way'; he said, 'Out, out!' and we were over the frontier without the slightest inspection of car or papers.

The trip, the idyll of a long stolen weekend, had shifted its emphasis. We had no dictionary in the car, but it was evident that what I clutched firmly between my hands was no dove. It required constant attention, and at last I gave up the tortoise, setting its flippers on a stony slope back to its origins, and threw out the bulbs. We gave in to the bird's imperatives and returned to Syria, irritably promising each other at least a moment of the original, cultivated itinerary on the defeated journey back.

No road led to this other, celebrated bastion. Cars had to be abandoned on the rim of the hill facing the ruin, while one climbed down a track to the dry wadi and then, painfully, up the other side, until the dungeons of the castle were at last attained. Hot and dusty, and accompanied by the usual horde of boys, shrieking. Not this time. There was silence as we locked the car and began the descent. A few boys raced down

8

the slope ahead of us and were halfway up the opposite one before we had reached the wadi. Presently they returned, carrying bats, some dead, some alive, which they held with their wings pinned back. The baby pigeon shrilled, a sound I had never heard before.

We followed bird and boys through fringing caper bushes and wild marjoram into a dark, deeply hollowed-out, cellar cum cave cut in the rock. Inside there was a stony mound, as long as a tall man's height.

Jaffa at the turn of the century. Nothing really, not even the simple, cheap and good life that grew to seem so full of essence, of sweetness like pomegranates, when one looks at it from the thin false comfort of international strings of hotels and convenience foods. This Platonic essence came so much later, after the second world war, with the euphoria of independence from the physically present foreigner and before the indigenous ruler grew to understand that his power was for real and could be used to control, to imprison, to maim intellectually and physically. But in 1910, say, Jaffa was a crummy sort of town, dustily or muddily combining the worst of every world that had ever impinged on the place. However glorious their past, none of the cities of the coast, from Antioch to Alexandria, can show much man-made physical beauty or unity, as though the desert, the wilderness, were necessary to compress builders' souls, to crystallise the jewelled facets of Jerusalem and Cairo and Damascus.

Jaffa was called a port although virtually no construction existed to support the claim. Ships' passengers scrambled awkwardly down rope ladders curving over the ship's sides, lurching against the small fishermen's rowing boats swelling and dropping away below, and jumped when they judged it safe, relatively. Women were bundled together and half-carried, half-dragged, then thrown like sacks. The stronger fishermen tried to catch them and sometimes succeeded.

'But I jumped.' Even at over seventy she looked capable of such a break with tradition, and Miss Alice had been seventeen when she arrived in the Holy Land. Her father intended to re-beatify the region by recalling its unholy, its infidel or heretic or schismatic peoples to the light. Miss Alice

11

also felt stirred by the call. 'And I longed to travel, the sun, the places of pilgrimage, Biblical sites. I felt so sorry for the poor people, cut off from the Truth although they lived at its sources: God assured me that I could do something to help, that they were waiting for me.' She snorted. 'He would have done better to tell me to go to Liverpool, although in that case I might not have listened so attentively.

'And the challenge. The Society had warned my father to consider the risks I might face. Moslem men understood as little of the sanctity of the family circle as they did the Truth that the Society wished to expound to them. The law of the Turk was made to be broken . . . uncontrollable . . . lustful . . . there was no bobby on the beat . . . the streets were ill-lit or not lit at all at night – that at least was true – the harem . . . the high price that white women could fetch (they really thought of Moslems as being black) . . . a lonely life. Hardship, physical difficulty of everyday life, disgusting food – I could not have been better prepared to love the place when I reached it. The real danger was the one they never mentioned, that I should never be able to leave it again, never bring myself to face the meannesses, the thin lips and emotions, the dreariness, the polite unkindnesses, the utter greyness of skies and hearts, of home.'

There had been, though, much trouble and difficulty at the start. The Ottoman authorities did not encourage foreigners to settle, there were laws against buying property. And the local authorities resented the idea of an alien presuming to change their satisfying religion for another of which they knew only that its adherents were seldom warm or generous or forgiving. The Moslem functionaries were on the whole indifferent to the Missionary Society's activities, but the Orthodox and Melkite and Latin hierarchies made endless difficulties, laid complaints, warned Istanbul of their strong resentment, made cabals and all but united forces to fight the alien. The Jews threatened to anathematise anyone who dealt with the gentile. The Society found it was obliged to temporise with the forces of darkness. It postponed the day, shelved the project of building the new temple which would irradiate the heathen, and opened a small school for girls in two rented rooms that an Armenian agreed to rent for eleven months, and later a makeshift clinic to teach hygiene to their mothers.

12

These were a relative success in that pupils did attend in some numbers, but not a great source for pride since at first they were all without exception Christian already. Idolatrous churches, but still Christian, and the original aim had not been simply to switch adherents from one denomination to another, but to restore the Founder's teachings to his homeland and thereby hasten the millennium. This was evidently further away than the scheme's originators had first planned for, but in the hiatus many people began to earn considerable sums of money, more found employment and prestige – bishoprics could be established for those left unsatisfied at home – and pragmatism won again. 'Render unto Abdel-Hamid ... as Our Lord would have said.'

Slowly both sides, or all seventeen sides, shifted their stance. Like true lovers who, after their final separation, find that they have each acquired the essential characteristics they most disliked in the other while losing the qualities that originally made them beloved, the Society and various native churches and administrations found themselves caught in a long slow waltz down the decades, through social and sectarian reversals, until a century later they found themselves frozen at diagonally opposite points from the ones they had started at. But when Miss Alice jumped from her ship, this saraband had only recently begun and Mr Rhodes had a difficult time ahead of him.

In Jaffa he rented, again from an Armenian (the intelligent usefulness of this community was reinforced by their reluctance to complain to Istanbul, no matter how well-founded the grievance), a house on the sea front. A perfect cube topped by an incongruously red-tiled pointed roof that gave it the look of a squat crystal. The tiles were imported from Marseilles and each one was stamped with a bee. 'Symbol of industry, not of Boney,' Mr Rhodes explained to the workmen he called in. They knew all they needed to of the first, and little of the second, except that he had once destroyed their town. The house was neatly sliced in two through its midriff; above were the living quarters, a huge central *dar* divided two thirds up its length by a triple arch, the gothic ogives filled in with sugary wooden curlicues at the apex, repeating those of the façade. Off this central meeting, sitting, eating, discussion space lay several rooms, to be used indifferently as necessity

13

arose for sleeping, cooking, writing reports to the Society, women's reunions. They were all large and slightly rectangular in shape, since the ceilings were high to allow hot air to rise and flies to circle well above the humans. Only one of them, giving on to the road at the northern corner – where the prevailing south-westerly wind could carry off the smells – was designed for a specific function, or rather, two functions, indissolubly linked. Here a small L-shape had been cut out from the basic cube, and within it there was a hole, two taps and a stone waist-high construction with steps, space for two copper *tishts* for hot and cold water, an arched niche in the wall for the silvered, lidded soap-bowl and the embroidered linen towels. In the remaining L-minus space, under the window placed to ensure a through draught from the south, there was a large charcoal range built of brick with seven different embrasures – some round, some rectangular; shelves, a long marble slab leading to the marble sink which – 'we are modern people, Mr Rhodes' – was sluiced by another tap, and the only cupboard in the house, made of sandalwood, built into the angle of the wall and constructed on the principle of a Lazy Susan in that it pivoted through its vertical axis revealing on one of its triangular sides dozens of tiny pigeon holes for spices and herbs, on another large rectangles for nuts, raisins, moderate quantities of rice, sugar, dried beans, chickpeas and pine kernels and, on the third, deep arched niches for pickles, jams, orange-blossom water.

Two large earthenware jars, glazed inside but not out, stood in the opposite corner, supplied (empty) with the house, as in London the furniture and fittings come with the contract. These were for olives, either black and green, or short and long pickled (*freek* and *mouni*).

'Of course I was appalled.' Miss Alice gave the same snort. 'There was nothing, nothing. White walls, a few utensils in what Mr Ohannes called the kitchen and bathroom. Even in those days I didn't pretend that we had come from a rich home, but I had grown up with beds and chairs and tables and pictures on the walls – whatever they were, they were *things* – and sheets on the beds and cloths on the tables and curtains at the windows and carpets on the floors. Everything I knew in a home had always been covered by something else. The lavatory had a lid, and so did all the saucepans. And here nothing was hidden, except the spices – because light took away their flavour – and in fact there was nothing to hide in the first place. I had enjoyed jumping into the boat, but this was different, this was going to be life, it was getting dark, there was *nothing*. Now I can see that this nothing was a presence, a something that might win, but then I felt only despair. I was so tired, I wanted some hot soup, a bath, to get out of dusty clothes worn all day, to get into clothes made especially for the night. I wanted a bed, and there was no bed in the house. My father seemed quite calm but then my father had been served all his life and wasn't likely to think where his next bed was coming from. A woman would always have made or unmade it for him and I suppose he thought it was just something that appeared when he wanted it – most of the magic in the *1001 Nights* is just men thinking of their ideal women and what they should be doing. The horror of Sindbad's tale is that the woman never turns up and he has to do the work himself, that's what has made him a legend. Of course I was stupid, I had thought of danger, of a moustache attached to a pasha, scimitars, gold epaulettes, I hadn't thought of plumbing and going to the market without knowing a word of the language, and more than this, I hadn't thought that it would be different from the poor homes that the Society encouraged me to visit before I left. There they had beds, even if there were bugs in the bedding, they had cloths covering tables and mugs and plates on the cloths, and a china dog, and firedogs; it was recognisable. And of course I never saw where they did their washing and peeing and cooking, not once.' She laughed instead of snorting this time. 'I'm not the first to be blind to what was lying under my nose and not the last either. At least I saw it before I lost it, that's more than most people can say. Anyway, that night Mr Ohannes said, "You must be tired, I'll show you where the beds are," and led me into one of the empty rooms. There was a *youk* carved in the thickness of the wall, and out of its recessed arch he pulled some *lahhafs* and, holding them bundled in his arms, asked where I would like to have them. I really did not understand, and while I stood there, thinking this was the lowest spot I would ever reach in an exciting life, a life to be different, there was a bang, a thud on the front door and Mrs Ohannes walked in, followed by several girls,

15

women, whatever – females, all carrying trays and copper dishes, one or two smoking charcoal hot. So we had supper, lots of little dishes, and a chicken and metres of thin bread and then Mrs Ohannes poured some warmed rose water over my hands and feet and made me wash my face with a hot linen towel and I fell on the *lahhafs* and slept. Ah! how I slept. I had been frozen to the end of my bowels, and then warmed again, no sleep like that one. In the morning I found two little girls squatting in the kitchen, blowing on the charcoal range, making coffee so the foreigners would not wake to the cold they had brought with them in their hearts, and from then on I began to learn what to do.'

She looked round the room. There were carpets now, some of them hanging from the doors (but not the windows) to keep out the draughts. There were no pictures on the walls, not even a silver-handled dagger, not a string of blue beads interspersed with alum, not a bedouin handbag with its tassels of silver niello fish. The walls rose uninterrupted to the round oeil-de-boeuf windows, three metres above, framing nothing but the sea and the rocks. They swelled slightly, out of true, bellied by the damp that had penetrated their earth. These irregular almost imperceptible curves were the only decoration of the interior, but through the fretted windows the sea, now a flat, hostile, metallic stare, reflected a complicated pattern of arabesque on the opposite wall.

Miss Alice said, 'It's not what you are here for, but I can tell you this house has no need of art, it is art. There,' she pointed at the centre of the floor, where the tiles formed a small concentric circle, 'at the August full moon, the light strikes its bullseye, right in the centre of the circle. Just one night a year for a few minutes – and if you're asleep, or at the governor's dinner, you can live here for years and never know it.'

I looked at her, shining with the pride of the housewife who controls the galaxies.

'Yes, he told me, but I had already found it out for myself. Perhaps that's why we understood each other. He must have been about fifteen then, although he never knew his age, how

16

could he? It shifted according to whether his mother wanted him to evade conscription in the Turkish Army, or whether his father wanted him to get a job. I don't think either of them knew themselves really. There were too many children to keep track of and of course nowhere near enough money. His being the eldest made it worse – once his mother came to ask my help: she was worried about him, worried that he might run away before finishing his education and deprive her of future earnings. "He's thinking it over, he sits at the table with his head in his hands and doesn't move. Pretends he's studying, but how can that be true when no page is ever turned? He says I don't understand, but is there really a book with all its wisdom on two pages?"

'She had a fine classical head with a broad forehead and winged eyebrows, but she was a slattern and their home was filthy, the neighbours used to complain that she bred mice and cockroaches as easily as children, and that they were overrun by all three.

'He missed school for a few days, so I went to see them, and he was sitting there, his elbows on the table, clutching his head in his hands and staring at the book, just as she had said. Children were running around the room, screaming, playing as usual, but I saw what the mother had not told me about: the curve of her belly as she reached for the coffee. A tenth child was on the way, the folly! Well of course I didn't mention it, but chatted about his reasons for missing school – bad headaches, fear of sickness – drank the coffee and said goodbye, with a hope to see him at his desk the next morning.

'She said brazenly, "O there's nothing wrong with him, he's only angry with me, he won't talk to me, the ill-bred thing." He pulled the book towards him and stared at it. "And what can I do? I tried everything to stop it, even the *jurn*, is it my fault if nothing worked?" The *jurn* is a large stone mortar that used to stand in every house or courtyard to pound meat or fish; I didn't understand what she meant – had she pounded enormous quantities of some herbal remedy, a magical recipe sold by the local *bassara*? She laughed and pushed at my arm in that extraordinarily Elizabethan stage gesture the women here employ – one expects them to cry in a foppish, courtly English, "Why, go to, sirrah, go to!" and the gesture does in fact mean just that even in a Jaffa hovel. She said, falsely coy, "You don't know about the *jurn*? Akh, you ingliz, one never knows when you are pretending or not."

' "I know enough," I said. "It is used to pound meat."

'She laughed and laughed, or rather she acted laughing and laughing, rocking towards me and go-toing again as though I were sillier than Osric. "Yes, yes, to pound meat, *every* sort of meat, *sittna*, you know what I mean."

'I still looked stupid. Tareq got up and went and stood in the doorway, looking at the courtyard. His mother wiped her dry eyes in large sweeping gestures to demonstrate how very amused she had been. "Akh, *sitt* Alice, perhaps I shouldn't tell you if you don't know. But after all, you are the teacher, you know everything really, it is you who tell us." Until then I had thought she liked me, or was grateful for the interest I took in her son – as the saying goes, "I am the slave for life of he who teaches me a single letter."

' "The *jurn* can pound babies too, not only lambs. You lie down at the foot of a staircase, with your face on a pillow. Neighbours, or" – she looked at Tareq's back – "strong sons, put the *jurn* on your back. Then the small children – not the older ones, they are too heavy – run down the steps and jump into the *jurn*, one after another. It often works, but it didn't this time." There was a silence; she added gravely, "The children who jump must be your own, otherwise there might be cause for feuds later on." '

Fifty years on, I looked as stupidly uncomprehending, incredulous, as Miss Alice must – may – have done then.

She smiled at the tape recorder. 'Pre-war missionary miss though I was, you must understand that we were not' – a hesitation – 'as, as idealistic as your generation.' She meant pampered as clearly as though she had said it out loud. 'Women were not as lucky then, even in countries with enough to eat and jobs with which to earn the food. And in Jaffa, although it was a richer town than others, the war caused much suffering. Conscription, the famine, the blockade, the collapse of the empire, it wasn't a good time to be alive, even for a man. And as for a woman in a city slum – the most she could hope for would be not too harsh a husband and the guaranteed love and care of her children when she grew old. If she survived to grow old. It was a wearing life. I don't think Um Tareq can have had such a bad time: she was a slut,

18

which shows that her husband didn't beat her, and he probably "loved" her for her splendid face: he never took another wife. People talk so much nowadays about women being badly treated, about the vote, about freedom' – she smiled again at the microphone – 'but the talkers usually earn 100 dinars a month and pay a woman 1 to clean their homes and buy their food. There's not much use in the vote if your husband brings home 40 dinars a year and you have ten children to wash and clothe and feed. Wouldn't be time to get to the polling booth before it closed, even if your husband let you. And who would you vote for anyway?

'No, it wasn't so much the *jurn* that shocked me, but the thought of her own small babes helping to murder their future brother or sister. And talking of it so brazenly in front of her son. I felt a horror of her, of the scene, something between us like a wall. No, a sheet of gelatine like those the grocer sells, that's it, something brittle and sharp but transparent through which we each distorted the other.'

Helpfully illustrating the sort of sound a sheet of gelatine might make if it were to be crumbled by a giant jelly-maker, the recorder switched off at the end of the spool. I thought of the human-sized wall, yellowy and crinkled, through which the two women, the two nations and experiences, blurredly stared at each other and their fatal influence on the boy.

'You've wasted your morning,' said Miss Alice, 'I've told you nothing of what you want to hear. Come back on Tuesday and I'll stick to the point . . .'

The lower part of the cubic house had housed the stables for donkey, mule, goats and cows and a horse while the back half, separated by a wall three metres thick and low semi-circular barrel vaults, held the winter stores. Plaster silos lined the walls, decorated by the last inhabitant's wife, who had scratched patterns on a dado two-thirds up and pressed her child's hand, dipped in blue paint, repeatedly over the front. In the fever of cleaning out, of planning the school cum church cum clinic, Mr Rhodes had had the patterns painted over but he kept the silos and the waist-high fat-bellied oil jars, with their grey-yellow tin glaze slurping over the thick

19

lip. They were made in a village in the foothills by a man walking slowly and evenly round a seated companion, feeding him over his shoulder the giant coil, like an immense python sinking to the ground from a branch, to be patted into permanence.

The summer was turning and Mr Ohannes took his tenant, but not his daughter, to market, to begin laying in the winter supplies before the hard months set in. Only the ropes of garlic and onions needed no processing but could be hung in the sun to harden off as they were. Everything else had to be dried and pounded and sieved and boiled and crushed and split open and dried again. The terrace was bright red with tomatoes, then a deep rich sienna, then brown with figs and raisins, yellow with boiled crushed wheat. The thick parapet sprouted large glass jars full of grapes stewing in the sun, turning to vinegar. An alembic was placed in one of the upper rooms and filled with fifty kilos of orange blossom. 'No, it's not too much,' said Mrs Ohannes impatiently. 'It's barely enough, after all you are a school and church and foreigners, you'll have a lot of visitors. Ten bottles will barely see you through the year.'

What Miss Alice felt was that ten years would hardly see them through the stores. Muleteers arrived and unloaded their sacks: rice and sugar and flour and lentils; and a servant brought the smaller, finer sacklets of pine kernels and walnuts and fresh pistachios and – 'I can't walk *anywhere*,' said Alice fretfully. 'I mean, food isn't everything and I haven't sat on the terrace and looked at the sea one single time this summer. And now my bedroom is full of pickles.'

This was quite true, she had gone in to find she could no longer reach the books in the alcove for serried ranks of glass jars filled with what looked like spleens, or worse, in formaldehyde.

'The heat makes you tired,' Mrs Ohannes said equably. 'Food is very important and you will be glad to have it when the hard days come. And you must also offer it, it isn't only for you. And you can't make pickles in winter.'

The next day the rows of unnameable horrors were reinforced by other jars squeezing down hundreds of vine-leaves, with small trumpet shells jamming them firmly under the surface of the brine, and the day after turnips not yet rosy

– by the time the *mouni* had been well and truly prepared there was little room for any human in the house and Mrs Ohannes was satisfied that she had got her tenants off to a good start in life.

'And she was right, as far as it went. Food *is* very important, not only to keep one alive, but to show warmth and generosity. And I grew to love this period of the year, because it was such a friendly time. Other women came to help and when I learnt, which took time, I used to go to them to help. We'd always be four or five working away, and tasting and having a cup of coffee and a gossip, it really was a village ethos. And the pride of producing everything and knowing that the ingredients were the best and had been prepared cleanly. ... Of course one doesn't do it any more, but I don't enjoy buying from a shop, there seems something almost immoral about it and I don't see that my friends' grand-daughters have so much more fun sitting behind a typewriter.

'Picking the green almonds – that was always a good day, the hills smelt so lovely at that time of the year, and the flowers and the earth turning a tender green – ah, it was such a beautiful country and its life was so right, in spite of the poverty and the ignorance and the injustice. As though it's any better now. Even then I felt we were ruining something worth saving. I could never argue convincingly enough with Tareq when he said we were on the wrong track. When the British came in force they were scornful of the peasants' way of farming, said it was biblical, and they meant no pious compliment. They introduced deep iron ploughs, paid selected farmers to use them as forerunners of the benighted mass. And they paid peasants to clear their fields of the stones that littered them in such visible profusion. You know the result? The stones had collected moisture all through the night and dripped it onto the earth; once they were cleared the earth dried out and the fields that had been so painfully cleared showed a sorry crop of grain, almost earless, compared to the stony medieval fields whose owners had refused to bother. And the iron ploughs broke on the stones and couldn't be repaired anywhere nearer than the cities, while the wooden ones could be righted by any village carpenter. And even when they worked they ploughed too deep, so again the earth lost its precious moisture and was useless – it wasn't a matter

21

of modernity, but of climate, and the iron was good for the earth of a land where it rained through the year and the earth was sodden, not for the rich, thirsty orange soil of Palestine. . . .

'Children were brought in shoals before the stable was anywhere near ready, they longed as much as their parents for education, for the magic that would change their lives and make them strong, and we had made it known that a meal would be given at noon, which was a great attraction. There were so many little boys among the applicants that Mr Rhodes changed the original plan to have a girls' school and accepted them. They were such funny little things, standing silently half behind their mothers, huge eyes and round heads, shaved for cleanliness. I liked them more than the little girls, who were too grown-up in their ways – sly, I used to think. Of course we had to segregate the sexes, although the first year all the children were under ten, but the two classes were taught by both my father and myself.

'Well, of course it was a difficult life in all sorts of ways. A lot of people made trouble, sometimes without intending to. But many did intend. They didn't want newcomers upsetting life – there were quite enough other things to upset them already. What were we teaching? What was the purpose behind our school? Were we really spies? And for whom? Or, much worse, were we going to convert the children and subvert the parents? Yes, trouble came and, strangely to me then, mainly from the Christian churches. The Latins were the worst, they thought that they should be the only foreigners in the land. The Jews never came near us – there were so few in Jaffa then, anyway – and the Sunnis seemed too secure to worry about our influence; although there were incidents with the administration, usually instigated by the Latins, I'm sorry to say. But most of the children were Orthodox, with a few Moslems. We were very careful to keep the curriculum pure of anything that might give the parents uneasiness. Mr Rhodes believed that a good education in the full sense of the word would lead the children out of their darkness into the light of the Anglican truth, that the example of our lives should be as important as reading the Gospel to them. He didn't mind about our enemies, he said that was what missionaries had to expect, hostility was a risk of their profession and a good man should expect to grapple with antagonists. As long as the school lasted he was a happy man. But many said we were wrong to come to a country where everyone belonged to a monotheistic faith – why not venture to teach the pagans and animists?

'Tareq came three years after we had started. I didn't notice anything in him at the start. He was taller than the others and I still think he was older, although his mother swore he was not yet ten. But Um Tareq's word ... He worked at his lessons, they all did, they all thought it a privilege to go to school and they were always there early in the morning, unless something terrible had happened at home. He worked, but he wasn't unusual, like them all he used to learn the lessons by heart and repeat whole chunks if I asked a question. It was difficult to cure them of the habit. I'd ask a boy, "Adham, does London have a river, and if so what is its name and length and where does it rise?" and in his reply the child would continue the paragraph in the book and recite shipping and tonnage figures for the Port of London and go on to the Clyde and the Forth unless I stopped him. It always irritated me, I used to tell them, "For heaven's sake think for yourselves." And one day, when he was fourteen according to his mother and fifteen by my reckoning, Tareq said, "But we do, Miss Alice, only not about things like this." "This" was the history of England, I think perhaps the Tudors, because we were careful in the subjects chosen – nothing about the Stuarts for instance; talk of armed rebellion against authority, the killing of kings, was not a good idea. He said it perfectly politely, no criticism implied, but it startled me all the same.

'"Then what do you think of, if not your lessons?"

'"If a man who knows all about a subject writes down his knowledge then we should learn from him, we don't know more than he does. When we have our own knowledge, then we can give it and others will trust our learning."

'This wasn't an answer of course but it made me curious and I paid more attention to him from then on.

'Don't think he was in any way exceptional. You journalists leap to things one never meant, you're the opposite of those solemn little students. You will write, "Even his foreign schoolteacher was astonished by him as a child," and make him out to be a prodigy of meditativeness. He did interest me

23

but in the way one pupil always interests his teacher more than the others. He was clever and quick at learning: although his marks for written work were never the best, they were never the worst either, except for the one fatal time. He was polite and well-behaved in class and noisy and rowdy out of it, like them all. The year before he left he suddenly became very good-looking and it helped that by then his hair was no longer shaved against the lice. He'd inherited his mother's classic profile, it's strange how those hellenistic features have lasted on this coast. They coarsen fast but they're so lovely while they last. Except for curly lips, like a horse's arse.' She looked at me.

I thanked her for her time and left. At home the smell of raw meat filled the hall and the baby kestrel flew past me, leaving an angry dropping on my shoulder. I turned on the radio, there was always news, at all hours now. 'We see through the conspiratorial moves of the hidden imperialist hands and shall foil their plots. We affirm that nothing can stop the victorious march of the noble masses on their road to freedom. This is the Voice of Freedom and Dignity.' There was a pause and the same voice said, 'Great sale now on at all branches of Lady Safia. Amazing reductions, twenty, thirty, fifty percent.' A choir burst into a jingle: 'Great sale, great sale. Lady Safia, Lady Safia.'

Looking through my transcribed notes it was evident that there was nothing there at all. There was no sign, no indication of fire, of revolt. All those gifts, that immense uprising, and the adolescent showed not a sign? Marks neither good nor, which was worse, bad. Miss Alice was either too cautious or forgetful.

Or I wasn't pinning her down, just taking gobbets of memories from her pinched-together fingers as the kestrel took meat from my gingerly extended ones. I went back. What was 'the one fatal time'?

Tareq had always been middling – mediocre – in his marks, difficult though this was to believe for another generation, magnetised by his memory. Until the last year of his schooling, and his last written examination, marked down on paper. When, according to what he had written down, he should have received over 95 out of 100 in every single subject, and 100 in three of them. No papers like these had ever been handed in in the history of schooling in Palestine, not even at Terra Sancta, with which the Rhodes did not attempt to compare their institution, enlarged though it was since its pickle-ridden début. They held a council of war with the three other teachers; the consensus was 'cheating'. 'I don't say geometry,' said Mr Rhodes. 'He does like it, he has an affinity for it. But never, never has he grasped the simplest form of mathematics – 6×7 still makes him hesitate – and now suddenly he's on the verge of higher calculus? I should mark this paper 98, but I will not.' Miss Alice, whose English papers had always been among Tareq's better efforts, was also surprised at the unexpected swansong.

The crisis was the more important in that the British Army was now in control of the Holy Land, transmuted for the moment into Occupied Enemy Territory, and Mr Rhodes expected a future paradise of linkage with greater schools than his own, and systems of education that might lead to a real future. When Tareq's only future prospect had been al-Azhar or Istanbul, he might not have worried so deeply. Or perhaps he would: who can tell more than a generation later whether there were some honest men among the British ranks? They were as discreet in their virtues as in their hypocrisy.

Tareq was interviewed first by Mr Rhodes alone. This was not a success and a plenum was held, Tareq opposite the massed line of outraged rectitude. He sat at one of the school desks whose probity he must have darkened, facing the accusers huddled together on the teaching dais, behind a table a little too small for the lot of them, but still above the disappointment that faced them. Naturally Mr Rhodes opened the proceedings, since the other teachers were natives and Miss Alice was a woman.

'The purpose of a school is to lead its pupils onto the road of life. The home teaches them affection, loyalty to the immediate family, warmth,' he paused, 'generosity to the weak, the old and those younger than oneself or to women. All are important and are the responsibility of the home and left to it for many years.' (Whatever Mr Rhodes may have been like in Bradford, decades in the Holy Land, reading the Bible and sitting through evenings of native life had convinced him of the importance of oral orotundity.) 'But there comes the time when the curtain falls on the haramlik and a man embarks on the hard way of the outside world. School is the hyphen between the two. It may begin its pupils with a gentle introduction,' he smiled at Miss Alice, 'but its purpose is to equip them for the difficult battle. They must be taught what they can never learn in the softness of the home: rectitude, a sense of honour, the inestimable value of an untarnished word, the importance of being a man. The marks that are given for a pupil's paper are only a passing indication to show that he has done his basic duty of coming to school and listening to his teacher and remembering what he has been taught. Attendance, and listening, attentiveness, and memory, are not what the school is most concerned about – uprightness, never giving in to the expedient, never mistaking the fugitive for the permanent good. ...' He continued for a little longer, always in generalities that few would have argued with, even in that classroom, while Tareq listened and gazed at him. Miss Alice had praised his neo-classic features. She had not mentioned that, attractive in profile, and saved from the everted curliness of scroll-like lips, Tareq's face was marred like so many of the third-century statues in the local museums by his eyes being too close to the good nose, so that, seeing him full on, a doubt set in, however much one admired the side view.

Then the local teachers spoke. Mr Rhodes thought them too concrete, too niggling in plaints of 6×7, not able to take the broad view of the disappointment that faced them, but it was better that they should do it than he, and perhaps it was necessary to delineate the crime. Then one of them lost his temper and shouted at the accused, 'You son of a dog, you could never answer me on this and this and this, and now you know it all?' Tareq didn't smile but his face relaxed, grew wider, his eye-sockets slid further apart from the narrow bridge of the good nose. A lock of newly grown hair fell of its own accord over his forehead.

'Alice,' said the headmaster, 'do you wish to say anything?'

'It's what I've always hoped for, but why did you hide it from us, Tareq? It was always my dream, the brilliance discovered where no one else thought of looking. O Tareq,

26

you know I'm not your enemy, how much pleasure it would have given me. Why hide it?' Huddled together on the dais, the slightest shrinking away could be felt. And seen. Tareq stared solemnly back and Miss Alice saw the child of the past and not the young man with close-set eyes.

Two or three months before this court of inquiry, he had stayed late – less than an hour – to help her when the muleteers arrived with the *mouni*. It wasn't that her Arabic was inadequate, but that Mr Rhodes was in Jerusalem and that a woman existed to be cheated if possible, whether she were liked or not. The presence of a man would automatically prevent the thought crossing the transporters' dulled minds.

While they waited he said, 'Rhodes, road, *tariq*,' and stopped.

She said, 'You're not called Tariq, but Tāreq, you said so yourself when I mentioned Gibraltar in a lesson and you said it was your own mountain.'

'Akh, Miss Alice, you're so literal that your knowledge slices our language as well as your own. You yourself said that in English they can't tell the difference between *tariq* and Tareq, when they're written down. If I go to London I can call myself Mr Road, yes? We have the same name?'

'No, we don't, we're many roads, not just one.' In spite of the sharpness she was pleased, she felt a compliment of some sort was lurking behind. And why not? She had always been kind to Tareq, and she was his teacher, his road however inadequate.

'Akh, Miss Alice, you should be called Miss Adela.' This did give her a jolt, it was her second name and she disliked it. She thought that the boy had found out, but she knew he couldn't possibly. British – English – records were not made available to Jaffa children, although the reverse was true. 'The just roads.' Not the good road, nor the only one, and in a society where generosity was so important justice didn't have quite the same connotation as elsewhere, it could almost be thought of as synonymous with coldness. Fortunately Alice was untranslatable.

It wasn't the first time that Tareq had stayed late, or said something perky and marginally unusual – not very unusual, everyone mused on words, was hooked on words, thought about semantics in a descriptive, adjectival way. Other people held pieces of paper in front of their eyes, sometimes marked with diamonds and hearts, the permanent opposites, or death and money; sometimes marked with uglily vertical and horizontal lines adding up – to nothing much, except that a man had failed to offer enough to get a woman to give birth to his children. In Jaffa they just tended to think aloud about words, it was neither better nor worse than any other city. Tareq was following in footsteps, no sign there of an unusual gift. Now supposing she were to introduce them to Trollope: that would create trouble. Not all of Trollope, but suppose she were to transcribe Miss Furnival's hesitations – what would Um Tareq make of those? Abu Tareq would ban the book the moment he understood what it was about, he would talk to the mukhtar and then get up a petition and they would all go to the governor and after digesting the plaint for a while – after getting an Armenian secretary to give him a précis – the governor would write to Istanbul outlining in less condensed form his worries about morality in his governorate; and eventually a beautifully written decree would arrive, signed with the multiple crescent moons of whatever *tughra* then reigned, and that would end Trollope Hawaga, regardless of whether he had written about the barbarian Americans or about Miss Furnival's immoral ways.

'What point in smiling at our stupidity now?' Miss Alice said. I had made the interviewer's unforgivable mistake of using future knowledge, of priggishness. 'And if you're so certain why interview me at all?'

(Because of facts, you silly old thing, facts, dates, confirmation of what we know. We know the essential, but you have all the surface facets, glinting in the setting sun, disappearing before we can build the memorial.)

'And then Tareq answered me, not any of the others. He said, "O teacher, believe me. I hid nothing. I didn't know myself. If I had told you, would you have believed me? All the papers tell the truth but I knew nothing until I saw the marks."

'My father answered at once. "If you didn't know yourself, how can you ask whether *sitt* Alice would have believed you?

What could you have told her before you knew?" '

For the first time in my visits, she got out of her chair and moved to the triple arched windows over the sea. It had the solid leaden weight of mid-afternoon at the end of summer, a pewter dullness. The fishermen were asleep in their own homes, the weekend bathers at work in the city, the tin sheet of water absorbed light undisturbed. The ripple of embryo waves hardly made a sound on the pebbles.

'You think we were blind, that we should have seen what is so clear to you. But do you see any better than we did? We saw a boy who had cheated at his exams, are you so certain that he didn't?'

After he left the room the war council discussed the case. Not for long. Miss Alice was grief stricken, not aggressive. There was no doubt whatsoever that the child had used external help, except that no member of the jury could think where from. No other boy was capable of anywhere close to those dazzling stars. How had Tareq done the trick? Short of carrying a couple of cabin trunks into the schoolroom and unpacking series of leather bound volumes? This line of enquiry was dropped. It was decided that instead of a scandal the boy's parents should be simply told that he had failed too many subjects to be granted a certificate. This was not too merciless a judgement, most of the population never dreamt of acquiring such a piece of paper. Work in the British administration, soon to become civilian, would be barred; the rest of life was open to him.

Whatever the disasters, life isn't broken off so easily in a small town before the general introduction of electricity and its divisive offshoots. Um Tareq remained in her home and continued to come to Miss Alice for free handouts of medicine and, if possible, money. Nine of her children survived, which proved she wasn't as utterly unhygienic a housewife as supposed, and several attended the school. Miss Alice asked regularly about Tareq, and was told he was too busy in the port, then too busy in Galilee, then too busy in Tyre, and then in Haifa, but earning money even if too busy to visit his teacher or, according to Um Tareq, his family.

'But didn't you hear the rumours?'

Apparently when there are no newspapers, at any rate of the kind Miss Alice might have read, and no television to deny the rumours spread by the newspapers, and a fear or reluctance on the part of the neighbours to spread rumours, however close they might have been when the figs ripened, then foreigners hear nothing of what is or may be about to happen. Because the rumours were all around.

One of them, which did not concern the Rhodes at all, said that an English pasha had given the land to the Jews. No one believed this in Jaffa. The land did not belong to an Englishman, whether the sultan had given him a pashalik or not, so he couldn't possibly give it away. Everyone knew to whom it belonged. Abu-Rustom had half a dunom in Manshiya, and a whole dunom near the fountain of Abu-Nabut, and he shared a nine-dunom piece of land, planted with orange trees, on the road to Sarona with his half-brother, the widowed second wife of his paternal uncle, the children of his half-brother (only one boy, fortunately, the others were all girls and would get less shares). Said effendi owned three buildings in the Hreish quarter and his younger brother had taken the almost equivalent share in the orange-packing warehouse where they crated the produce to be sent to thirsty Egypt; the Umbarjis, too large a lot to be distinguished by name, owned – every piece of land was accounted for and the only English who so much as rented a part of it were the Rhodes in their schoolhouse. If the pasha wanted to give that to the Jews, let him. There was enough left for everyone else.

And the British themselves soon scotched the absurd story and showed the young hotheads at the Umma Club how foolish they had been to believe it. The British, through their highest man, delegated to Palestine to tell the truth, swore on their word that it was nonsense, a vile lie put around by irreverent and godless liars who had seized power, by force and without any right to it, and who had even killed the Sultan of Russia and his wife and daughters. Men who slaughtered women could be expected to put about any form of untruth.

But there were other rumours, closer to home, that were not so easily laughed away. 'They were all true, too.' And Miss Alice laughed. 'At the time we thought they were lies and they were more accurate than anything one reads in the papers nowadays. How to explain the way people get hold of the hidden truth and repeat it without distorting it? It's the game we used to play, Telephones, where every sentence was changed into its opposite before reaching the last player, that was the lie. The British were lying, and the Jews were lying and the French – only the Arabs and Turks told the truth but we never paid attention to them because they were liars by race, by nature. It is funny to think back on now but I suppose not for them. And Tareq did come back and I too lied about that, and to his own family.'

Mr Rhodes was in Jerusalem, arguing about changes in his syllabus with the newly consecrated bishop, when Tareq walked in through the front door that remained open at night until the household went to bed. As it happened Miss Alice was sitting alone on the terrace overlooking the sea, which, exceptionally that evening, was choppy even within the small bay, playing at breakers, foam, stormy waters within the narrow channel. He walked through the empty house, the dar, and sat down next to her, facing the sea, on one of the straight-backed wooden chairs that were still made in every market town at the time I interviewed her. 'May God preserve your peacefulness,' she said, in the greeting that conventionally met a traveller. But she was nervy. A student who cheated at his exams was unique in her experience; a boy who left his family was unheard of in all Palestine.

According to convention, Tareq should have replied with an equally conventional wish. Not to do so was a rudeness, boorishness, that could create a feud without blood being spilt. Instead he said, 'This is a magic house.' It was then that he told her about the moon striking through its navel, once a year, and only once. And something that she hadn't noticed: that its axis echoed the sun's at the same point of the year, which was why it stood at an angle from the other houses of the neighbourhood, all built on a true north-south axis. 'But this one is the August house, the building of the eagle.'

Of course houses, walls, foundations, absorb what their builders and owners pour into them. Some people say you can tell at once where a fine ram has been slaughtered over the first foundation stone and another over the first wall, and where the owner has been mean and only used a goat, and sometimes a female at that. Those of my generation are more likely to ascribe it to a good love or to music soaking the walls for a decade or more. Tareq said, and Miss Alice believed him, that the house had found its given orientation and that its occupants could not, ever, influence or alter that. It would always be radiant, and those who occupied it might have to leave if they could not adapt. 'Your father' (he called him Abu Alice, which sounded wrong) 'will leave it long before he dies.'

But what he had really come to tell her was that he had not cheated, that whatever he had been before, at the moment of the examinations he had found his own orientation or it had found him, and he had written down all he knew 'of the books' and had been as surprised as his teachers at the result. 'You mean you know more?' Miss Alice was struck by his reference to the books.

Even before the consumer society imposed its absurd standards, people judged other people, on the whole, by outward physical signs. The writing was on the wall: those who inscribed their material yearnings with an eighteenth-century bokhara or a Schwitters received, expected, different treatment from those who hung up saucepans or a quartet of china ducks. Even the revolutionaries found a little man to upholster their three-piece cane suite. Tareq had been born in a house whose aesthetic was to become the most élitist of all – but 50 years later. Simplicity, bareness, pale straw mats, a few copper utensils adorning the whitewashed walls. Interior decorators were to make their fortunes by turning palaces on the coast into expensive approximations of a peasant home, but Miss Alice never knew them, while she did know homes well-run, with forks and knives, a table to eat at. Whatever her contempt for Liverpool, she thought of Tareq as the bright boy out of a slum. Admired his unusual remarks in that context. Bright did not mean genius. The infant Mozart was not only the son of a man acceptable, up to a point, in circles that Mr Rhodes could not hope to penetrate, but was a European. The local context was abysmal.

Tareq told her that he did know much more. 'They speak to me,' he said, sitting on his straight-backed rush chair.

'The stars?' At the moment he was looking upwards.

'No, those behind the stars.'

It was the sort of answer an interesting adolescent might give to a sympathetic teacher. Miss Alice was not disappointed, she was intelligent and grasped some of the problems a bright ambitious boy might face with a family such as Tareq's.

'My teacher, I swear I did not cheat, I will surprise you and you will be happy you knew me.'

Impertinence, the British colony told each other regularly, had to be checked at the start. Treat an Arab like a friend and he might – would – respond as an equal. He had no grasp on reality, no sense of inherent differences.

She knew better than to ask the question she longed to hear answered: *how* had he cheated?

'But you agree that the results were so much better than anything you'd ever done in class?'

'Yes, much better.'

'And in some papers your work was so different from what it had been before that we find it hard to understand?'

'Yes.'

'So there are only two explanations, either you were pretending all through the year to know less than you did, which is really just another form of cheating, even if it was senseless, or you got outside help during the exams.'

'Yes.' And he let out his breath, almost like a sigh. 'I got outside help.'

The little waves chopped and foamed, playing at being breakers, slapping the sides of a fisherman's dinghy. The house, the town, were asleep; in the silence their low words carried over the water, brisk though it was. There was no moon and in the thick velvet darkness the Milky Way trailed over the sea and the little white scuts of waves like a branch of jasmine reflected fitfully and inaccurately in an agitated fountain. The light of the one lamp still lit in the house streamed past Tareq's face and drowned in the sea. She felt too disappointed to speak.

'Miss, I did work hard for the exams, I wanted to succeed, I thought I would, even by myself. I didn't know that help would come at that time.' He turned in his chair to look at the black sky, so that the light fell on the back of his head. 'Perhaps it was wrong, too much, so that instead of being a help it has harmed me and now I cannot find work in an office

33

with the English and am worse off than if I had only come out in my true place.'

This was a curious excuse, but she had lost her curiosity, didn't want to listen. She didn't reply and they listened to the wavelets for a few moments while she waited for him to leave.

Then he said, 'It's hard to explain. Let me show you something.'

The dinghy was bobbing up and down, jerking at its rope halter, swinging round ungracefully. 'Look at it: Abu Selim is such a lazy . . . all the other men have beached their boats, and he hasn't even bothered to anchor both ends. As though he were worn out by the heaviness of his catch, instead of always going out late and coming back early. Look at his boat!'

She was so used to seeing it that her irritation at the man's slovenliness and illcare for his family (Selim was one of her pupils) had worn away. He would lose his boat one day and beg the town to help him regain his livelihood. She looked again, uninterested, and then again. He *had* lost his boat, before her eyes. It had been there, with the sea going slip-slap at its blue sides, and now it was not there and the sounds had stopped.

Tareq went into the dar and unhooked the oil lamp, raising it on the balcony so that light fell on the sea and she saw that the dinghy, roped to the seabed at both ends, was now sunk in the water to its gunwales. The fishermen often did this to a leaky vessel at the end of summer, in October and November when the sea slides into an oily golden calm, falling away from the rocks where parched seaweed turns black in the low sun, as though the winds and breakers of August had skimmed off half a metre of the mass of the Mediterranean. A boat would be filled with stones until it floated just below the clear unmoving surface and would lie there until the timbers had swollen out to caulk the leaks. A simple operation, but how had it happened now? Abu Selim, with his eternal skimping of work, hadn't weighted it down sufficiently and it had suddenly settled of its own accord? She didn't know enough of the action of water on wood to judge whether this was possible, but it was certain that there had not been two mooring ropes and now there were.

The light was trembling. Tareq took it back to its nail on the wall and returned to stand by her.

34

'You saw: it is easier to show than to explain.'

Of course Miss Alice had been trained to believe in miracles, in the suspension of physical laws. It was virtually an occupational necessity in her home and her work. Still, it took her several seconds before she understood that she had really seen what she had seen and, much worse, that her pupil was claiming responsibility. Her pulse (her heart?) begun thumping unpleasantly, it was difficult to speak.

'*You* did that?'

He opened his hands, the palms towards her, in the gesture that means 'it is not my fault', or 'what can I do about it?'

'But I don't understand. How did you do it? Why? How did you arrange it? Tareq, I will not have you laughing at me. Mr Rhodes will be very angry with you.' It was the first time since the school opened that she had ever invoked the power of her father's name, the authority of the male head, to ensure that she was respected by her pupils. But the thumping was in her throat, her head.

'No, no please, O Miss Alice.' He had crouched beside her, one knee on the ground but not exactly kneeling. 'I beg you, don't tell Mr Rhodes, don't tell anyone. I beg you, I beg you. No one must be told, I only showed you because you thought I had cheated and I am leaving and you would have thought that for ever. No one must know, please. Not even my parents.'

It was so plaintive, so childish, the child's earnestness about its unimportant little secrets, its magic world that must be hidden from the everyday world, that she felt easier, the thumping subsided into a tremor, a twitch in an eyelid.

'Yes, but I don't know what you mean Tareq. You haven't told me anything. How did you do it?'

'I was helped. It's just like the exams, except that there I didn't ask for help and now I did. I don't know how it's done, but I ask for something to happen, I mean very hard, with everything in me, it's not like saying I wish it would rain, of course that doesn't work, how could it? But I think and think: let this happen and sometimes it does. I swear to you I didn't do it for the exams but I felt it happening, I sat down and wrote and wrote without thinking and I knew all the answers, even though I didn't.'

Tareq was a good-looking male, his hair fell well on a wide

forehead, his features and figure were almost at a peak, his eyes shone and their shifting colour, hazel, gold or greenish, was surrounded by an unusually thick black rim to the iris which intensified the gaze. He had one of those thick clear skins so common on the coast, burnt a deep honey in summer, paler yellowy red like an apricot or a peach in the winter, which pick up the setting sunlight like the antique stones do, and turn, for a few moments of the day, a radiant warm colour, like copper dipped briefly in gold. If he had been pasty, had flabby folds, black hairs covering the backs of hands and shoulders – another common type – Miss Alice might have accepted less and, perhaps, understood more.

'Who helps? Why?'

It was like pulling the heavy stones out of the sunken boat. He couldn't tell her who, that was certain. Behind unawareness of why lay a hesitation, evasiveness that she ascribed to shyness and ignorance. How was quite simply explained, although in the days before electricity was understood by the general public it was impossible to grasp. When the first power flickered into Jaffa streets and homes, Miss Alice remembered and comprehended easily what Tareq had been using as an analogy. He was plugged in to a generator: if he turned the switch, power came, sometimes strongly, sometimes weakly or in unpredictable bursts so that actions went wrong. Sometimes the switch stuck: apparently it was turned on but the lights did not click on at all. Sometimes – either the generator had temporarily run out of fuel or it had a will of its own.

But when he first told her he seemed mad rather than incomprehensible and her fright, terror, the thumping, were soothed away into sorrow for a pupil she loved. Miss Alice was fourteen years older than Tareq and had matured much later.

So she listened, she gave her word 'and we all know that the English do not break their word,' she reminded him – not to repeat what she had learnt, and he left, slipping away after lifting her hand in the conventional manner towards his forehead, although, well-brought up by the Brits, the gesture stopped a millimetre away from actual contact. She did not accompany him through the dar to the front door, as she would have done for a compatriot, because that might have looked as though she were ensuring that he stole nothing (the oil-lamp, for example) on the way out through the sleeping house. Intra-racial etiquette is often the opposite of homogenous politeness. And she sat on, gazing at the frenzied little sea, for several minutes after he left, trying to make out the outlines of the dinghy and failing.

And in one sense, Miss Alice sat there forever, narrowing her eyes onto an agitated liquid dark, trying to see. In our interviews, or at one point, I thought to myself that she had died there, choked by her thumping blood, and in some way – a switch that had clicked without being turned on – I had managed to interview someone who had been dead for years, who had appeared only to tell what she knew.

At least she tried to see. Whatever the time at which she finally went to her room and slept, she woke about half an hour before dawn, when the light was already quite clear, a hard grey, and the fishermen's clunkings and thumpings marked the end of what they called a storm, really a mildly heavy swell, easy to slide over, outside the narrow bay. Her bed lay alongside the ridiculously tall windows. She sat up and looked at the activity. The sunken boat was still there and her pulse flickered and transferred its own throb to her eyelid, which began twitching again. The fishermen chugged out to sea, strung out one after another in a long line to the close horizon. They all easily avoided Abu Selim's boat. Were they surprised at his unseasonal diligence? The fishermen never talked much, they smiled, they gave the price of their catch, they were the nicest people in Jaffa. Some of their little boys, having helped to shove the boats down to the water, were now swimming around the sunken one, sliding their tummies smoothly over the gunwales, standing for a moment upright before the dinghy settled lower in the water, falling over the side with a shriek and a crow of triumph, as though they had performed the most exacting of dives. Abu Selim appeared. Strangled shouts, gruff and hating, were addressed to the children who slid silkily over the rim of the boat and wriggled through the water to the promontory at the mouth of the bay. Abu Selim stood on the beach, more foolish than usual, shouting all the commonest curses. Then he turned round and went up to the town, apparently disappointed that his boat hadn't surged to the surface and beached itself at his feet.

Miss Alice, smiling again, rose, dressed, still watching the beach, and told the servant who had also risen to light the charcoal range to serve her breakfast on the balcony, since Mr Rhodes and his insistence on using what he called the dining room were still in Jerusalem.

Abu Selim returned, with Selim trotting behind him. Miss Alice frowned, or if not, she was displeased. (Could she frown? At seventy she had a calm, justice-dispensing forehead.) Selim was due behind his desk in twenty-five minutes. He peeled off his clothes, keeping on, since he was nearly twelve, his empty sagging white pants, and swam out to the boat, while his father stood on the beach and cursed his mother, his house, his sisters, the boat, the sea. Selim removed, one by one, the heavy stones that kept the boat underwater, but it didn't rise. He dived, rose to the surface, shouted: 'The anchors are too heavy for me, shall I cut the ropes?'

Abu Selim cursed the anchors, the ropes, his son, the general situation of life, the – 'Yes, cut them.'

Selim obediently swam back to shore and was handed the knife, with more curses on his head were he to drop it, were the knife not to cut, were the rope. . . . He swam back, dived, vanished. The boat swung abruptly in a curve of almost 180 degrees. Selim reappeared and yelled, 'The other rope is new.'

A new rope cost 5 piastres a metre, quite a bit more than Abu Selim got for a kilo of fish. A little more, had he not been in such a rage, than two kilos of any but the most sought-after fish. And unless the monster, the stewer in his sister's menstrual blood, who had done this to him had chanced upon one of the triangular stones with a convenient hole through the apex (Phoenician anchors, welcomed with historical ignorance but deep gratitude by the fishermen), then over a metre, at least, was wound around some rock.

Miss Alice gave up her fascinated post and went to school to teach. Selim arrived an hour and a half late, and she said nothing to him until class had ended. Then she asked him to stay behind. He described, fairly accurately, what she had already seen.

'But why did your father soak the boat at this time of the year?'

Selim explained that he hadn't, that the 'storm' must have filled it, although as far as they had noticed the boat had not been leaking at all before that night. Miss Alice waited for him to say something about the second mooring rope, then she realised that it would not be mentioned. A new rope was too valuable not to be hidden from envious, or perhaps legally righteous eyes, ears.

Instead of scolding him, she sent off the surprised little boy without a word.

Time lets things settle and after days and weeks, months, Miss Alice had let the sediment rise over such a disturbing, inexplicable event. Tareq had vanished, his mother stopped mentioning him, but the everyday continued, day in, day out. The sea smoothed itself into the metallic reflection of autumn, new children appeared at school, some clever, some beautiful, all eager.

'We have to give a dinner,' said Mr Rhodes. The bishop had a new assistant, the archbishop was to vist Jaffa, Miss Alice sent messengers to members of the community who were suitable to talk to dignitaries. The head of the CID, the Orthodox archimandrite, the district commissioner, wives. None of them were Arabs: perhaps because wives were included, perhaps because Arabs were not really suitable. It was a party as well as a dinner: the guests, the host, wished to relax, to be natural. The archimandrite was a Greek, and a merry man, not at all hampered by his habit, his bun of hair. They were all used to seeing each other, to eating well, to more physical comfort than the Rhodes house provided. It was lucky that a journalist sent by, although not of, the Society's house organ should have arrived with an introduction in time to be invited, to supply the grit of alien dust that enabled the too familiar group to coalesce against and with him to create a shining pearly interest. Extraordinary stories from those hills, he said during a silence at table. They all looked at him. He jerked his head in a roughly north-easterly direction. What stories?

It was now nearly a year since Tareq had shown Miss Alice what he could not explain.

'Ah, they make such a fuss about nothing.' The head of the CID in Jaffa was a gingery man with rough reddened large-pored skin. Small piggy eyes without eyelashes and a weak straggle of eyebrows, thinly scattered hairs over the eyebrow arch. He ran to flab and the British fashion for cutting hair militarily short over ugly necks unkindly showed fatty flesh oozing over the tight collar. He was himself unkind to better formed men and Jaffa feared his cruelty even before its extent was known. Miss Alice disliked him, without knowing the worst of the rumours – who would tell a Brit about another? Except to praise?

'It must be a trouble to you.'

'In Sierra Leone we always said *they* were just like children, sweet but so noisy. Lord, the stories! But since I've been here I must say I regret those children. The Arabs aren't even children – they'd be nicer if they were. Sly, they are, they put their hand on their forehead and tell you they love us, are glad we're here, welcome, my house is yours, and the next minute they're in the street demonstrating and shouting and if one of them gets shot they look as though they hated us. Puberty, I suppose.' He looked at his freckled hand lying by the knife. 'Still, they're better than the Yid.' And he gave his high surprising giggle that had led the suq to call him Abu Dahk. 'Not as cunning, thank the Lord, and they don't whine from here to Whitehall.'

'I think in some ways we understood them better,' said the archimandrite. 'Byzantium is the only European power that really controlled this country without too much trouble.'

'How interesting, Beatitude, you don't believe then that Islam made a difference to their character?'

'*I* think it's because the Arabs and Greeks are so alike.'

'And so different.' The archimandrite was not flattered.

Mr Rhodes diverted the conversation: 'I don't think I've heard of any trouble recently. Is it serious, Challis?'

'Of course not, can you ever get anything serious out of them? Chickens who don't know their heads have been cut off and go running around as though they're still alive. But anything like this can turn dangerous. Does one ever know in advance? We have to take it seriously.'

'Will you arrest the man?' asked the journalist.

'Don't know yet, it all depends. We're watching him now, we'll see the lie of the land, whether he'll listen to us, it's perfectly possible. If he's stubborn, we'll see. Arresting him might not be wise, unless there's a good excuse, a common crime, something that'll stop the hens from running after him clucking and cackling.'

A man had appeared in villages, a magician. This was not unusual in the week after the pilgrimage, when those who could not leave for Mecca celebrated Abraham's near-sacrifice by slaughtering a sheep and eating it, sometimes the only meat they tasted all year, by dressing their children in new clothes and giving them whatever treat they could devise. A magician got good audiences at this time and was nothing for the CID to watch over.

But the countryside informers, who regularly sent in reports of all events, ordinary or not, mentioned that he was a most remarkable conjuror. Instead of pulling silk block-stamped scarves out of his sleeves and giving one of them to the girl who was due to be married during the feast and later selling the rest, or eggs out of his nostrils, or baby quails out of his ears, he walked through walls of houses, 'where there's no door,' added a report painstakingly. Some brushwood blaze had got out of hand in one village and threatened the mounds of unthreshed and as yet unallotted wheat: he had put it out in a flash, from a long way away, without buckets of water. He had told it to go out. There was an olive tree, a line of olive trees, that for undiscoverable reasons had ceased to bear for the past seven years. The owners had dug to the roots and found nothing, the trees were bewitched, but they were reluctant to cut them down and there was bad blood in the village, luckier owners fearing that the devil who had fouled the trees might move to their property. He had sat under the accursed grove for a day or two in the winter, and the following year they blossomed and now the young fruit was set, a good, though not exceptional crop. He had. . . .

'It's all rubbish,' said Challis. 'If we gave him a portable radio set they'd all start twittering that he calls up the jinn from the deep and talks to them. Lucky that he can't get his hands on one.'

'It's a story though. Makes a change from riots and complaints and Commissions. I never seem to get much on local life,' said the journalist. 'Miracles are happening again on those green hills not so far away . . . I'd like to see him in action.' The Greek laughed, there was a pained silence.

'Sorry, sir,' the journalist said to Mr Rhodes. 'No comparison of course, but you know how Fleet Street likes to tart things up.'

'Some things should be sacred,' said Mrs Challis. She was a silent woman by nature but her husband had often explained to her that to be head of the CID, even in Jaffa, was a great thing for a man of his age and largely due to his army experience. Men with higher educations, even graduates, were now attracted to a country pacified and held for the foreseeable future, men with connections of power, able to get their godsons, nephews, second cousins, into interesting positions in an interesting land. 'They can send their aunts pressed flowers, descriptions of the Vale of Sharon,' Challis explained. She had to help him get on before the younger, more presentable candidates occupied future promotion, and a wife who pleased others, church and state, was essential. Challis was himself still young, notably so for his post, and he aimed at becoming head of all the CID in Palestine long before he retired. It was a variety of ambition that neither his wife nor Miss Alice would have questioned at the time, but which today makes me, and thousands like me, scratch their sluggish minds in vain to understand, whether in Latin America or in Asia, some special category exists which, at the age when most children dream of becoming TIR drivers, or space astronauts, or computer programmers, dreams only of the black room, and flesh that can be altered.

So Mrs Challis sang for her supper. She had learnt that it was her duty to join in the conversation, not to be a great milky sack of silence, to prove to her hosts, her fellow guests, and to show the servants that the wife of the head of the hidden room was an asset, had also chosen an asset.

In fact the journalist was a good example of the kind of future man Challis feared, or thought about. He signed his reports 'Frank Egerton', which sounded chummy enough in hotel bars in the Levant as well as on a byline in a fervently Britannic middle newspaper, and he was chummy – heavy drinking – enough for his colleagues and sources such as Challis not to fear him. But, without the coldness of choosing, he was an asset in himself, linked to many of those who could make or ruin Challis, and, for that matter, Palestine.

He was also well trained, by his nanny rather than by his ravingly populist paper, to smile easily at the tight middle-brown sausage curls: 'My dear, nothing is sacred to the great unwashed. It's Gutenberg, not Galileo, who should have been forced to recant. The world as we know it ended when the monks laid down their pens, although fortunately,' he turned to the archimandrite, 'they did not lay down their muskets.'

Everyone was pleased. Challis thought to himself that with steady training his Nettie might do well, instead of giving such a good imitation of a housemaid who has found the beds made by the kitchen staff while she was changing the water in the vases. Mrs Challis, was, simply, charmed, and thought of how gentlemen had looked at her, sometimes twice, when she had gone shopping in Guildford at the age of seventeen.

Mr Rhodes was relieved that a delicate moment had been averted, above all by the manner. His servants had been educated in his school and understood English quite well; and of course they had converted, convinced of Anglican superiority. But their old habits wavered on, and they would have been deeply offended by airy levity if they had understood what was being referred to.

'Tell me, sir,' said Egerton, 'would it be very difficult, do you think, for me to go and have a look at what this galla-galla man is doing?'

Challis thought about it. Even in the days before the movies became a popular activity, an ambitious man used histrionic tricks, leaned forward, took a slow sip of wine, leaned back in his chair, took off his glasses and breathed on them or, if he were not at a dinner with ladies present, relit his pipe with urgent concentration, frowned, showed in two or three basic courses how much mental activity was required to survey the risks and consequences of an action impinging on his kingdom.

He would then normally say, 'Sorry, old man, can't be done, too risky. Never know how they'll react – you wouldn't want me to have to call out the entire Jaffa police force to rescue you?' Egerton, however, was definitely related, albeit collaterally, to Lord Seth, not a quiescent member of the House of Lords, and rumour was now spreading (faster among the Arabs than among the Brits, but still percolating up) of a relationship to the next, civilian, High Commissioner, not yet appointed but whose name was already known even to the British community. Challis' problem was a difficult one. He was clever enough to know that a relationship did not connote friendship or even liking, that it might be as dangerous to favour a black sheep as to ignore a white one.

'I don't see why not,' he said. 'Give me a little time and I'll see what I can do, but for heaven's sake don't go charging in on your own. I'll look at the reports again and ask around; if he's going to a safe area it can probably be arranged.'

A serious flaw that undercut the ease of British life in a subjugated country was that social distinctions between themselves were, if not nullified, threaded with unease. By virtue of the salaries paid to them for living abroad, they were all at a level with, almost, the richest in the land, and barred from mixing with the clerks and grocers who had formed their original milieu at home. The power their army and administration wielded meant that they could not meet the natives on any level except that of power – educational as well as legislative. Their clubs, nominally for the exercise of sports, excluded the natives, were assemblies of the ruling power to relax in. But of course once among themselves, their own social distinctions were reasserted, and the Mrs Challises suffered, although they were surrounded by Mrs Abd al Majids with whom they would have found much in common, and been happier.

Christ, however, was a virtually absolute abolisher of original class, whatever his own background had been, and missionaries, as well as all men of the Churches, were accepted at all levels and learnt an ease of manner and authority of their Lord well enough to hold their own with the High Commissioners' ADCs. Miss Alice liked Egerton and her father never suggested to her that she should please him, so he liked her too. A week or more after the dinner he called on her, carrying three magnolia buds knotted with shreds of palm-leaves to keep them closed, as an apology for not having thanked her sooner.

'I went to Jerusalem the next morning.' He watched as she arranged the buds in a wide low bowl of bubbly blue glass.

44

They bobbed clumsily in the width, but in an hour or so they would open and overflow their container. 'That man! Do you know what he's done? Given orders that no ingliz are to enter the area where the magician is practising. No one, not even a doctor, unless he works there already. He's done it to keep me out.'

'But why? He said he'd do what he can. It must be dangerous, there may be trouble. People often get excited during the Feast, they might take you for a Jew. Challis worries about his people, he understands what alarms them.'

'Miss Rhodes, you are too kind to understand a man like that. There's no trouble, I've never had any, wherever I've been. I can speak the language a little and people like to talk to me, they think I might help them in their trouble. That's what Challis is worried about, he thinks I might write too sympathetic a report, might get the public asking questions about what he's doing here. And perhaps he's right.'

'What he's doing here? He's a policeman, he's keeping the peace.'

'If that's all, then he has nothing to fear from reporters. Censorship always means something unpleasant is happening. You wouldn't stop me from sitting at the back of a classroom and writing about your school, would you?'

'No,' she said reluctantly. 'But it would embarrass me, I shouldn't like to think you were watching us. I wouldn't teach as well, and the children would get excited and self-conscious and behave sillily.'

He laughed. 'Challis would have put it exactly like that, if he had thought of it. But are they children? I'm certain he's not a teacher, not of the good, the true, at any rate.'

'They're not children in other matters, of course not, but in something quite new to them, I don't know, I think they might say things to attract your attention, or to please you, or even to laugh at you. I don't know, but it would be an unusual thing for them, they wouldn't quite know how to fit you in, how to deal with you. . . .'

'Like the magician.' Egerton moved to the balcony and looked out. 'What a view to live with, to *hear* every day.'

'Yes, it's lovely, though in the end one doesn't hear it at all any more, unless one wants to.' She looked at the sea, dull in the vertical midday sun; for a moment she felt heavy, her life seemed tedious.

Egerton did not tell her this, but his trip to Jerusalem had not ended when he learnt that the area was closed. One of the High Commissioner's aides was his friend or long acquaintance from county and school. He had given him dinner and complained. Kit Farren had said he'd see what he could do. HE was to visit Jaffa on Wednesday. Kit would accompany him and if necessary introduce Egerton to ask the favour for himself. HE was due to visit the Rhodeses' school on Thursday afternoon, at the end of the day's classes. It was official policy not to stint external, verbal graciousness, encouragement towards privately-funded schools; a visit by the highest, even though unofficial, unannounced beforehand in the press, was virtually equivalent in the goodwill thus acquired to the founding of a school or a classroom by the Mandatory and cost less.

Mr Rhodes had of course been told, and an amount of tidying, clearing and cleaning had been done, although to be fair the school was admirably run and could have passed an unexpected visit. Miss Alice refused, upholding the spirit of the Reformation, to change the little girls' blue pinafores three days early, arguing that this would cause rumours, flutter, falsity (although all the citizens of Jaffa knew that the Mandoub was coming; that according to custom he would visit at least two schools, one governmental, one private; and that among the latter the Rhodeses' establishment would naturally be higher on the list than the Lutherans'). The little boys' khaki shirts and pants, chosen as so much more practical than white, could anyway last the week.

The impeccable, immense, brass-decorated cars drew up. Smiling, surprised Mr Rhodes appeared at the door and welcomed the honour. Miss Alice, as agreed, continued to hold her class in check until the door opened and the gods smiled at a little girl stretched earnestly upwards to the blackboard chalking 'Wellcum', blinking as she looked sideways at them. They also smiled on Miss Alice.

Kit Farren was then very beautiful, or at least young and tall (which counted as the same in a country, a region, stunted by famines and privation and overwork at too early an age), with features that appeared regular from a short distance, an ease of manner and smile that contrasted with the nervously reined-in attitudes of lower men catapulted into power over other humans, a skin that took the sun gratefully instead of reddening. He was four years younger than Miss Alice, and belonged to experiences, landed, scholastic, worldly, that she would never have encountered in a lifetime in their own country. But at that time she was very pretty, in the English fashion, with a little nose that tilted up in a question like her upper lip, a little mouth, a little waist over a long bell skirt, a forehead whose outward curve repeated exactly, inversely, the concave line of her nose, faint fair eyebrows whose faintness turned them into another questioning plaint, as though all she saw bewildered her and a man was needed to explain. A mask of fragility was the most misleading she could have worn, and the most attractive in a country where ferociously strong, large, assertive features were the norm. Kit Farren's position meant that the women he met were the thickening wives of already successful or half-successful men, and instead of a question their nostrils held complaint, resentment of slights, notice of bad placing (his fault) at dinner tables. Or the daughters accompanying their totally successful mothers and aunts, on a temerarious visit to the sights. Grumbles at the inefficiency of muleteers, the horrors of sanitary arrangements at the Cook tent at Petra, were mixed with probes as to his relationship to the Farrens of, to his mother's maiden name, and with manoeuverings round HE to discover what his future career might be.

He felt that in contrast Miss Alice was the maiden (later lamenting, although he did not think of that) who is discovered by the eighteenth-century gallant in a vale, spinning while she tends her flock: tranquillity, loveliness, *not a nuisance*. Perhaps he also felt, unconsciously because he was not a villain, that an idyll would only be enhanced by distance and that a love so many hours from Jerusalem, so many steps away from quotidian dinners and their placings, could last without reproaches. This may be unjust. It may be that he fell in love with her as spontaneously as she did with him and that it was simply due to his shallower nature that he fell out again sideways, obliquely, having climbed back into his natural milieu. And how would I know, anyway? Miss Alice certainly had no wish to talk about him, except where his impingement on the gist was unavoidable. Research gave some facts: he did this, he went there, he married the duke's daughter, if only the second of a brotherless progeny. The real facts aren't known now and never will be. Nor does it matter. Smiling, he took her hand and held it towards the group entering behind him, to the shorter chubbier man in pinstripe, like a well-flattered donor holding St Catherine's trembling fluttering fingers to the roly-poly babe.

'Miss Rhodes, sir.'

The advantage of knowing someone's name, profession, position, when they know nothing of you! Whatever one's religion or race, one acknowledges the divinity of knowledge, of the smiler who approaches with the dossier. The mistake of Challis, and of all the inquisitioners, the rulers of the Moscobiya, then and later, was to show by their questioning that they did not know, were at a disadvantage and lowered by their ignorance of events, names, dates. It was Farren who should have run the CID: his training in the nursery, at table with his parents, let alone Eton or Magdalen, fitted him beyond nightmares to extract the truth. There was no need for physical brutality, though its rumoured existence was what prevented him and his like from entering such degraded and degrading work, thereby ensuring that it was left to brutes who knew no alternative, whose efforts were not only wasteful of lives, limbs, teeth and nails, but unproductive.

Miss Alice nearly curtseyed, but the High Commissioner was shorter than she was, and she was saved from mortal error. 'Let me join in!' he cried. 'Do let's play a game.' Miss Alice failed to grasp the moment. Farren had organised a gentle scrum in the courtyard in less than a minute. The children kicked a ball east and west, HE, chuckling with a smile still on his face, dribbled it towards the kitchen tap kept out of doors for convenience. A tiny, dark-brown little girl hurled herself at his legs, brought him down in the dust before he reached the drip and ran off with the ball. There was a hiss from the adults, standing round, their smiles wiped off. 'You little – you little *Arab*,' he said as he rose. Farren and Mr Rhodes rushed up and surrounded him towards the door.

Next day, when the official party was attending the Friday service, Farren called. First he told her how impressed HE had been by the school: 'so clean,' he had said. Then he explained away the incident. 'It's not at all because he's Jewish. HE leans over backwards to be fair – the trouble we have with the Jews, you wouldn't think it, but they expect him to favour them and he won't.'

This was, in short, the first time HE had been publicly known to make an anti-Arab remark. So it should be forgotten. Ignored, certainly not repeated. If the little girl had repeated it to her parents, then – well, then, Miss Alice had forgotten her duty to her country and the parents would have to pay for this forgetfulness. Farren did not phrase the problem in this crudely underdeveloped way, his job was to smooth away prickliness. Nor did Miss Alice quite understand what he was saying. Whatever light the little girl had accidentally thrown on the Mandate's official policy towards five-sixths of their flock, she had acted as a beacon for Kit Farren's love, or expression of his love. The first call was followed by two more, not motivated by official reasons.

The same expedition had allowed him, perhaps mellowed by a flash of lightning, to obtain Egerton's pass. Succinct, this allowed the bearer, named, to travel wherever he wished and asked, in English, for all to help him in his aims as far as lay within their power, if not their ability. Miss Alice still had it, showed it to me, with its cagily correct generosity, and in return I showed her the too-used paper, this time in Arabic, that had allowed me to reach her without fearing curfew or kidnapping. A paper that twenty years after the Mandate had ended, was still needed by anyone who wished to cross 'the lines'. Only the organisers, the signers, the language and the implications were different: the cause of it all remained the same.

For all his pass, Egerton did not find his magician for some time. When he got to the little village in the hinterland of Nablus, where he had been told the man was – practising? exercising? – his craft, his art, his gift, when he got there, the man had gone. Had he been there? Yes, or perhaps no: depending on who answered the questions. He had been there, was now elsewhere. He had not been there, never had, no one had heard of him. Egerton's paper worked with the British soldiers; the mukhtars could not read English and were less inclined to bow to high orders.

But as he said, he knew how to make friends. And dealing with people who at that time still trusted, it was a quicker process than in, say, South Kensington. A few meals eaten on the floor with people whose annual income equalled a day of Egerton's alcoholic outlay, led the hosts, drunk with their own generosity and imagining that this intoxication was reciprocal, to direct him, not to the man, but to his compass bearing.

He had never covered his tracks. It wasn't only that at that time people – all of us, not only Miss Alice – were innocent of treachery, didn't think of it except at the level of salt or gravel in the *rutl* of sugar, chalk in the sack of flour, thought of Westerners as so many Rhodeses, bearing an anti-Ottoman banner, believing in an integrity not only of character and relationship to the land, its products, its fertility, but also a scrupulousness of behaviour to those feebler, more helpless in terms of guns and learning than themselves, which explained and excused their coldness and material meanness towards the weak, their belief that anyone reduced to begging in streets was malingering, refusing to work, therefore unworthy of alms.

It wasn't only that, although no one among his people would have blamed him or held him at fault if that had been the only reason.

Stupidity? Hubris? The sly angels of Rilke rather than the earthier, less snobbish ones of Blake? Holding my grubby piece of paper, my 'pass', how could I grasp what they had thought in those days? Let alone what Miss Alice, protected by a more lasting piece of buckram, ever understood?

Egerton could not only cross his legs when he sat down without a grimace to chew on the honouring, fatty, tasteless but smokey ruminant, without querying whether it was sheep or goat; he could sit there without shifting, twitching, fidgeting or even boasting of his abilities later. If he meant to succeed in a job that exempted him from the war, this was a gift as valuable as his family connections. Not many guest-houses after he started he was told, 'The man is in Tarshiha this week.'

As we all know, Tarshiha is now a well-ordered, swimming-pooled, lawn-sprinklered victim renamed Maalot, whose cement bungalows were bloodily violated by the outer hordes. But at that time it was a village like any other, stone-cut, whose vaulted domes rose huddling into the hillside, on foundations that had existed for centuries, whose inhabitants, then natives rather than spreaders of terror, lived for the seasons, quite unaware of High Commissioner or his thun-der. They were far from even the seediest centre of manda-tory power, being in fact much closer to what came to be called 'Syria proper', than to what was to be their dispersal and ruin. The mountains, hills, on which it sheltered, rose in a series of balconies from the coastal plain, stepping up to the ultimate sweep of the great mountain with its hermetic altars. The seer who established himself there never saw that it would be so utterly destroyed that even when it was partially avenged its name would never be mentioned, nor the fate of its inhabitants. Slaughtered, driven like the bony sheep they cherished for the feast, obliterated in the most exact sense of the term – wiped off the earth – and replaced, like Carthage, by the salt of the same planet, there was to be neither mercy nor understanding for the children of Tarsh-iha, guilty of living in a vineyard coveted by others.

The magician told them nothing of their future. He told them – he told them that glory lay ahead.

Difficult to know when or whether a Palestinian villager believes in you or in what you say. Politeness, breeding, fear? A ready agreement, which may be sincere or oblique. He was fed, his hands and feet were washed, the guesthouse was his, a certain amount of orange-blossom water was expended. Belief? Perhaps. Dread, certainly. Then Egerton arrived. He had backtracked from Nablus; in Jerusalem he had, discreetly or journalistically, used his contacts. Challis suddenly called on him, alone at home, and offered to take him on 'a trip to the high Galilee', offered pleasantly, as though he were asking a friend to join him on a human journey. Egerton accepted. They drove to Safad, not such a pleasant trip. Challis found fault with everything en route, worked – at what? – in every town or large village, and complained every evening of the food served. Egerton was forced into a position of agreeing and adding to complaints, or of defending what often was indefensible, and antagonising Challis even further. Because at the end of the first day it became clear that he had not been invited out of camaraderie or even the most passing feeling of sympathy. Nor did Challis explain the ends of the journey.

Tarshiha was too small for Challis to disappear on his business. The mukhtar met the car, together they were led to the guesthouse, together drank the coffee of arrival. The sun hung over a glassy sliver of distant sea; the village was still at work or preparing the guests' food.

The mukhtar said, 'We have another guest, he will be honoured to share the night with such eminence.' He did not look overjoyed at the prospect.

Challis pulled his lips over his teeth, grinning at Egerton.

'All good quests,' he said in English, and in Arabic, 'your guests reflect their light on us.'

The mukhtar looked depressed, Egerton asked what Challis meant.

'Journey's end. We've run him to ground. I shall read your story with interest, saves me listening to his gibberish.'

In a single rubbery movement the mukhtar rose, apparently from his ankles, refolded his *abaya* over his white robe as though to conceal some inadmissible revelation of flesh, wished peace on them and left the house.

Egerton had risen, more slowly, to thank him for hospitality. He stood looking at his camel-haired back, at the identical robed brown silhouette over the same silk-striped silvery under-robe approaching, facing him with a different face under the same headdress. Behind him the sun set with its mythical green flash and the face was for a moment invisible.

'Sir!' said the double-faced figure in reasonable English. 'Welcome, twice welcome, have you been washed? Shall I call for the women?'

He was taller than Challis, a strong face, although the cheeks were too full, and large glowing eyes, shining against the lamp. He slipped off the cloak, sank gracefully to the floor without an unnecessary movement and clapped his hands sharply. 'I fear they have kept you waiting for your food,' he said politely. 'Had I known you had already arrived I should

52

have returned sooner.'

'We made better time than expected,' replied Egerton, to assure him that no remissness was held against him, 'we hadn't planned at all on getting here before dark.'

Then he saw the look of fury on Challis' face and understood. This was not another host, previously informed of their travelling plans: this was a game that he had caused Challis to lose, at least its opening move.

The food was carried in, spread on the large round straw trays, strongly coloured in purples and oranges that the women make to echo their embroidered dresses. 'Chicken's older than the mukhtar,' muttered Challis, tearing vainly at an ancient breast, as flat and juiceless as an old woman's.

He had grumbled in English. Tareq smiled deprecatingly, said smoothly but loudly in Arabic, 'Forgive the poverty of Tarshiha, which in no way reflects the warmth of the welcome we wish to show you, Challis bey. It is a misfortune all the inhabitants feel, that because of the fines and the taxes there are so few animals left that this was the only food that could be found. For tonight, I mean, only for tonight, tomorrow messengers will be sent to find worthier meats to offer you and your honoured,' he bowed his head at Egerton, 'colleague.'

Outside the guesthouse, in the unlit night, a woman's voice rose hoarsely for a phrase of anger and stopped abruptly. Egerton hadn't caught at all what she said, but he replied, embarrassed at Challis' boorishness, 'I'm not a colleague, I'm a journalist.'

'An even greater honour; to my knowledge, which is of course less than Challis bey's, Tarshiha has never received the graciousness of a journalist before. They will be overwhelmed.'

He was smiling widely, engagingly. Was he laughing at them? All the more interesting if he were. Egerton did a rash thing: he reached into the kitbag supporting his spine and dug out his silver flask. Unscrewed it for the smelling and offered it to the smiler. Challis pushed the tray back roughly. But Tareq, still smiling, put his hand out and held Egerton's wrist gently, touching his own chest and forehead lightly with his right hand. 'You are very kind, you return our hospitality. Believe me, I am grateful, even if – no . . .' He took the flask,

53

raised it above his open mouth and let one drop fall in. 'There, I have accepted your generosity.'

Challis' scowl went. 'Have some more,' he urged.

'Thank you, perhaps tomorrow evening, if the bey is kind enough to offer again.'

Then the mukhtar returned, followed by women carrying trays of coffee. He handed round the cups, Egerton noting without too much attention that he now appeared to be several inches shorter than the other man, that the mistake was really a mistake, a confusion of the sun. Coffee, polite conversation, the women returned, pulled out the *lahhafs*, removed the dirty cups. The mukhtar made his second speech of the evening expressing the honour done to the village by Challis' visit, and the accompaniment of, of Challis bey's colleague. He left; the three men slept.

More food in the morning, food indeed taking the place of comfortable beds, of hot or for that matter cold water to wash in, of the daily newspaper, of all that the two men took for granted as comfort. Instead, the replacement consisted of olives, fresh bread, tomatoes, *labni*. And the deep pleasure of breaking with habit, of not returning the manservant's greeting every morning, of rising, washing, shaving, putting on, if not choosing, the clean shirt, the uncrumpled trousers. The joy of breaking the lunging rein at least for a moment, of rising, unalcoholised, with or before the morning light, with the new unbreathed air of the dawn's hills. As the sun rose it struck the earth at an acute angle, every orange clod stood picked out by light, the dew still ran off the stones, hung on spiders' webs among the olive branches. Round the guest-house the pots of basil breathed out their scent for the last time until the evening sun again glanced at the same, opposite angle; the multi-coloured flowers of succulents had not yet opened. Even Challis' ill humour had not yet unbudded.

Tareq was not there.

The two ingliz ate, their beds of night still lying rumpled behind their moving elbows, washed at the well, tidied their clothes.

Egerton said he would go for a walk. Politeness, reluctance to witness how his government transacted the business that kept him in a way of life he took for granted. The reddish path still held shadows, but the heat grew sharper, struck at his morning freshness. Quarter, less than quarter, geodes, failed half-crystals, appeared under his feet occasionally, so glintingly beautiful that at first he picked them up, then made a cairn to collect on his return, then ignored. Sides of hills still lying against the light were velvety blue-green, high though they were; a mountain swept away to the north high and snowy, or just white, above them. Hermon? Egerton recited a psalm to himself, uncertain of what exactly he saw. The noise of the village, accentuated by the silent hills, rose up to give him the happy image of the philosopher above the turmoil of everyday living.

The problem of these exhilarating walks is that the descent, slipping, stumbling on pebbles unnoticed on the climb, so slithery on the downward path, is dangerous as well as undignified. As Egerton's left leg shot out, landing a buttock or half hard on the gravel for the third or fourth time, Tareq appeared on the upward climb, smiling, holding out a hand to help without an apparent sense of superiority.

Egerton took it.

More self-destroying than hilly descents are the endless daylight hours on trips such as these. The excitement of the dark arrival, the rush and bustle, the culminating comfort of oil-lamps and food and then sleep of fatigue; the pleasure of a dawn unbreathed by buildings, of exploration, are cancelled by the unending tedium of the day, with nothing to do but kick stones around until the evening, or even the midday, meal, arrives again. Interview people? The men are in the fields, or with the flocks, or at market. Impossible to tackle the women. Three, six, seven days are needed to found friendships strong enough to bear the weight of ordinary life – interviews, the exchange of hesitant probes called conversation, are reserved for the night. Egerton had never yet visited a village unseeded by earlier acquaintance; he knew the impossibility of rushing at trust, the uselessness of relying on Challis.

'This afternoon, I talk to the people,' said the magician. 'I shall be honoured if you attend.'

The immediate unpleasantness over, Farren had called again,

and yet again to say goodbye before the hard climb up from Bab al-Wad back to Jerusalem was embarked on. Whether he loved Miss Alice, whether it was a soothing to his conceit, she believed that they understood one another and would continue to do so when he was back at Government House. She talked to him of her life, of her pupils, of those who had made an impression on her.

'One has to be careful,' he told her. 'They're always out to get something. Things have changed since your father started the school. They change when they leave school and try to get at us.'

'I started at the same time as my father, and I've never noticed that they want anything except what we've offered to give. And remain grateful after they leave.'

'Cheats,' he said sadly. 'They all cheat, it's their nature. Themselves and each other as well as us, but we don't know them as well, we make easier targets.' He smiled at her. 'You're too good to understand, it's a defence in a way.'

The remark caused her unease. No one had ever suggested that her life was not a useful, a fundamental one; her own conceit, so tenuous as to be almost unnoticeable, fed on the thought that she was helping to improve the future, laying a few stones in the foundation ditch of the country that was to be. The children did not seem to her to be hypocrites or sly, on the contrary they appeared to love as well as respect her and to follow her teaching with a thirst to learn that proved their belief in her.

But Farren talked mainly of other things, of England, his home there, the beauty of green summers, of lawns in June when the coastal plain surrounding Jaffa turned ochre dust. His family's house was beautiful, small enough not to frighten her off day-dreaming, the lands extensive and held long enough to encourage him to think of Westminster as a probable future. A distant one, since he had to earn ready money first, that lacked. In one way, a good lack, driving him to work and experiences that would help his planned career. 'Foreign policy committees,' he laughed gently. 'Very useful line to specialise in. All the others do agriculture, too many of them to rise, I'll be the Palestine man. Very useful.' He played with the fanion of HE's car, which he had removed after parking at the school. 'There aren't many here, Egypt would be harder,' he burbled on, dreaming as much as Miss Alice, listening entranced.

'He wrote as soon as he returned to Jerusalem.' She stared at the other sea we sat by and stopped, broke off as I shall break off – evidently he wrote that he missed her, that he thought of her; she answered, more letters followed, then other visits, and so on. The details are unimportant, anyone can fill them in.

Nor did Miss Alice ever talk of Farren much. What I heard of their story came from others, peripheral to the essence and reviving ancient gossip, sourer after the years, for the unnourishing pleasure of gabbling away the hours, even more emptied of content by the explosions around us, the anarchy that threatened their homes stuffed with treasures – souvenirs! – relentlessly acquired, collected, polished and repaired and burnished, until these carpets and silver ewers and framed embroidered sleeves cut out from the dress some woman had made pulsing for her wedding, had acquired their human owners more certainly and permanently – till the end of their lives, literally – than the other way round. Had anchored them to the anarchy, so that their reaction to the bombs, the shells, was not to flee for their lives but to pad and wrap and hide their possessions yet more securely. It was these people, apprehensive not of what they might reveal of their souls, but of whether I might have glimpsed too much rashly displayed silver, who spoke to me of Farren – 'Kit', to assert their social standing – and 'that poor teacher'. They had heard of Tareq, dimly, but common, *baladi* people were not of interest; nor were their actions, however historically determining, to be followed down the years as though they were the sterile encounter of emotions between people like us. Even though the consequences of some of those disinherited acts were being lived through, today, at the moment of our interviews.

But if she did not talk of him to me, she had talked to him then, and written. And when Egerton returned she wrote an account in her letter that Kit made a copy of, omitting the personal references, keeping the meat.

The assembly gathered in what was not so much the village

square as a space, stony and dusty, where the cubed domed
entity of the domestic honeycomb broke off to face the hills
and sky unprotected. The unwalled courtyard of the lowest
house formed a platform above the space where all the village
had assembled. In front, just below the step up to the
platform, a row of straw-woven chairs had been aligned, and
where the feet of the notables were to rest lay a couple of
blond reed mats. The men crowded, giggling and shoving,
behind the chairs; the women silently ringed the men, cuffing
or grabbing a noisy child, readjusting their white head-
coverings or fanning the flies away.

The mukhtar appeared, escorting Challis and Egerton and
followed by the four or five men who with him constituted the
governing assembly of the village. They sat on the chairs,
waiting for the English to seat themselves first on either side
of the mukhtar, and then arranged themselves in descending
order of precedence. The mukhtar lifted his chin from a
compliment to Challis:

'Let the children come closer,' he shouted, 'they can see
nothing from the back, is the *'eid* only for us?'

Scuffling, hoarse little cries, pushing, squeaks: what
seemed like a mountain river of innumerable children filled
the space between the notables' feet and the dais without an
inch of earth showing between their knobbly little brown
knees poking out akimbo. Egerton felt several skinny little
buttocks wobbling precariously on and off his large and solid
boots. He tried to move a foot out from under, and a great
heaving and bubbling, like a too-thick white sauce finally
coming to the boil, took place around his shins until his feet
were cleared, just, but prevented from any further
movement.

He was still smiling widely at the children, trying to show
gratitude and good-will and emotional distance, difference,
from Challis, when Tareq appeared, quite suddenly, on the
platform. He wore a shiningly clean and new *qumbaz*, silvery,
silky, without the usual thin black stripe, and a white shawl
wound into a floppy turban that suited his looks. He looked
solemn, imposing.

'In the name of God, the Forgiver, the Merciful.' The
crowd shifted and relaxed. A pious magician, not one of the
godless gypsies who sometimes appeared at festivities. He

spoke for a minute or so about the feast, about how Abraham had loved his God more than even his son, had been willing to sacrifice his child in obedience, what this meant for devout believers. Challis said, quite audibly, to the mukhtar: 'Is the imam ill? No sermon tomorrow?' The imam, sitting on his other side, leant towards him and said earnestly, 'No, no, your honour, I will of course lead the prayers tomorrow.' A sycophantic titter went up from the men standing in Challis' line of sight.

Tareq had stopped, then, raising his voice, he called, 'Children! Remember the Sacrifice! Remember that Abraham loved God more than his own son, though the love for a son is the greatest that a man can feel. And so God rewarded his obedience. Now watch!'

He murmured some words too low to be heard, turned his back on the audience and appeared to be fighting or scratching himself. Turned again to face them and out of the wide sleeves of his robe produced a gangling newborn lamb. The children shrieked with joy. He held it high, turning proudly from side to side so that all could see it, its tender little hooves swinging feebly, and then knelt at the platform's edge to give it to the children. 'Pass it to the English officer,' he said, 'it is the feast-meat he asked for.' Stroking the lamb as it was passed among them, the children handed it back till one last little boy stood up politely and placed it carefully in Challis' lap, its weakly-muscled forelegs dangling over his putteed calves. He said nothing at all. His ears and the fold of thick skin at the back of his neck grew congested with blood but his face remained as impassive as the mukhtar's.

The magician then turned to more usual tricks. Gossamer scarves, one of which he did offer to a pretty girl standing not far from him, eggs, a glass of well water which turned vermilion after he had turned his back on the audience, a pack of cards – Egerton understood that they were watching all the time-honoured trade of a feast. There was nothing in the reports save a wish on the part of the informants to make themselves important, to justify the money they hoped to continue earning. The lamb was a more difficult piece of legerdemain and must have needed some hard planning; Egerton decided to inspect the room behind the dais after the show, just to see how it had been done.

The children, though, loved their treat and their excited squeaks and squirms and burbles infused the village with a radiant good humour. The men smiled and cuffed them tenderly.

After the show the magician settled on the ground among them and told them stories of his travels and the far cities he had known. Egerton sat on in his chair of honour and listened too.

By the nature of their practice, magicians had to be itinerant and there was nothing surprising or unusual in the extent of the man's travels, nor in what he recounted to the children. The obligation of the pilgrimage has only reinforced, modernised, the antique impulse to leave home, to range the desert and the sea and observe how other men live, sometimes for ever, to gaze at exotic monsters and customs, to hold up one's hands and exclaim in wonder at the inexhaustible imagination, whimsicality, of the Creator, who has made other people so extraordinary in habit and custom. All the same Egerton was taken aback when he heard the magician describe a city of fog and soot, where the sun rose for only a few hours of unequal struggle before it set again, sometimes without having been seen at all through the mists of its brief 'day'. The hearts of its inhabitants had been permanently chilled by the greyness they lived in; they were cold to children, ungenerous to the poor and maimed. Each lived alone, in a house closed against the elements; they were obsessed by time and constantly observed its passing, giving it an importance that could be explained by their fugitive sun.

That evening it was Challis who was late and the magician who waited on the cushions when Egerton arrived. He paid him a compliment on the afternoon's entertainment. 'No no, never. It was to please the children, a few tricks I learnt in the cafés of Beirut, a nothing, but it amuses.'

This silenced Egerton, as a remark will which agrees too exactly with one's own opinion, conversation consisting as it so largely does of polite exchanges of disagreement.

'Is there trouble in the area?'

Egerton looked up, surprised, not understanding.

'A journalist, I mean, travelling with Challis bey? There must be something bigger than the troubles of Jerusalem, or Jaffa? I had not heard of anything in my travelling, I wondered whether it would be dangerous for me to continue on the road.' He smiled.

'No, there's no trouble that I know of. I just wanted a change from the cities and Challis mentioned he was going north, so I attached myself to him. It's difficult to set out on one's own.'

'Ah.' A silence in which the words seemed more foolish than when spoken. 'It may be easier than you imagine. Challis bey, we welcome you. Tonight it is we who wait hungrily for your arrival.'

'And for your delicious lamb, I expect. Hope it won't have returned to thin air when you took your spell off it.'

But a lamb there was, at least until they had finished licking the bones and thrown them out to the village dogs. The policeman did not mention the afternoon's entertainment at all and none of the men spoke until they had finished eating, except for the mukhtar's ritual offering of scraps of meat to his guests.

After he had at last gone and they were pulling out the cotton mattresses for the night, Egerton fished out his flask and with a smile offered it again. This time the magician put his head back and poured a generous stream into his swallowing throat. Challis raised the hairless bony arches that framed his mingy eye-sockets.

'With thanks.' The flask was handed back and Egerton took a swig himself and gulped. Instead of brandy he had swallowed a sweet sharp liquid – mulberry? – someone had found the forbidden liquor and replaced it with a more lawful one. It was possible but surprising. The villagers would be too frightened of Challis to rummage among visitors' belongings, even supposing them to include potential thieves, on the whole unusual outside the large towns. And the substitution was odd: a snooper enraged in his piety would be more likely to empty the flask and stamp on it to show what he thought of the insult.

He looked up into the magician's smiling gaze. An extraordinary thought hit him and he shivered, furious with himself. Saying nothing, he arranged the bedding and lay down with his back to the other men.

In the morning, after the magician left, he did say something.

'I say, Challis.'

A grunt.

'Something rather odd. Don't mind if I ask but did you happen to fill my flask with mulberry juice yesterday?'

'*What*?'

'Well, you see, it was almost full of brandy, and yet last night when we had a drink it was mulberry juice and I was wondering who on earth could have switched it.'

'I don't care for the stuff myself,' Challis said coldly. 'If I did I'd carry my own supplies. If you really think that I swill in secret. . . .' Getting angrier the more he thought the accusation over, he added, 'And I wouldn't try to cover my tracks with any bloody juice, either. *Mulberry*, indeed.'

His skin was mottling with rage. Egerton tried to apologise. It was not easy to get his feeble excuses accepted. But then Challis thought beyond his anger; his little eyes stopped blinking redly. 'Where did you keep the bloody flask?'

'In my pocket.' Egerton's pockets were indeed always heavily weighted on both sides so that the garment sagged almost equally into two thick handkerchief points, like anchors keeping his thin height on the ground.

'Where did you leave your bloody jacket?'

'Well, I didn't. I wore it all day.' And as he spoke the shiver ran through his spine again.

'You must have taken it off at some point.'

'Well, when I went into the yard to wash, but you were both in the room then. And I used it as a pillow to sleep on, so it couldn't have been snitched at night.'

'When you went to wash.'

Egerton felt for the first time that Challis was probably very good at his job. A power of concentration came from him, exuded.

'You went out to the yard and I sat around watching that bloody charlatan saying his prayers. Now,' he was thinking out loud, 'could he have reached your jacket while he was bowing and scraping? Sleight of hand is his business. . . .' He looked disappointed. 'Don't see how he could, I was between him and your *lahhaf*. You're sure you didn't drop the jacket near him before you left the room?'

'Quite sure.'

'Yes,' said Challis regretfully, 'I remember it was still rolled up. I thought to myself that it's lucky you can afford plenty of clothes. Treating them like that's not for a poor man.' He gave him a lethal look. And then a great snigger.

'I know what you're thinking; you're thinking this is another miracle, wine into water this time round. Eh?'

'Well, I can't see how anyone could have.'

'And if you can't see it, it must be supernatural? Not that I'm surprised, all the rot you journalists believe, this isn't any odder. Some of the stuff you've written, just as nonsensical.'

'What stuff?'

'Read a thing of yours the other day, you were going on about self-determination for these poor beasts, on and on, as though they were capable of running a village council by themselves. Look at them yesterday, all gawping at the crudest sort of sham. These are the people you want to give the country to?'

'It was a children's treat,' Egerton said slowly. 'We have the same things at home. You don't say we can't rule ourselves because people go to pantomimes or watch a Punch and Judy show.'

'Ah, but here they *all* believe in frauds like this man, whether they call them leaders or conjurers. We take our children to the panto, right, but we don't believe that you can never grow up. At any rate, my sort don't. But in this bloody country there aren't any of our sort, that's the problem. They're all like the mukhtar and his cronies, from the top, such as it is, to the bottom.'

'You don't know that the mukhtar believed in it; he was just enjoying a feast day and giving the children a little fun. He didn't say anything about believing it to you.'

'Saw it on his face. Part of my job is to watch what it is that people believe in. Watched their faces more than the sham man.'

Unpersuaded, Egerton had no wish to argue with a man he would see and resee as long as he was based in Jerusalem; a man whom, if he did not actively need him, was still necessary as an absence of ill-will and with whom he was to travel back to at least the nearest city. He said nothing. His face showed a vague benevolence although he did not compromise his feeling so far as to smile.

'Look,' said Challis. 'Nothing is easier than for a man like

63

that to switch drinks. The quickness of the hand deceives the eye, you know? He may have done it as a pun, guessing you would be impressed. Cana is so near that it probably gave him the idea. He was brought up in a mission school, you know.'

'I didn't. You know about him?'

'That much at least. Wouldn't be doing my job if I didn't. It's not particularly important – most of the trouble we have is with the bloody mission schoolboys: they think they know it all. The villager is all right until he's got at: works at his crops and thinks of suq prices and thanks the High Commissioner when it rains. Much too sensible to make trouble. It's these half-baked schoolboys who sting us in the foot.'

Softened by Egerton's silent acquiescence, he added: 'I'm not against improving them, poor little beggars. But we're going about it the wrong way. What's the use of all these village schools? The teacher can hardly read himself and we go and tell him to teach the children about Themistocles!' He giggled. 'I ask you! Don't know who the chap is myself! You know, once I asked one of the wretches, told him out loud in front of his class that I didn't have a clue: would he kindly explain to me exactly who the man was? Of course he couldn't, he got red and said something silly and his class was enchanted. Poor little beggars. What's the use of it? They're all going to be wiped out anyway, unless they learn how to shoot. Told them I'd got where I had without knowing a thing about Themistocles or any of his club. Not to bother about nonsense. It wasn't for them any more than it is for me *or* the Palestine Police.' He stopped talking for a moment, still grinning. 'But you know, the teacher was livid? I mean, for once an official visitor was taking a practical interest in their flea-bitten education, telling them something practical, something they needed to know, just as useful as the rotation of crops, and instead of being grateful the silly sod was angry? They're quite useless, the lot of them. I don't care for the Yid myself, but at least he grabs an idea and chews it over.'

'Yes,' said Egerton. It was the sort of speech he heard at most British dinners, a little grittier in substance, but the gist was the same. It bored him, without making him ask whether there was any truth in the view.

'Turning brandy into water! What's the good of that? Even supposing he did it, what's the *point*? Turning it into bullets would be more useful.'

'I suppose the point would be that he has an unusual control of physical laws.'

'Rubbish,' said Challis, 'he switched things around when we were asleep and you felt nothing because that's his job, the sly and snaky hand.'

Before they drove off the following morning, Egerton invited the magician, who seemed to have settled in the village, to accompany him on a walk. They started up the reddish path, in silence until they reached the little semi-circle of rocks that overhung the noises of the village. Egerton sat on a rock and stared at the view, the magician stood slightly behind him; he thought, not seriously, how easy it would be for the man to give him a gentle shove and send him arcing down into the huddled roofs, at present a rich burnt sienna from the grapes turning into raisins on every flat surface.

'I was very interested in your performance,' he said lumpishly, after having discarded other openings.

'Sir! Will you do me the honour of writing about my poor gifts?'

Egerton did not wish to turn round to see. He felt certain that the man was laughing at him.

'I think I'd have to watch them again before writing, haven't seen enough.'

'It's one of the many sorrows that accompany the techniques, the arts. Now if I had fired a gun – bang – and killed a man, you would have written about me without needing to watch a second show.'

Egerton felt really frightened. The extent of his sweaty terror showed how much he had been humouring himself before, with shivers and scary feelings at the nape and neck. With courage, he turned and faced the man, who looked perfectly unintimidating and almost servile.

'Did you change the brandy?'

'It is a forbidden drink here. We are not in Challis bey's home now.'

'I wasn't going to offer it round the village. It is not forbidden to me.'

The magician said, in English, 'When in Rome. ...' His accent and robe made the pert schoolboy remark even more incongruous, incredible.

'Nonsense.' Egerton thought to himself that he was catching Challis' ways of dealing with the natives and that Challis would point out that this was the only way in which they could be dealt with. 'I can do what I like in private, nobody's business.'

'But you offered it to me, so it was my business.'

'You talk like a Jew,' said Egerton, exasperated. 'How did you switch the drinks? That's what I want to know.'

'*Sidi*, come and watch my tricks again, by yourself, and perhaps I will be able to show you.' He smiled at him. 'Alone.'

'Perhaps I will.' Egerton got up and started down the path without saying goodbye. The conjurer called after him, 'It would be better if I could act like a Jew, is that not so? Talking is useless.'

'Well,' said Challis as they bumped down the track that led ultimately to the Jaffa road. 'Did he cast a spell on you and make you promise to write about him?'

A little later he added, 'Tell you something. If you do decide to go and gape at him again without the dead eye of the CID cramping your style, just let me know when you start off, will you? I might be able to fill in some gaps for your story.'

Background information is always useful, but Challis was back in Jerusalem, whispering to the higher-ups, when Egerton decided to return to Tarshiha, so he was alone and unfortified by police knowledge. Always supposing that it would have been given without an unacceptable quid pro quo.

Of course there are great gaps in this account. And, I expect, incrustations of nacreous lumps that have nothing to do with the matter. It isn't only that years have passed, that so little was written down, that the survivors, such as they are, have no wish to talk, and that I myself find it more difficult every day to survive in a city maddened by self-destruction.

There are the silences surrounding Miss Alice and Farren, so that one can only guess at their relationship, so alien to us today, even supposing the militias weren't holding us all to ransom. Was she, for instance, really intoxicated by love? If she was, it is evident from the way she refers to him that she was unable to respond, to grasp the night-side of her self, essence of any dialogue between a sexually- or emotionally-linked couple, more binding or more primary than children. He was a charming man, aquatic, light, with a habit of agreeing, soothing, oiling without grease; HE congratulated himself on his acquisition. But there were moments when Miss Alice was more ruffled than flattered by his graceful easiness of compliment. Oddly, for someone apparently so strong, she did not believe that she could change or influence Farren. She saw him as an unworshipped image whose good or bad actions had to be experienced rather than redirected or averted. At least, this is the impression she gave me in the little she said of him in her interviews, perhaps undermined by age and distrust.

And Challis: everyone – and I've interviewed many who remember him at work – speaks of him with loathing. In the mythology of that particular episode of empire, he has become an archetypal villain. When I visit London I look at the *Daily Telegraph* readers, the still-pinstriped short-back-and-sides pursed-mouth London Transport riders, and wonder how many nipped-in-bud Challises ride among them, whether he would have been remembered kindly had he lived in the suburbs and dug his garden strip. Mostly, people play at their roles; change the script and unsuspected sides of their character (if there is such a thing and not just public and private parts) come under the lights and are commented on by critics. Even the falcon is at present playing the unexpected and unwilling role of domesticated bird. He's not as good at it as a bulbul, but he plays it quite well, all the same.

Egerton did return alone. He wrote, and his paper published, a short piece, saving himself from ridicule by a muffled use of irony, and describing village life at harvest time in that part of the Holy Land as the ostensible and headlined subject of the article. However, he risked enough to say that the man, while practising the most threadbare conjuring tricks, also knew some that would puzzle many practitioners in the West.

He gave as an example an eye-witness account of the magician appearing in a room without, apparently, going through the door, a room whose hewn stone walls were patent proof that no secret trapdoor could possibly be hidden in their unplastered surfaces.

The article roused some interest when read in Jerusalem. Christmas was not too far off, children's parties required galla-galla men as well as the cracked and worn prints of Charlie Chaplin shorts that made the annual rounds.

'Do put Mr Egerton's name down for dinner soon, Kit,' said the High Commissioner's wife. 'A little dinner, not an official one.'

So Egerton was soon on her left at one of the more relaxing evenings at Government House, all English together and hair let down, comparatively speaking, as far as its length would allow.

'Well,' said Egerton, a little taken aback, 'I don't see why he should refuse. It would be a great feather in his cap to have performed for the Mandoub's guests.'

'And how would we go about finding him?'

'Why not ask Challis? His men keep track of what goes on in the villages, they'll know where to find the man easily enough.'

'Ah yes.' She turned to her other side and explained that Mr Egerton had written a fascinating piece on a conjuror who was enchanting the villages.

'Glad to hear it,' said the man, a visiting MP with strongly pro-Zionist views. 'Give them something to amuse them, poor things, take their minds off the sort of nonsense some of their leaders are giving them. I'm sure half the trouble in this sort of country comes from boredom. They can't think what to do to entertain themselves so they go out and attack their neighbours. All these feuds and vendettas one keeps on reading about – boredom, that's what most of it is.'

'You don't say idleness,' murmured Egerton, who was professionally if not personally irritated by hearing *Palestine Post* leaders quoted back at him undigested.

'Of course idleness isn't their besetting sin,' Kit said, smoothing before a crack should show. 'They work like anything, poor devils, not their fault if the results are so feeble. But you must agree they deserve a little entertainment now and again. Their lives *are* dull, all work and no play, you know.' He gave his charming smile and looked at the guest of honour with admiring respect.

'Silly old dullard himself,' he said later in his own small sitting room, having a nightcap with Egerton while the MP withdrew to HE's study for a briefing. 'Talk about boredom! I had to spend the day with him, taking him round kibbutz after beefcake kibbutz, listening to him going into ecstasies over every single water-sprinkler. Really, some of our masters know less about the place after they've been here than when they just sit in Westminster. If you *can* know less than nothing, that is. Really Francis, I sometimes wonder what I'm doing in this job. HE's not a bad sort and she is tolerable, but some of the people one meets! My dear!' He flapped his wrist at Egerton and laughed.

'You love every minute of it, meeting the great and then tearing them apart.'

'No,' said Farren thoughtfully. 'I used to love it. I think I'm getting a tiny bit tired of it. But I simply cannot think of what to do next. Money is the most boring thing of all.'

'Marry it, your charm must be worth about a couple of hundred thousand at least.'

'Yes, but I haven't met the girl yet, have I?' He got up and stood at the window, looking at the immense stars over the Old City. 'At least I love the place. What a country it is! I shall be sorry to leave. If only all the people crawling around it weren't so awful.'

Farren was usually lighter and better company. Egerton, who did not then know about the idyll with Miss Alice, put it down to two days of squiring the MP.

'They talk a lot of rubbish about money, you know.'

'In what way?' Egerton was fond of Kit, he found this sudden portentousness endearing.

'Oh I don't know. They say silly things, like the best things in life are free, when as we know all too well it costs a fortune to run a couple of hunters or to pop over to Paris or pay one's tailor now and then, which one simply has to do, or to love. Love is the most expensive thing in the world, though you wouldn't think it to hear idiots talk. And I don't expect marriage is any cheaper, though it might be if the girl had enough.'

'Kit! In a minute you are really going to amaze me and announce that you love.'

Farren came back from the blazing night sky and sat down to his whisky. 'No, I won't go as far as that. I'm just saying *if* one were to love, which no ADC in his senses would do, it would be damned expensive, beyond my means, at any rate.'

'ADCs meet the right girls, all the ones who come out here have enough to be useful. You're in the right job at the right time.'

'Yes,' said Farren, 'I suppose I am.'

At this point the always weak electricity supply of Jerusalem failed utterly and in the kerfuffle of finding the matches, and knocking over an almost empty whisky glass and insisting on refilling it for the road as soon as the oil lamp could be found and lit, Farren's unusual mood of thoughtfulness passed and the moment for talking about Miss Alice passed, if, that is, it had ever really approached and if Farren had not been engaged in prodding his friend further into incomprehension so that he could reassure himself that he had done all he could, and if Egerton had understood, not been dense, not diverted the track, then he, Kit, would undoubtedly have confided in him, received advice, acted differently. Kit was very adept at approaching a tricky subject obliquely, veering away when his ambiguities were taken at face value, and then justifying himself: 'But I did try to tell you and you didn't want to listen. I couldn't *insist*, could I?'

So Egerton left after the very last whisky of all, and that was really the end of Miss Alice, although neither she nor, overtly, Kit, knew it then or later. (And if it seems as though I had no means of knowing it either, and must have invented the conversation, the explanation is the obvious one: Egerton, like any conscientious journalist, nightly kept an abbreviated account of all conversations and events of the day, and even cross-filed them, fairly efficiently. His papers, personal as well as published or publishable, are now in the archives of the Middle East Centre and can easily be consulted, since he had no issue to dispute the picture that might be left of him.)

. . .

The request for help in tracing the magician was polite but mandatory. It wasn't its non-refusability that irritated Challis, but its subject. For reasons too complex for a simple Arab to grasp, the British in Egypt and Palestine, and for all I know in Africa and India as well, were easily threatened in their self-esteem by self-possession in their subject races. Of course this is as inaccurate as any sweeping generalisation. Restate it: at many levels of administration there were men, almost invariably those who had made a lifelong career of working in colonies or mandates or protectorates or friendlily-ruled countries, who reacted to dignity or even indifference as though it were some personal threat, and who used the bureaucratic advantages in their power to limit or destroy such men. I can't think of a single case where women presented a similar danger, which makes me wonder whether buggery was not a latent explanation, as well as the more obvious answer of the British class system. Men at the top rarely deigned to engage in personal vendettas, but Challis was not at the top, either of his native caste system or of his job in Palestine. Tareq had become his shadow-self; he had no wish to see him received at the High Commissioner's Christmas party. A ridiculous way of taking revenge, but then the whole structure of colonialism was ridiculous, though not, it seems, at the time. Since the request could not be refused he took, for him, an unwisely simple way of negating it. People usually come to grief when they step outside their natural mode of action: the cunning of the serpent wasn't at all Challis' approach; a nocturnal rock spider, weaving invisibly, was more his style. And the result of his insolent message to Tareq to attend him for 'a children's entertainment' was not, as he had hoped, an equally insolent refusal, but the unannounced visit of the conjuror to Jerusalem to try and discover why he had been summoned.

'You're a made man,' said his second cousin, who was nearly a generation older and still struggling. 'The Mandoub wants to entertain his guests. After that you'll be asked for by them all. They can't even amuse themselves, we have to do everything for them. *And* pay their wages.' Rates in the Old City had just been raised.

The matter was not so important as to be on everyone's

lips, but a Jaffa newspaper had learnt – how? – that Tareq was a native of the city and had reprinted Egerton's article, rather oddly distorted in translation, together with a few lines about his family and his education at the Rhodes school. The editor, a rigidly pious Moslem, had himself titled the piece 'A missionary education can be useful'.

They were sitting in a café near the Damascus Gate, generally patronised by Jaffawis and which furnished their local papers, if they could read, with the coffee. Tareq re-read the article and returned the paper to the counter. 'The son of a dog. What has a missionary school got to do with it? He just wants to blacken my fame.'

'He's getting at the ingliz, why should it bother you?' A compatriot pulled up a straw-seated stool and sat with them. 'He's laughing at the preachers, that's all. *They* can't be pleased at your work.'

'Perhaps they will be, if I am invited by the Mandoub.' But he still looked sulky.

'And have you been?' asked the compatriot, blandly ignoring the fact that he had read the article.

'Yes.'

'May God bless you. I want you to help me: one of those mackerel policemen gave me a contravention yesterday because he said my goods were impinging on the pavement and preventing passers-by from passing. Mackerel and son of a mackerel! Where does he expect me to put the sacks? Passers-by are meant to stop, otherwise they might forget what they had come out to buy. Tell the High Commissioner this, please, tell him in all frankness: is it a suq? – or is it a public garden? Until now it has been a suq and I have to display my goods to sell them, not so? Just tell him this, O man, and ask him to explain life and the ways of the city to his imbecile policeman.'

'I will do all I can.'

'They come to our country uninvited, they impose their mad laws, and then they make us pay them for their presence.'

The cousin ordered coffee, and with it the server offered a tric-trac board. 'O no, O no,' said the Jaffawi, pushing out his hand. 'Never will I play with you again, man.'

Tareq, who enjoyed the game, as did every man he had ever known, was surprised.

'O no. You will bewitch the dice *and* the counters and beat me in double games, one after another. I play with any man, not with the jinn, no no.' He finished the coffee and rose, smiling. 'Remember to give the High Commissioner my message. Tell him to think about it.'

Challis, who had asked the Jerusalem HQ to pass him copies of anything to do with Jaffawis in general and with Tareq in particular, received a copy of this conversation. Talk of free speech and the iniquity of secret police is a fairly recent phenomenon in the West; generally it follows by a few years the end of their last dominions or other 'possessions' and the consequent uselessness to them of such methods. He filed the account, not under the name of the outraged shopkeeper, but in a file headed 'Conjuror – Tricks'.

For the first time in her life Miss Alice was going to Jerusalem. The harshness of the long journey by *hantur* was compounded by the lack of women who undertook it. Mr Rhodes had not considered hiring the entire coach for himself in order to protect his daughter, but an invitation from Government House, coinciding with the feast of their Lord's Nativity and also with a general assembly of the Church Mission Society, softened the awkwardness of taking her with him. And as it turned out, two of the other passengers were to be women; with a little urging, they shared the cost of the unoccupied seat between themselves, buying comfort as well as the certainty that no strange man would gaze at them for the hours of the journey. Because the climb up to Jerusalem was arduous and winding and necessitated a long rest and meal and change of horses at Bab al-Wad before the hills were engaged. Grimy and ruffled, at last the passengers made ritual exclamations as the view of the city appeared. It was the first time that Miss Alice had seen it. Mr Rhodes was not an especially thoughtless father by the standards of his world and time, but his kindness functioned more readily after some prodding. The treat had come about like this:

'I shall be attending the CMS meeting on December 31st, my dear.'

'Ah?'

'So, as I would like to talk to a few people in Jerusalem while I am there, I shall spend Christmas with you and travel up the next morning. I'll be back the night of the 2nd or early on the 3rd, DV, so I must ask you to look after the school by yourself for those two days.'

'Yes, father.'

She thought it over in bed, looking at the gleam of the waves.

The next morning she said, 'Father?'

'Mm.'

'If you weren't staying here for Christmas, you could go to Jerusalem and finish your work before the meeting and travel back on the 1st, couldn't you?'

'I wouldn't dream of leaving you alone for the feast of the Nativity, Alice. The whole meaning of the celebration is to be with one's family.'

'I thought perhaps I might accompany you. I've never seen Jerusalem. Or Bethlehem. I *would* like to go to Bethlehem for the midnight service. Couldn't I?'

Mr Rhodes' eyebrows came down in perfect Ls of surprise and potential 'of course nots'. Before his slower tongue began to express them, she said, 'And really, I *should* see Jerusalem. I always feel embarrassed teaching the children about their capital and not really knowing more about it than they do. Mrs Khoury was amazed that I hadn't made the pilgrimage – she says all her daughters have been there twice and three times to Nazareth and she plans to.'

'Alice, Mrs Khoury's life is hers to arrange as she chooses, and ours is ours.'

'Well, but why not? I'm sure the CMS wouldn't mind and they can easily put a *lahhaf* in your room and I could help look after the children at their Christmas party and do take me with you, please, father. And the 22nd is a Sunday so we could explain to the parents that we don't want to open the school for just one day and then we could leave on Saturday after lunch and—'

'*Alice*! Are you suggesting we travel on the Sabbath?'

'It won't be the Sabbath. We'll be travelling on Saturday and then on Sunday we'll be arriving in the Holy City in time for church. It's not travelling when people drive to church.'

'*Alice* ... you'd better stay with the Jesuits in Jerusalem.'

So there she was, on the crest of the hill (and of her heart) gazing at the domes and spires. Such a *little* Holy City, the buildings so low and in such harmony with the naked hills surrounding that they hardly showed except for their orifices, black olives embedded in the dun stones. One immense and sublime dome eclipsed every other building raised by man.

'No, it's a mosque,' said Mr Rhodes. 'The Holy Sepulchre is to its left, there.'

By the puritanical bleakness of its physical life-style Jerusalem reminds the soul that man does not live by comfort at all. Cold stone walls, cold stone floors, whistling wind through the keyholes, cold water in the tap ('and throw your slops there my dear,' said the CMS cicerone to Alice, 'it's been a very dry November, the cistern is almost down to rationing level and we'll use your washing water for the flowerbeds'; Kit wasn't there to murmur that the flowers could only be more beautiful for such dew), thin cotton rag rugs to check, vainly, the cold seeping up one's ankle bones from the icy floor. Scrubbed cheeks, hair pulled back in buns, complexions pink with incipient chilblains, a faint smell of sewage ('don't throw in more than half the bucket, will you dear? *That* water can't be used again, more's the pity'). Thick slices of doughy white bread, bleak plates of leather, over-cooked in clarified mutton-fat, accompanied by brown pieces of potatoes so hardened by fierce frying that they shot off the plate into neighbours' laps if one tried to spear them, and some peas that had missed their vocation and would have been worth their weight in brass to the resistance fighters now hovering on time's horizon. Even the olives weren't particularly good, although how one could fail with olives was beyond Miss Alice's comprehension.

But she noted these things at such a subsidiary level that they only added to her intoxication. The leather was a Jerusalem cutlet! and the potatoes were fried to extinction in Jerusalem! and the peas skidding in trajectories that would have enthralled a physicist were – and she herself was eating them – in Jerusalem! Her cheeks were pink, but not with cold, and her profile, as appealing as that of a duck – curved convex forehead, curved concave nose or bill – shone upwards over the food she was too excited to eat.

'We *are* so pleased you were able to bring your daughter, Mr Rhodes. And to come so early yourself. No trouble leaving the school, eh?' She had been too confused, excitement and shyness not being the most explicit of godmothers during presentation to a roomful of mainly unknown names and faces, to know who he was. The bishop? The administrator? The delegate from home? Whoever, he was not so pleased as he emphasised.

'High time she saw Jerusalem,' said Mr Rhodes. No churchman ever muttered; years of practice ensured a clear delivery, aurally if not psychically. But he was not unaware of hostility. 'Alice runs our Sunday school; she should know what she talks about at Christmastide.'

'Of course, the sooner the better. What a good thing you could arrange to bring her this year, after such a long time.'

More than charity, background knowledge needs to be shared if one wishes to present a united front and conquer the enemy, or at least keep him out of the heart. But Mr Rhodes and Alice hadn't pooled their respectively marriageable pieces of the jigsaw. He knew Dr and Mrs Moneypenny had four daughters and an ecclesiastical income; she knew that Kit liked to linger after the tea things had been cleared away. Separate, their respective information was useless.

How did ladies manifest themselves, in the days before the telephoned 'Hallo, it's me. I'm here'? By simply being there.

Miss Alice attended midnight mass at Bethlehem. So did Kit Farren, accompanying HE. She saw him first, since they all had to wait in the courtyard where the icy winds smashed from wall to wall, playing some celestial game of squash with their sinuses, until HE arrived, accompanied by the carefully chosen cortège (the Crimean War having started over precisely this kind of oversight in this very place) of Latins (a minority, but one which celebrated Christmas at the same time as the Protestants, who were themselves an even smaller minority, but one which happened to have the largest army in the country that year), Armenians, Copts (other minorities, whose Christmas was yet to come, but who would be damned rather than be omitted from their rightful places, on the whole precedent of the Latins), the Orthodox Jews (loathing the whole rigmarole, but wishing to remind the High Commissioner of his ancestors' creed and anxious to check that he did not in any way give credence to the rumour that he had converted to the religion of his ostensible nation in order to ease administrative problems), the unorthodox Jews, there to remind the HC that he was one of them, whether he liked it or, even better, whether he hated it, in which case they would really give him hell; the Moslem holder of the keys of the Holy Sepulchre, whose family had held them at a time when the Brits were painting themselves in interestingly pre-op art patterns, and continued to hold them however strained their Sunni tolerance of the antics of other 'believers' might become, the Mufti – but I have omitted, another war in the offing, the power behind the star – the Orthodox hierarchy, not to celebrate true Christmas for another fortnight, but there to remind the world that they had always been there, ever since Christ was born, on whichever date that might have been, there before Rome heard of Him, there before Europe had dragged itself out of the swamps sufficiently to start fighting itself, there before the start of Holy Time. Not busybodies like the Protestants, not whiners like the Jews, not worldly troublemakers like the Latins, just there, checking from time to time that the bun of hair was still in place, smiling at Power, knowing that Power comes and goes and the Church remains. On the whole, the only two peoples or religions in HE's unholy train who understood each other were the Orthodox and the Sunnis (which means Orthodox), and they both found the same sort of things pained them, ruffled them, made them think it would be better to retire to one's own study until this horrible era was past and peace and good will should prevail again, as it had done for centuries apart from some hiccups before the tribes of mist and fog had arrived to inject their ineptness, inaptitude for life.

First is the wrong word, since Kit did not see her at all, nor would have, had Mrs Bishop not been addressed by HE while his ADC let his eyes roam over her retinue. Cries of joy. 'Where are you staying? For how long? I must come and call,

77

may I?'

When they sang 'O come all ye faithful', throwing their throats back exultantly to swallow the stars above their sectarianly muddled heads, he caught her eye and winked.

In the late afternoon of Christmas Day, after the bloated lunch at Government House and the no more ascetic but cooler one at the CMS, Farren called, flushed with brandy-snaps and accompanied by Egerton.

'O Miss Rhodes, how splendid to have you here!'

The right thing to say, assuring her of his pleasure, happiness, assuring Egerton and the assorted CMS dignitaries that his feelings were above suspicion, since they could be declared so openly. Only she felt a slight twinge at her heart, or stomach; she would have preferred a less appropriate declaration.

Egerton sat next to her, Kit flitted from dignitary to dignitary's wife, burbling. 'He's really happy to have you in Jerusalem,' said Egerton, smiling at Kit's erratic movements.

'I'm happy to be here, I've never been before.'

But there were hitches in arranging her, or their, happiness. Christmas week was a busy one. Official calls had to be paid, several to Jews and Moslems to reassure them that the Mandoub was not inclining towards what was after all the smallest minority in the country he was delegated to rule over. The Christians, retaliating as fiercely as though the gospel had never transcended the Old Law, gave as many dinners and lunches as they could be certain of acquiring the Mandoub's presence for.

'Rush, rush,' said Kit. 'But we'll squeeze you in, willy-nilly.'

And he did, it was the sort of activity he was good at.

'Little Kit,' said SHE, 'are you possibly *épris*?'

Kit smiled and waved and explained that they were a lady short and the girl had a sad time of it, Jaffa was . . . , and that if they asked the daughter of Mrs Larsson there would be trouble with all the other daughters of the Swedish-American community – Miss Alice possessing the pearl-like quality of being the only one.

'Well, but we can't ask her father without offending the Dean.'

'Father's busy that night, that's why I thought of her.'

'Ah, Kit, what should I do without you? You think of

everything.'

Smirk.

The real problem wasn't the father nor even shyness or unsuitability, it was one of clothes. This could not be explained or mentioned to Kit and he did not think of it. Miss Alice was not fundamentally vain; had she had anything approaching the income of the other ladies invited to the same evenings she would neither have spent as much, nor as unprofitably, on clothes and trinkets, nor thought of it. But to have only one possible dress for a dinner, when invited to five or six, all bundled together in the same week of one's life, at which she was bound to meet and be seen by the same people, or permutations of the same people, and above all, at which she hoped to shine in the eyes of a worldly young man – although she was not vain enough to refuse the invitations, she was not completely happy.

Then quite unexpectedly, Mr Rhodes said to her, at breakfast on the day after Boxing Day: 'My dear, I haven't given you your Christmas present yet. Since you are in Jerusalem the Golden,' he smiled a little, 'for the first time, I think you should choose something for yourself, as a souvenir.' He opened his wallet and counted out a couple of *majidiyas*, hesitated and added another.

It was the first time he had ever given her money as a present, or for that matter as a salary, or for any other purpose than a strictly circumscribed one of housekeeping. And in a way it was a chilling action, implying that he had had neither the time nor the imagination to think of something she might like.

However, it delighted her. It was, more than anything, what she liked at that moment.

'You can come with us, Alice,' said Lucy Snape. 'I'm taking the Visitors' ladies round the Old City.'

Jerusalem was full of Visitors, or Pilgrims, or Tourists, that week, depending on whether one belonged to an official or quasi-official establishment, or to a convent, or to a hotel. Whatever their status, they were generally a trouble, a thorn in the flesh of those delegated to care for them.

'No, really, Mrs Manning-Brown, I don't advise it. They look delightful hanging there in rows, but the skins aren't properly cured, the smell is ineradicable.'

'Well you see, Miss Gunterssen, the reason the Hebronites have such a generally – what shall I say? – *oblique* reputation is because they charge rather more than anyone else for goods that, er, are not *quite as good*.'

'I'm awfully sorry about it, Canon, but Mrs Reading simply insisted on buying it. I did try to dissuade her, but she said she knew you would like it. No, I don't really think Batanjian understands about sale or return, nor about customer satisfaction, it's his own he tends to bear in mind.'

Lucy was quite glad to add Alice to her charges. Not for long.

'Alice! You can't possibly be serious. Whatever would you do with it?'

'Wear it,' said Alice, holding it up before the small triangular scrap of broken mirror and bowing and curving to take in every aspect of the stuff held over her body.

'But you can't, I mean, *where*? At home?' Lucy had heard the Rhodes home was rather native in style.

'I'll mend it a bit and wear it to dinner tomorrow.'

The point about Jerusalem suqs is that – apart from their architectural and human beauty – you can find anything there. Could find anything, before the city was 'liberated' from its past as a centre of world pilgrimage and became a sort of delayed image of a 1920s Lithuanian slum. Christian pilgrims brought ikons and Russian silver and early nineteenth-century French furniture and silver-topped bottles in leather dressing-cases and odds and ends of Western jewellery; Eastern ones brought daggers and ancient muskets, needed on the hard road and discarded when the Rock had been reached, polished cairngorms and quartzes from the plain of Arafat, elaborate amber mouthpieces for narguilehs, inlaid marble plates, massive silver and coral necklaces from the Yemen, and any spare clothes they had, or that the dying had left, odorous of sanctity. Miss Alice had picked one of these, a wedding dress from the Hijaz, sky-blue silk inlaid with mirrors and embossed with silver thread so that the original background colour only glinted through like a sky overlaid with cirrus clouds. The little that showed was the colour of her eyes.

'Five pounds,' said the shopkeeper. 'Only for *you*, of course, and because it is so beautiful on you lady. I swear, on

80

my mother's head, that it would be seven for anyone else.'

Alice's face fell.

'Thank the Lord,' said Lucy Snape. 'It is *wholly* unsuitable and I don't know what Mr Rhodes would have thought of me had you gone home with it.'

'I love it, it's just what I want.' She looked beseechingly at the shopkeeper.

'Only for you lady, four and a half, and I won't be making any profit on it at all.'

In Jaffa Alice would have haggled, pointed out that a poor teacher couldn't afford, that it was a ridiculous price for a bit of finery, that it needed mending. But she was over-inhibited by the capital and a fear that perhaps they did not behave as in provincial cities. The people of Jerusalem, she had heard for years, thought they lived in the centre of the universe and that only their city conferred value on the world.

'I'll think about it,' she said regretfully and turned back into the street.

Tareq, beaming, overwhelmed, grabbed her hand. 'Teacher! Miss Alice! What are you doing in Jerusalem? What a joy.' He corrected himself. 'What an honour. Where are you staying? May I come and visit you?'

For a moment she didn't recognise him. He had filled out, the torso and cheeks were solid, fleshed, no trace of the fragile sapling. And he was much taller, or the immaculate white robe and turban enlarged him. Leaning over her, he smiled and smiled.

Shops in the suq are glorified cupboards, doorless spaces, niches opening off the street, which is often invaded by enthusiastic sellers spreading their goods across the passage-way for better viewing. The shopkeeper, separated from this reunion by a few inches, entered into it.

'This lady is your friend, *sayyidna*?'

'No, she is my teacher.'

In the Arab world the words 'my teacher' carry connotations undreamt of in countries where teachers are only another branch of the civil service, ill-paid and despised. The words imply a debt of gratitude that can never be repaid, a debt that only death discharges. Even 'my mother' or 'my father' are not so heavily loaded, since in those cases one can repay by caring for aged and helpless parents, who indeed generated one for this specific purpose, while one can never teach one's teacher, who laid the foundations of all subsequently acquired knowledge, wealth, success.

The shopkeeper bowed to Miss Alice. 'I beg you, lady, honour me, accept this little thing,' he glared at it, 'this rag. Let me add this veil that matches it'; he grabbed irritably at an immense cloud of paler blue gauze that billowed into the street. 'I had no idea. ... His teacher. ...'

'I don't understand, I still can't afford it,' and 'What?' said Miss Alice and Tareq together.

Mrs Snape, who now felt certain that all the tales of the Rhodeses' way of life were well-founded, took Miss Alice's arm and said, 'Alice, we must go, we shall be late for lunch.'

Tareq put out his hand at her. With his height, his glowing apricot skin, the metres of flowing white, he looked so much the Englishwoman's dream of the stage Arab that Lucy Snape gulped a sharp word back into her glottis.

'What is this? Anything my teacher wishes to have she shall have.'

'It is hers, *sayyidi*.' He finished wrapping up the glittering metaphor of the firmament in a worn and fraying newspaper, tied it firmly and tightly in the middle with a rough piece of hemp and handed the bulging sausage to Mrs Snape. Teachers were too exalted to carry their own parcels.

Miss Alice produced her three gold coins. Exclamations of horror and shame and gestures of pushing away such sordid methods of dealing.

'Give him two,' said Tareq and, as she hesitated, took them from her and handed them to the shopkeeper.

'May God send you back to me.' He sounded as though he meant it, the capacity for acting being the first requirement of trade, well ahead of book-keeping.

'But Tareq, I can't, he wanted—'

'He was cheating you, of course you can. Whatever you pay, it will be more than it's worth.'

'But he wanted – are you related to him?'

'I?' Contempt. 'Of course not.'

'So why?'

'Ah, Miss Alice, you haven't changed, what joy, what pleasure to see you here. Where are you staying? For how long?'

It was agreed that he would come and see her and tell her what he had been doing since his last apparition.

She was too busy telling him when not to come to ask him what he himself was doing in Jerusalem. Mrs Snape said nothing at all. The Visitors' ladies talked, as they usually did, among themselves.

At the gate, Tareq took Miss Alice's hand, held it in both of his and raised it halfway to his forehead. Then he bowed towards Mrs Snape and the Visitor's ladies and went away.

'And who was *that*?'

'Oh, one of my pupils.'

'Well I'll leave you to sort things out with your father. I don't interfere in your Jaffa stories.'

Nor as it happened, did Mr Rhodes.

'Tareq, was it? And what did he have to say for himself?'

That was that.

The children's party, which incorporated a gymkhana, was always held in the week of Christmas but never on a day that any sect could possibly interpret as showing a bias to one rather than the others. Its origins lay in some primaeval stroke of luck, when at least the three main streams had coincided on one starry day and the Governor of what was then OET had said, pinkly exuberant, 'Let's have a party for the poor little blighters, Aidan.' His successors had faced nothing but headaches ever since.

'Show me the calendar again, will you? There must be one day. . . .'

Somehow they managed, empire's demands raising the individual to the level of the task that faced him, and a children's party there was, without bloody riots, yet.

'This magician of yours, Farren? Still haven't interviewed him.'

'What about the donkeys, Abu Issa? We'd better have our vet look at them before some ass gets bitten in the calf and everyone starts yelling bloody rabies.'

'Ismail, please try to remember, I've told you so many times: no potted meats of any kind whatsoever. One whisper of pig and—'

'No, they *cannot* stable their mules in HE's garage, once and for all.'

'If the Jewish Agency rings me up one more time to ask how we are deciding the confessional mix I, in person, will abrogate the terms of the Mandate. Just tell them that, Giles, do you mind?'

'Look, enough is enough. If there's another word about the segregation of pissers, SHE has said she'll take off for a lively holiday at the Dead Sea. Got that, everybody? Just sort it out between yourselves and better segregate yourselves while doing it.'

'*Kit*. Your conjuror is the star attraction and where the devil is he? Do something, will you?'

'Yes, I am looking worried,' said Kit to Alice after he had charmed higher ladies. 'In a fit of madness I promised to produce a superior magician for their unspeakable party and now the man hasn't turned up and everyone is blaming me.'

'Well, where did you find him first? Can't you ask your contact to deliver him?'

'Egerton told me about him. He saw him peform in some benighted village and raved so that I thought of him for the garden party. And now Egerton says he hasn't the least idea where to lay his hands on the man.'

'Oh dear, what a problem. Is he still in his village?'

'The last I heard he was in Jerusalem, unless he had his throat cut on the way. Wouldn't mind doing it myself. Palestine is probably full of people who feel just as I do and who unluckily for me got their knife in first.'

Alice giggled and then stopped. Kit looked so serious about such a ridiculous, normal, contretemps.

'I wish I could help.'

Then Kit chatted of other, less humiliating subjects, showed himself in a shinier light and at last left.

The next morning, so early that in spite of being early risers most people were not yet down, Mrs Snape entered Alice's room.

'That man is outside, asking for you.'

'What man?'

'The one of the shop, of that unsuitable garment. He wants to speak to you. Perhaps he has thought better of it, even if you haven't.'

Alice finished dressing and ran down the stony stairs. There was no one in the entrance hall. 'He's at the kitchen door,' called Mrs Snape, leaning over. Alice went through the kitchen into the courtyard, expecting to see the shopkeeper, asking for more money for his magic dress. Tareq was standing there instead, smiling.

'But come in, come in.'

'They don't mind?'

She felt even more embarrassed. Of course they would mind: a man wearing a *qumbaz* was not to be shown in to the front of the house; even though it had been built for such a man, by others who wore the same clothes, it was now to be inhabited only by men in khaki shorts or European suits, or priests in robes that were the direct descendants of the *qumbaz*, but preserved from disdain by their long association with the West. All the same, she took him into the sitting room and en route asked the girl to bring them coffee.

'It's lovely to see you again, Tareq. What are you doing now?'

'I'm travelling, Miss Alice. Travelling all over the country. I didn't know it at all, and now I'm learning. I've been north as far as Beirut, and I hope to go even further in the south. Gaza, and then perhaps Egypt and along the coast to the ocean.'

'Yes,' said Miss Alice, 'travel is a great achievement, but how are you living? Are you helping your parents?'

'A little, not as much as they would wish. I don't earn much over my own needs.'

'It was such a pity, that story.' She was talking almost to herself. 'I had hoped you would find a place.'

'With the British?'

'Yes, Tareq. Something with a future, something to stretch you.' She didn't say 'where you would have worn western clothes and not have been treated like an illiterate'.

'I have found something with a future, and with a past as well, which is more than the government offers.'

'I'm so glad,' she said. 'Do tell me about it.'

The coffee arrived. Instead of handing the tray to Miss

Alice to offer her guest, the girl rudely placed a cup in front of Tareq.

After she had left the room he said, 'Well, I travel the country, and I talk to the people.'

'But what about?'

'I interest them.' He hesitated. 'I entertain them, and I then teach them or try to teach them while they are enjoying themselves.'

This was puzzling. 'But what are you teaching?'

He looked after the servant-girl. 'In a way, Miss Alice, I show them the laws of physics that Mr Rhodes taught me.' Again he hesitated. 'In a simple way. How they can be broken, which shows more clearly what they are.'

Miss Alice didn't understand at all, but she felt that to insist would be as rude as the servant's behaviour. He was no longer a shaven-headed little pupil.

'The shopkeeper yesterday must admire your teaching. I'm so happy with the dress, so glad you came by then. I'm going to wear it tomorrow at Government House.'

Lucy Snape entered the sitting room and stopped by the door.

'Alice, when you have the time, I'd be grateful if you could join me.'

Tareq rose and bowed. 'It was an honour to see you, Miss Alice.' He bowed to Mrs Snape and left the room to her lecture: 'Alice, I must ask you, would you mind not bringing people, people whom not everybody might wish to meet, into this side of the house?'

Lucy Snape was Challis' sister, although luckily for her she did not resemble him physically. Her colouring was the same, but tempered perhaps by hormones into an attractive foxiness: she had small pointed eyes and nose and lips and narrow wrists and ankles. Her husband was in the Church and she herself taught English in a CMS school for girls in the Old City.

Perched up here, watching the centre of the capital burn, the manifest idiocy of hatreds that do not even know their target, the whole story seems fairly simple, straightforward, except for two underlying mysteries. One of which is: why did Challis hate Tareq so fiercely? Follow him like my little hawk does a scrap of charred paper, floating up from the blazing offices, that he mistakes, skittering along the windy terrace, for a cockroach? Not that there seems, from what everyone has to say of him, anything of the hawk in Challis – a predator too, but an ugly one, repellent, hyena. Miss Alice doesn't know. 'His job, perhaps? Perhaps he just disliked him. It happens.'

Yes, but why? Her generation doesn't think in those terms, they were secure, no inflation or civil wars or the unbelievable crumbling of the whole fabric of life. They thought life was lived in peace, unless one was in the army; it never occurred to them they were laying the foundations of another hundred years' war, with its wreckage, mattresses and stoves and babies piled into wheelbarrows and pushed by stunned women from danger-zone to danger-zone.

It sounds a little silly: my explanation of Challis' hunt is a physical jealousy. One of those 'well-informed sources' once told me that the real reason for the insane British invasion of Suez could be traced to the first, unofficial meeting between Anthony Eden and Gamal Abdal-Nasser. As fatal as though Brangaene had offered the two men, or one of them, the potion of eternal enmity. 'And,' he said, 'if only they had met elsewhere, at some place where protocol required them both to be seated, it might never have happened at all. But in a private house, where it was all meant to pass as a friendly, non-official meeting of importance – Gamal arrived early, out of courtesy to an admired British statesman, and leapt to his feet when Eden arrived, coming forward to meet him with his hand outstretched, smiling warmly. He *felt*, you see, the correct attitude: Eden had a long and great past as a man, Britain had ruled Egypt for decades, whatever the rights and wrongs of that story, the representative of the new Egypt owed respect whatever the soreness among his people. And Gamal was always punctilious over debts of the spirit – let me show you the photograph, so touching, of him bent over double, kissing the hand of a tiny bowed old man who, stateless, penniless after the revolution in his own country had deprived him of even his civil service pension, had yet founded, before Gamal was born, an educational system to be used throughout the *mashriq*. It doesn't show in the photo, but he wept when the President of Egypt, the man who was then at the height of all his powers, leader of the Arab world, who had just accorded him asylum and a new, more generous pension, insisted on paying him homage before all the official photographers, so that he would be respected to the end of his days. Luckily for him, he died before Gamal. I tell you this to explain, not Gamal's generosity, although I think the British and the Americans were fools – but then, when and in what Arab country have they not been fools? – but his feeling towards Eden. A flicker of warmth, on the part of that 'Arabist', and the history of the Middle East would have been so different.' He paused and added, 'As you see, I'm no follower of Tolstoy. What did happen, when Gamal rushed up, like some great Kurdish lion-dog longing to be friendly and playful, was that, absurdly, he was *taller* than the Englishman. And bigger – he was a big man, shoulders, chest, with the habit of a massive man of bending down to others, as though to hear them better from a height they could not attain. Like the Sphinx looking over the heads of the crowds come to admire him. And Eden wasn't only a tall man himself, used to doing much the same, but was also accustomed to little Egyptians, fatly pear-shaped, balding, physically inferior. And here was this great thing looming over him, corporeally condescending to him, and young and radiant with life. And Eden had married a young wife. . . .' He sighed. 'It all sounds very silly, but you'd be surprised to find how often politics are played by silly men. The clever ones go into business or the professions, and the lunatics into the arts. I'm quite convinced that the Suez fiasco was a matter of inches, in one part of the body or another, and that's what I told my PM in my report.'

If I hadn't paid much attention to this at the time, believing in causes and ideologies, or perhaps just influenced by Tolstoy, it came back as a possible explanation of why Tareq had been so hounded by a man smaller, older, an ugly man, his surface too clearly reflecting his soul. The deepest reasons are usually physical: loathing the smell of a man, for instance. I sometimes think that one of the reasons Europeans and Asians are so baffled by the USA is the smell-lessness of its deodorised human packages. Our senses can't cope with laboratory scents, have no way of decoding them. Because at the start there was no other explanation. Tareq and his conjuring had posed no threat to the safety of the realm. Unless Challis himself had been the more far-sighted, the better seer of the two. Or unless every Palestinian was a danger to the British Empire once he went beyond eating and sleeping and stupefying himself with manual labour.

The Christmas party at Government House lasted all day in one form or another. It started at midday, with the grounds thrown open to the children. Under the straggly young trees various treats were placed, tubs full of sawdust in which treasures were hidden to be fished out with hook and line and screams, coconut shies, well-groomed donkeys in polished 'English' harness (leather, no blue beads or tassels or dangling brass hands of Fatma) to be ridden, a real camel, borrowed from the Bedu for the occasion, an open air cinema showing 3-D shorts in which custard pies were repeatedly thrown at the red-and-green-goggled audience, several large trestle tables covered in varicoloured paper and thick white china dishes of sandwiches, jellies, trifle and custards. There was a paper-chase and an archery stand (rubber-tipped arrows) for the little boys and a Karagoz puppet show for everyone. In order to save time, preparations for later, more adult stages (jumble stalls in particular) were going on among the pandemonium. A sad young lady, over-punctual, wandered around in a tiered and flounced pink crêpe paper dress, accompanied by a sulky little girl. The young lady's function was to offer, charmingly, painstakingly cut-up and numbered slips of paper which would later be drawn as lots, entitling the winner to a roast sheep which he would then be expected to offer to the company, having paid rather more than double its market price for the privilege. There were, however, no takers yet and the little girl, whose less attractive function was to ask for the money after the enchanted buyer had taken a slip, was busy following her leader with a pair of scissors and snipping triangles off the pretty pink flounces. On the other side of a field, preparations were being made for the gymkhana in which older children would compete after lunch. The wooden stage for the promised magician was already constructed, but masked at present by the cinema screen ('not SHE's damask tablecloths, my dear, use one of the servant's sheets, there must be one without a hole').

Dotted around, smiling painfully, stood the members of HE's staff, accompanied where possible by wives. HE himself had shot through once, patted any child he could catch, grabbed with relief an unfortunate member of the Arab Higher Committee whose children had insisted on coming and whose wife, even more persistently, had refused to unveil for the occasion ('but then they'll all look at me, Abu Faisal') and, saying loudly, 'Glad you could find a moment, Auni bey, something I simply must talk over with you,' had fled with his alibi-hostage into his study at the other side of the immense stone building.

At the CMS the ladies had divided up the day's tasks between them, as equitably as they could. Those who were invited to the dinner that night would shoulder the morning's burden, which was the heavier since it consisted mostly of native children; those not invited to the accolade would still be able to share, after the gymkhana, in tea, shading into drinks for the men, with many of those coming for the dinner. So Miss Alice set off at ten, carrying with her her evening dress, the scarf, evening shoes, her pair of earrings and a brush, a comb and a face flannel with which to prepare herself for the night. The journey was too long to be made twice in the same day after a tiring spell at the bran-tubs.

At past two o'clock she was free and eating sandwiches at the long table. Kit came up. 'He still hasn't appeared. He's going to let me down, just like an Arab.'

'Who?'

'My magic man. He's supposed to perform straight after the gymkhana. Or is it before? I can't bear to think about it any more.'

'I'm sure he'll turn up. He won't want to disturb you at lunchtime.' Alice was full of the comfortable happiness of knowing that her great moment was yet to come. A syce whispered to Kit, he ran.

Tareq was sitting in one of the pantries. He was wearing his white robes but not the turban. A tin suitcase, painted with blowsy purple and red zinnias, stood at his knee.

'Thank the Lord,' said Kit. 'I thought you were never

coming.'

'You told me not before 2 p.m.'

'Yes, well. Do you want a room to, er, change in or anything?'

'That would be excellent.'

Tareq's turn was after the gymkhana, to mark the end of the children's side of the day and give any awkwardly bridging adults a motive to stay in the gardens instead of charging into the house and dragging SHE from a few moments' rest. The sun had not yet set but in the east the sky was turning into the amethyst that preceded night. An immense planet, without a flicker of rotation, hung steady over the mountains of Moab and a slice of the Dead Sea showed cold and green. The shadows gave the landscape its characteristic aspect of being a maquette of the earth's bones, set up in some universal museum of geology.

Tareq began his show.

Afterwards everyone agreed on one point: the first part, which lasted until nearly the end, was the usual sort of thing. Under the naked light bulbs strung between the insecurely rooted trees, the magician made passes in the air, produced the standard products to the joy of children while the adults, arriving or leaving or halfway between, paid little attention or stepped forward politely to choose a card he held out to them. They applauded each trick and went on chatting to each other.

And then he did something quite different. '*If* it was he,' Miss Alice told me. 'Or if it was done at all and we weren't all just victims of some mass illusion, a trick of the lights.' It had grown quite dark by then, except for an acid lemon streak in the west, and the stars were out overhead. Over the conjuror's white turban rose the huge immobile star – 'planet,' Miss Alice corrected herself; HE came out on to the flood-lit steps of the house, showered, talcumed, rested, ready for the next lap. The lights all went out and the star – 'so it couldn't really have been a planet, could it?' – flashed downwards, leaving a comet's trail over the conjuror's head. By its light HE was visible, stripped naked as he came down the stairs. He seemed to hesitate and some people said later they heard him cry out. Others denied this. Then the lights glowed on, the magician bowed, bringing his hand up from chest to forehead in the usual sign of ending a speech or a show, invoked the blessings of God upon them all and stepped down into the night. Not one pair of hands clapped him goodbye.

HE joined his guests, unruffled and amiable.

Several guests had seen nothing at all. Either they had grown tired of the show and turned their backs to it or they were impervious to whatever spell had been cast or nothing had happened to be seen. Unease grew as those who had seen sounded out, in as glancingly oblique a manner as they could, fellow guests who were quite uninterested in discussing a boringly run-of-the-mill galla-galla man.

'It spoilt the dinner, really. Though everyone made a tremendous effort and of course several guests had arrived much later and heard nothing.'

Alice herself forgot or stopped thinking about the scene. Her dress was admired: 'I've never seen anything so beautiful,' Kit told her. 'If only these old hens would dress like that, instead of their eternal gamboge lace.' But he said it absently, the courteous young ADC there to please and reassure, while his mind was on serious matters. At table she was placed next to him and watched him grow gloomier as the end of dinner approached. 'O Kit, please don't look so sad.' The first time she had called him that. 'It'll all be forgotten tomorrow.'

He looked at her. 'You saw it, did you?'

'Well of course.'

'No "of course" about it. I've done a spot of checking this evening, you'd be surprised how many people didn't see a thing. Most of the women, to start with.' He gave a snort that was meant to be a laugh. 'Perhaps that, that *man* spared their modesty. Can't insult the ladies. It's odd that you should have seen it . . . not even married. . . .'

'Perhaps it's because I was his teacher.'

'You were *what*?'

She explained, while Kit looked at her with real attention for the first time that evening. 'Did he do this sort of thing in class?'

'No, no of course he didn't.' And then she remembered Abu Selim's boat. For a second she hesitated, thought better of it and said nothing. Kit saw the hesitation. After dinner, when the gentlemen had rejoined the ladies, he took her for a walk in the starry garden. Miss Alice did not detail it for me, but I gathered that his depression, his fear of losing his post, his self-pity, evoked hers and she admitted to him that she loved him. Or did he make a declaration? It would have been out of character for him to tie himself down to a penniless schoolteacher, however magical she looked in her Hijazi dress. I imagine that, after an anguished wail, she had burst out with some spontaneous indiscretion and he had probably kissed her and told her how beautiful she looked and after that Miss Alice assumed they were engaged and Kit assumed nothing of the sort.

Among those who had had eyes to see was Challis. He joined some of the groups of fellow eyes, listened to their perturbation as they moved slowly back to the ladies, stopping to discuss the experience in the high white vaulted corridors. He looked calm, but this was misleading.

'I don't say that clothes make a man,' Miss Alice said to me. 'This is a good town to see that, where the passion for expensive clothes and natty Italian shoes and gold cufflinks and sleekest of grooming never quite manages to hide the hollowness and, frankly, the criminality underneath. Whatever a heart of straw wears, it will never be mistaken for oak. But I do think that clothes have a ceremonial importance as an outer sign. It's hard for the young to understand how strict the symbols used to be, until not so very long ago. And it had a pleasant side. When you walked through the suqs you knew at a glance where people were from, which particular village as well as the region, and often you could see what they did in life. Their place in life, socially and geographically, was signalled very clearly because they liked others to know, it was a confirmation, an affirmation of a sense of security, of a meaning to their lives.'

'But not for the women.'

'O yes, just the same. The village women were splendidly dressed when they came to market, as proud as peacocks of their embroidery and its declaration of origin, truer than any passport. And the city women were swathed in black to make them invisible because they were not meant to be in the market-place at all, it was a come-down, it meant they had no men to do the marketing for them, so the black signalled, 'Don't look, I'm not here.' At home they dressed magnificently and were covered in jewels, because they were queens

93

of the house.'

'Um.'

'It's true, though. I don't think they were unhappier then than they are now. Perhaps I'm wrong. But you know, when the young dress in this extraordinary way, all jumbled up fancy dress and torn trousers and feathers in their hair, they're being just as accurate a reflection as the most pompous old dragoman ever was. They're saying as clear as clear can be that the beliefs and traditions of centuries have collapsed and that there's no meaning in the past or present any longer and that nothing matters any more. And the British dressed with such tight emphasis because they had to remind themselves as well as their subjects that they held authority and power over them and not a hairpin could stick out of place without suggesting a carelessness, an incompetence, that could undermine the empire.'

She gave her charming, young laugh.

'Really, I just meant to give you an idea of what a shock it was to see HE come down the stairs without his boiled shirt and medals and black patent-leather pumps, a plumpish man with tufts of gingery hair sprouting out of his armpits and stringy hams under his belly and. ...' We both laughed.

'You see, that was precisely why Challis was so worried. That was what he feared most of all, that the natives would start laughing at us. And you know, what made it worse was that HE naturally made no attempt to er, hide his nakedness. He just came springily down the stairs, smiling at us, and the men behind him, who had preserved their evening dress, added to the impression of some naked Parisian dancer escorted by a chorus of eager young men.'

Challis had cause for worry. Although many of the British had seen nothing, he soon found out that every single Arab present had – the servants, the housemaids, the syces, the chauffeurs. (He did not ask the one Arab guest invited to dinner.) He knew what this meant and he was right: the next morning there was only one subject of conversation wherever two men met in the streets of Jerusalem.

He also had cause for triumph. His promotion had been

confirmed and at the start of the second quarter he was to be transferred to the CID HQ in Jerusalem. Not yet as the head, but as the potential one. Neith was due for retirement, Challis was fairly certain of his own chances.

'Would you tell Neith bey I am here to see him.'

When he was shown in he saw no point in discussing their respective futures, or even referring to them.

'Good to have you with us, Challis.'

'Thank you, I look forward to Jerusalem.'

Then he went to work.

Like many men whose physical appearance repelled men and women alike, Challis could nourish hatred for as long as he had not had his revenge. He was too sharp not to realise that no one found his appearance of a gingery, hairless toad attractive in any way, but his knife-like resentment was kept for those who openly showed their disgust. One of his village informers had told him that Tareq had once referred to the ingliz policeman who looked like the yolk of a fried egg, bald and glistening.

Farren gave a lunch to say goodbye to the Rhodes in the Polish convent on the hilltop of the Old City. None of the guests referred to the High Commissioner's party, even indirectly. They talked of the CMS, of the Rhodes' school, of living in Jaffa as compared to the dry neurotic intensity of Jerusalem. Much of the conversation was as plain as the food, but after most goodbyes had been said Kit took Alice up to the roof of the convent for a private view. The city sloped away below them in serrated gradations of duns, pale ochres and gazelle-skin rectangles with vaulted domes faintly shadowed by the afternoon sun but still reflecting a glare that drove the eye to the darker lead domes of the more important holy sites for relief. The stone-flagged terraces curved with age, the Moslem homes could easily be picked out by their dense rows of earthen pots, spilling with jasmine and basil and rosemary, tight-furled little roses, so dark a red as to be blue, some superstition-defying frangipanis and here and there an un-happy little olive tree, cramped and sterile. A few cypresses marked ancient and almost overwhelmed burying grounds, but there was no park, no relief or assuagement for the smarting exhausted eye until the great space surrounding the mosque at the last corner of the city walls, when suddenly the fretful flood of material life was checked, reminded of another truth, before the bare and stony hills swept up and down again to the further mountains beyond which lay, uninterrupted, the deserts and steppes and the whole continent of Asia, looming over the last and first outpost of the spirit. It was a view that never failed to recall the circumscription, the puniness of human ambition: the intact walls, facing the wilderness, enclosing such a small noisy futility, delineating the other, the beyond, more clearly than any holy writ, causing a sinking of the spirit beyond any kind of salvation, or salvaging. Nothing so bare of hope, of illusion, existed on the coast, with its face turned towards the sea and its background of fertility and orange groves.

Kit, whose reaction was to fit a pair of sunglasses onto his little nose, thought it a lovely view. 'I shall miss you dreadfully,' he said.

Then he made a mundanely oblique declaration, overt enough for the girl to respond but not so explicit as to commit himself for ever. 'It has made all the difference, having you here, I don't know what I shall do with myself once you've gone.' There was a short pause and he added, 'May I come and see you when I can?'

Alice now entered that short blissful continuum that runs between the time when one longs, uncertain and hopeless, for the lover to come when called, and the longer period when he will do so even when one doesn't want him to, bringing nothing but trouble with his arrival: the brief moment when one is certain that he will come if called and still wishes him to do so. Not that she thought of that when she invited him to visit the missionary school as often as his duties would allow.

The British hung together. Whatever their individual foibles, idiosyncrasies or worse, the most that would be said was an uncertainly Viennese explanation. 'He's not really a thief, poor man: he just can't resist wallets ever since he saved himself from caning at school by padding his knickers with a billfold.' '*Poor* Laura, she never got over her father's remarriage, that's why one must take care not to leave her alone with anyone in trousers – and she's so short-sighted, poor

96

dear, which doesn't help.' The French have a better word than liar for Kit: a mythomaniac. Not a simple, nor a pathological liar, he created a situation in which he could move at ease, buoyed by a total environment as nourishing as water, however tangential it might have been to reality, which he called 'boring old things'.

His myth at present was his deep sweet love for a girl who could give him nothing of what he wanted, but whom, in spite of sacrifice, he was determined to adore, having recognised her nature when worldlier men (such as he was afraid of becoming for ever) would have shrugged her off with a 'charming'. The myth was at any rate enough to envelop and persuade Alice.

'I've never seen anything as beautiful as you the other night. They all looked like dried chick-peas beside you. How I wish, O Alice, *how* I wish you lived here, you'd do so much to pep them all up. And it would make me so happy into the bargain.' Then he hinted at how unhappy, golden appearances notwithstanding, he really was. This was more difficult. No incurable malady, no danger to be faced on the battlefield, no threat of poverty or unemployment. Still, he managed quite well. HE was an angel but had difficult days. Colleagues were utterly impossible and always out to get him, Kit. Things were turning sour in the country. 'They're all living in a fools' paradise, but you mark my words, Alice, things aren't going well and they may get worse.' All the responsibility lay on his shoulders, he saw clearly but no one wanted to listen to him. 'Woe to him who ...' and so on. If only he had beautiful Alice to listen to him and to shine in her starry dress it would be a comfort beyond expressing. Alice had never heard this sort of thing before, nor, I suppose, would she again. It went straight to her head. Her skin glowed, her eyes grew larger and the pupils darkened; she looked almost as lovely as Kit's description of her. When he politely preceded her down the narrow stone stairs he was full of earned gaiety and she of love. He kissed her respectfully but movingly on her cheek.

Alice was not a fool. She expected Abu Selim to lie to her if he felt it necessary and she knew enough of her pupils' parents not to be disappointed or surprised by deviations from a strict rectitude. But she did think the British were different and had a duty to show the natives another attitude to the difficulties

97

of life. Mr Rhodes and the little she had seen of the CMS missionaries had upheld this view. She believed all the words Kit had said to her and, more dangerously, the total pattern of feeling they seemed to weave.

After his triumph Tareq left Jerusalem, politely refusing the many invitations to perform that Arab notables sent him. He was honoured, he was regretful, he had urgent business in the north. But, in fact, he only went as far as the Nablus area, where he stayed in the guesthouse of a small village near Sebastaea. A line of minor Roman columns marched, more than half-buried in the ploughed loam, across the olive grove in the vale at the foot of the village; otherwise it had nothing to distinguish it from a hundred others.

The day after his arrival the mukhtar said to him, 'I know nothing about it. Nor does anyone in the village. One of the children will show you the way.' Tareq inclined his head; to show his readiness to spare the village involvement he spent the morning by himself in the olive groves.

In the middle of the afternoon, when the village men had returned to their fields, a very small boy came and stood silently before him. Tareq rose and climbed the mountain path behind him until they reached a large grey rock, precariously balanced on an eroded pinnacle. The child turned and ran back down the path. Tareq rounded the rock and saw a group of ten or eleven men, sitting on the ground. He bowed to them, they greeted him with respect.

It was nearly dark when he cautiously side-stepped down the goat track, planting a foot sideways against the slithering stones, and returned to the guesthouse, leaving the men sitting unmoving behind him. None was from the village. The next day, at the evening meal, he told the mukhtar, 'I should like to thank you for your hospitality. Perhaps the people would care to watch a few poor tricks to amuse the children?'

The mukhtar looked unhappy. 'We are honoured,' he said cautiously, 'the fame of the spells has spread through the country.'

There was a long silence. The village men gathered in the

room played with their beads, looked at the floor, shifted their hams.

At last Tareq bent forward slightly from the waist, his hand on his heart. 'Perhaps it should be another time,' he said slowly. 'They will wish to work until dark and I must reach Nablus before sunset.'

'For the sake of God,' said the mukhtar warmly, 'they will all regret it but it is true that they must be in the fields all afternoon. What a pity that it cannot be arranged.'

He left early the next morning. The women going to the spring to fetch water turned away from him. They would be able to swear convincingly that they had never seen him.

At the trial Challis offered dates and addresses and men who had attended meetings to prove that Tareq spent nearly a month in Nablus, giving no performances and living without money earned.

Then Tareq travelled. For several months he kept to the bony spine of hills overlooking the coastal plain. The villages here were strung along the ridge of the country on infertile eroded ground, their fields in the rich soil of the coast below. The villagers climbed down every day to cultivate the fields and up every evening, accepting the weariness for the sake of leaving every arable inch free for growth. Their pleasure came at harvest time, or just before, when they looked down on the wheat and barley coming into ear, bending in the gentle south-westerly that carried the scent of poppies and lupins up to them. Or the deep waves of orange blossom, sweeping up the parched slopes of the mountain side, cloying and heavy against the other symbol of the country. If you live among olive trees you discover that the trivial blossom does have a scent of its own, dry and powdery and curiously negative, almost an anti-scent that hovers behind the mind, cancelling stronger flowers, as its puny bitter fruit overpowers richer tastes. It brought no luck to Palestine to have two such wildly contrasting symbols of its nature, the austere, mythically gnarled reminder of time lasting, eternity, and the luxuriant green and juicy gold blowsy abundance of fruit and flower, simultaneity.

Tareq moved, zigzagged, from one stone village to another. He earned his keep by sharing in some of the work, though not regularly, since, he explained, he had to preserve the suppleness of his hands and wrists. He offered shows, to amuse the children. But their mothers came too and watched enthralled. They fed him, they begged him to stay on and not to move to an inferior neighbour. Sometimes he would throw the cowrie shells for a favoured admirer and prophesy a good husband, fat goats and a well-watered field. In the early days it wasn't noticed that favour usually went to physical grace, a fat-cheeked slanting-eyebrowed girl bouncing with life.

Challis, though, did notice. Born before the binary, his passion for tracking down, stripping the quarry to bare bones, undistracted by flesh, hair or least of all clothing, kept him sifting through, recoding, endlessly cross-referenced cards. His colleagues might relax with a recorder, plaintively piping through the astonished evening, or handle prefabricated cards, brightly coloured, in nightly permutations; Challis enjoyed drawing his steel chair up to the index file after his secretary had left, and browsing, playing through the subdivisions as though they were a solitaire. The man must be *something*, was what he thought. Not necessarily one or the other, most of the buggers are both. But there must be something, and it would trip him up. The women were too admiring, trouble could sooner or later be made.

His informers, who were as simple as the population from which they were drawn, had to be pointed in the right direction. 'Watch the women.' It was a tricky thing to do. A villager did not mind reporting on strangers who arrived for no reason, stayed too long and left. Since he had to share the burden of hospitality he might be happy to speed the guest even if it meant involving the British. He would earn money for doing so and save guesthouse expenses. But watching the women, apart from its practical difficulty – *how* could he do so without being accused of sin? – suggested dangerous possibilities. Watch his own wife? Or daughters/sisters/nieces/cousins or, if he was very young, his *mother*? Most men would prefer to abjure their unearned income rather than have it suggested that disgrace lay at hand. Those who accepted such work were often unreliable in character and information. Challis was lucky. The general strike was declared before he had solved the woman problem.

It began in Jaffa, but to Miss Alice it was just a part of the outside world, the irritating hindrances and foolishness that invaded real life, held it up, caused housekeeping and school-keeping problems. I have already said that she wasn't stupid; nor was she callous. The suffering, the daily problems raised by the strike were close to her daily work. There were many solid households in Jerusalem and Haifa and even in Jaffa to whom this was only a cause for more grumbling, already a way of life in prosperous families. The Rhodes school was linked to the port, the families of the port and the orange groves and the old city, and the repercussions were immediate: weeping mothers, and hungry children whose concentration levels dropped measurably. But all the same Alice didn't then understand what it meant. We would probably have been quite as impervious. It's only time that has shown us something, not our own acuteness. I never meant to impinge, the preeningly better-informed hindsight, but nothing has ended at all. I sometimes think that time has been caught here in some extraordinary spring-trap, and by spring I mean just that: a spiral coil that goes up and down as forces tread on it or walk past, so that we are caught until we can find the unknown release in a recurrently helical trap where the same events are touched off each time the coil is pressed down – a general strike, a revolt, a repression, a moment to draw breath and then crush, the weight comes down again, the rusting wires touch each other and off again into – I mean, two days ago I was supposed to go out and see Miss Alice again, to ask her some details about the Jaffa strike and its terrible consequences. Well, I couldn't, and I still can't. Because a couple of hours before I was due to set out a bomb was thrown – here, not in Jaffa, which doesn't really exist any more – in the largest square of our city, the one space that from a height might correspond to the Haram silence in Jerusalem but which here doesn't enclose a space for prayer and thought but an assemblage of all the cinemas, popular and élitist, and a hub for all the transport system that covers not only the country and the city but stretches to Aleppo and Istanbul and

Damascus and Amman and Baghdad and Teheran. But no longer to Jaffa. And the cafés and restaurants, and the flea market and the brothel quarter, and the gold suq and the lovely suq of anything you can think of from blue beads to axes and hosepipes and herbal remedies and live geese waiting for their throats to be cut. And all this came to a silent stop because the bomb hit a tram as it slowly and grindingly inched its way round the Gaumont Palace corner through the disdainful American cars that never give way to a tram. And its passengers, crammed sweatily and crossly, cursing the traffic and the drivers, were scattered in bloody lumps, many still clothed in a ripped sleeve or a glove, far and wide, so that even people sitting quite a bit away in the middle of their bundles aimed at a mountain village, found themselves hit in the eye by a purple jammy big toe, still surrounded by a leather strap, of a man in a hurry to book tickets at the Empire for Brigitte Bardot's new film, or, for all I know, hit on the toe by a brownish bloodshot eyeball.

And as a result there is now a general strike, separated by over twenty years from that very first one that was staged in Jaffa, caused by the same reasons. Of course ours is much more efficient: experience does help. When Abu Selim and Abu Tareq and Abu Hanna called their first, no one knew how to go about it, there was no union and no union funds, everyone simply stayed away from work and the food-vendors explained to the housewives that no food would now be trundled through the streets: the women would have to walk out early every morning to the city perimeter, carrying their household brass weights, to buy vegetables and fruit and meat and chicken. 'I don't see how this will make the ingliz change,' said most of the women. 'It's me, as usual, who has to do extra work. How can I give Abu Hassan his breakfast if I'm out at Salima looking for cheese?' 'Ah,' said the man who ran the vendors and who therefore ran the strike. 'But Abu Hassan can breakfast late as he isn't working anyway.' No woman asked, 'But why should I walk three kilometres to you and three kilometres back?' They said, 'If he doesn't go to work there's no money. Is there a strike on payment too?'

And that was the trouble. There wasn't.

But once it had started, no one wanted to stop. The reasons had not altered, the ingliz were taking more and more away of what had been so insufficient to start with. To stop would have been to admit that one was beaten, and who would be the first to make that admission?

So men grew poorer and poorer and their families suffered. If there is no work, no possibility of work, no self-enlightened attempts to prevent despair, the Minister talking and talking, the safety net stretched by the social welfare system which the ingliz were at last able to afford for themselves with the blood money of Palestine and Egypt and India and the Caribbean and much of Africa, then comes the gun. Rifles, flintlocks, old mother-of-pearl-inlaid yards of danger to the firer. The revolt. It was a very simple affair. Men who had never been to Hebron, even. No talk of Cuban or Vietnamese exemplars, no knowledge of the enemy. Pamphlets, commissars, cadres – undreamt of. A man would pay five Palestinian pounds for a gun, or unhook his father's immemorial matchlock from the wall, and tramp through the hills, looking for other men like himself. The extraordinary thing is that it worked for four years, by the end of which half of the largest imperial army in the world was bogged down in a bare, tiny country without natural cover or allies.

'He's in it up to his neck,' Challis told Neith. 'If he isn't actually running the whole bloody mess.'

'Mm,' said Neith. 'It seems to be fairly widespread, wouldn't you say? He doesn't strike me as that important, somehow.'

A subaltern district officer had been killed the day before on the road to Qibya. Challis began stabbing at the wall-map with his thonged leather swagger-stick.

'He was seen here, sir at 4 p.m. Tuesday. Afternoon,' he added kindly. 'Sutton was attacked *here* at 9.50 the next morning. Just as his car turned the bend to come up the hill. It suggests a lot.'

'It suggests to me that Sutton took his time about getting to work on field duty. *Nil nisi*, of course.' Challis was going mottled at the neck.

'All he had to do was go down this hill, spend the night in the valley and be up the other slope waiting for Sutton in plenty of time next morning. He wasn't seen in Qibya at all that night. So where did he go?'

'Look, Reginald,' said his superior, though not for long. 'If he'd been planning anything of the kind no one would have seen him within a twenty-mile radius for a week before. You know that as well as I do. If you ask around you'll find he was sitting peacefully in a café fifty miles away when poor Sutton got it. And joking apart, *was* there a reason for the wretched chap being so late? He should have started out at seven at the latest. Have you asked whether some petitioner turned up and held on to the hem of his puttees until the rendez-vous was set up? They're always late off the mark, the Arabs, even for assassination.'

'All the usual enquiries have been set on foot, of course,' said Challis stiffly. 'But you know, sir, he *is* quite involved in the general picture. I think these conjuring shows are just a blind for his real business. Wherever he goes there seems to be trouble.'

'Well,' said Neith in as reasonable a tone as he could manage. 'There *is* trouble anyway. It rather seems to me we're arguing about the chicken and the egg, and a piddling little egg at that. And we know that he's been at his conjuring for ages, don't we?' Both men thought of the Government House party.

'I'll look at his file, if you like,' Neith added. 'See if he makes inflammatory speeches while pulling the quail out of his sleeve.'

'He doesn't,' said Challis. 'He's not a fool. But he has a curious trick at the end of his show.'

'What?'

'He produces a hat and waves it around and then turns it into a keffiya.'

Neith burst out laughing. 'Really, Challis, what's wrong with that? It's the commonest trick in the book.'

'Yes, in other circumstances. But it does seem a bit subversive when the hat is a silver Homburg with a black ribbon round it. Just like the one HE always wears. And the keffiya is what all the rebels wear.'

'You mean he's suggesting they'll defeat us?'

'It always gets a tremendous hand. I'm told the women ululate when he waves the keffiya in the air.'

'I said all along it was extremely foolish to ban it, but no one would listen to me.'

A month or so earlier, the British had passed an emergency decree banning the wearing of the keffiya and ordering the arrest for questioning of anyone seen wearing it. Until then it had been worn mainly by peasants, but on the morning following the decree the city Palestinians appeared in the streets of Jerusalem and other main towns defiantly wearing the headdress that hitherto they had looked down upon as a sign of poverty and backwardness. In the face of these multitudes the police had been unable to arrest anyone at all and the order had been silently allowed to lapse.

At last Neith agreed to authorise a CID watch on Tareq.

'Just for a month, though, Challis. You know as well as I do how thinly we're spread. If nothing turns up by the end of the month you'll have to call it off.'

Challis agreed with pleasure. At any rate surveillance could not be thorough since the conjuror could hardly be followed on his actual journeys when he walked from one village to another through empty country lanes. The British had only just begun to build roads across the country, to facilitate troop movements, but few had been completed and there was still little motorised traffic. Nor could a stranger appear in a village without explanation, and even if it could be done once or twice, Challis agreed that it would be too dangerous to alert the quarry. A market day, or a performance commissioned for the celebration of a rich farmer's marrying off his daughter, were possible, and so were the larger villages like Qalqilya or Ramallah that were close to becoming towns. And the towns themselves. So Challis did not get the minutely detailed observation that his heart longed for. But he did learn something that seemed significant: Tareq often took a day and a night to travel a distance of six or ten kilometres. He would perform in a village, spend a night resting, leave the following morning for an announced, neighbouring destination, and only arrive the morning or even the afternoon after. Sometimes it took him two full days.

Challis ordered a large-scale and completely blank map of Palestine, with only the cities and villages marked on it, drawn on tracing paper. Once a week, usually after office hours, when the building grew quieter, he would pin this carefully over a fully detailed contour map that hung behind his desk and chart Tareq's movements. He used different colours for each week, and related them to a fairly complex key referring to outbreaks of violence, either before or after the magician's appearance, to the vicinity of Zionist settlements and whether these in their turn were known to be linked to armed groups, to the location of British army camps or to regular forays by British soldiers, to the relative wealth and poverty of the areas on his route, to the presence of known Palestinian politicians or social links with such. He placed purple dots at places where the man had vanished overnight, and, more slowly, vermilion ones where the CID men reported 'contacts with a woman'.

He kept the key locked in his desk, so that even when he was interrupted at his game no one else could decipher it. And he thought about it, musing over the streaks and moons that dotted it more and more closely and yet which never coalesced into a rationally consecutive pattern. He was certain that a pattern did exist. Challis was an obsessive: he arranged his papers and his pencils just so, his pipe jar so many centimetres away from his wife's photograph (which was there not because he enjoyed gazing at her pointed nose which had twitched into blurriness even at the studio photographer's but to show that he had a wife, wasn't a dubious man, or a gadabout, as though the thought would ever have crossed a single mind after five minutes' conversation, but then Challis wasn't sure), and like so many who had ceased, without acknowledging it, to believe in divinity, he had to deny anything, such as coincidence, the inexplicable, that might have suggested a playful power. There was an answer to the world, human, mineral, vegetable, if only one approached it tidily enough, with a tidy mind, and docketed, filed and cross-referenced its phenomena.

Here hindsight must break in again: what never occurred to him was a fact that every child learns today: the system is only as good as the questions you ask of it. And perhaps it isn't hindsight: had Challis' parents been able to afford, had they even thought of sending him to the universities of his time, he would have learnt the lesson of Delphi – if you don't ask the computer exactly, precisely, what you need to know, the answer will destroy. Challis thought that myths were games for the rich, like polo or gin rummy, and that a Simple Man could show the Neiths and Farrens just where they got off.

So although he was right and there was indeed a pattern, he didn't find it in time because he thought of the wrong questions.

'Contacts with women' posed difficulties. It was natural that they should be frequent, women being prone to believe in folly and superstition. The CID men in the field proved quite incapable of sifting the wheat from the chaff, they reported every incident of mothers or grandmothers bringing sweet-meats and eggs to the magician, every telling of a fortune. Challis issued a new directive: only women under twenty-five need be watched. But he was forced hurriedly to amend this in the flurry of bewildered questions, and after one man, who was withdrawn immediately, had actually asked a girl how old she was. 'Young women but not children' brought better results, but although the conjuror enjoyed talking to them there was apparently no more to it than that. Nor did any village men complain of indiscreet behaviour.

Then Tareq began to speak. At first it was difficult to pin down sufficiently to interest Government House. The glancing allusions to those 'who loved their honour,' or their country, or even their home, proved to Challis beyond any doubt that the man had dropped any pretence of loyalty, that he was agitating against the rule of law. To love one's own home was to run against imperatives of British policy. Government House did not exactly disagree, but as an aide pointed out at the Club, it would be difficult to protect, defend such a charge in Westminster. Where men, drawing their comfortable way of life from the indefensible, would actually refuse to defend it were concrete aspects to be drawn to their attention, or to their constituents' or worse their opponents' constituents' attention, by an irresponsible segment of the press. 'Disadvantage of democracy,' he said cheerily. 'Come on, Challis, you know as well as I do how many backwoodsmen would be happy to go for the jugular. Can't change it, so live with it.

'Of *course* I agree with you,' he said wearily some time later. 'And I can tell you, between ourselves, that HE thinks you're the right man for the job. But that's neither here nor there, is it?

'Look,' he said around midnight. 'I've simply got to go. Some nebi's day tomorrow, we have to be on parade at dawn. But do believe me, old man, you've got to produce something more damning. Get him to say publicly that all the ingliz should have their throats cut, something like that. Then we can move. The great unwashed get upset by blood, unless it's spilt by a Sten. Can't you arrange something? I thought your boys were up to all sorts of things under the rose. Or should I say the jasmine?'

Buthaina's father was highly considered in Anabta. He had multiplied the five dunums he had inherited after his father's death and now owned the land around the spring, two pack-camels to transport his produce as well as a substantial flock of sheep and a few nanny goats for milk and *laban* and cheese. His olive groves were well-tended and he had a light hand with pruning and harvesting so that his production of olive oil justified the installation of a small crushing-mill and he could deal with the Masris' factory, selling them his surplus for soap. From them he had bought a black woman under forty who had resold herself after a year or so of manumitted life; he had married her off to the vineyard watchman and then employed her to keep an eye on his daughters. Fortunate though he was, the poorest villager didn't envy him and no *hijab* against the evil eye was needed. He had produced three daughters and then, against his love, had married another woman for the sake of the future of his fields. She had duly produced a son, but the child had been touched by God, and after that Abu Hikmat desisted out of piety. So his hard work, his cunning, were a living example of the saying, 'Do not fear, God will always provide,' which was generally interpreted as, 'Don't exert yourself, all is futility at last.'

He adored Buthaina, she had all his spirit and none of his looks except for his immense radiant eyes and well-formed chin. Her cheeks were rounder than her mother's had ever been, and their flush burnt through the brown and her eyebrows slanted upwards like a falling star. She stood like a cypress and moved like a gazelle, in accordance with the most hackneyed and best-known lyric poetry. 'Is this your face: is it

the face of the crescent moon?' Every young villager sighed
the lines, aside, as she came and went in the village street.

She didn't do this often. Abu Hikmat only displayed his
material wealth in the ostentatious supplying of attendants to
his daughters. They never drew water unless the whim for
gossip seized them, they never picked the olives until the last
day of all, when they joined in the final spreading of the linen
cloths, and the triumphant ceremonial stamping of the
ground under the silver leaves, released and trembling with
air once more. If they wanted a new distraction, one of them
would appear in the wheatfields with the porous jug of cool
water and the bread and white cheese for their father's lunch.
The three would never appear until the giant mound of grain,
winnowed and crumbly, was to be measured and partitioned,
and at the end of the long tense day, arguments resolved,
allocations made, the harvesters, reassured that blood was not
to be spilt this year, would join hands and follow the waving
exultant scarf, weaving in and out of the stubble, heads and
knees bending to thank the earth as they sang to it, 'O you
spoilt one, O see the spoilt one as she smiles and beckons to
me,' before they left it to rest until the November rains. Abu
Hikmat had so often hummed it to Buthaina when she was a
little girl that she thought of the immemorial song as created,
addressed to her.

She did not even have to work in the kitchen gardens that
surrounded the house. She could order one of the women to
fetch her a bunch of purslane or coriander, to pick the lemons
which grew so near the kitchen that she could easily have leant
out of the small square window to reach for herself. Of course
she cooked; no prospecting mother-in-law would have finished the sweet coffee had the girl not known how to prepare
the long list of dishes that the groom expected throughout his
life, though she never went out on the early morning chore of
collecting scrubwood for the oven, nor did she pat the dung
into cakes that gave the bread its inimitable flavour. She
embroidered her seven dresses for the future, daringly and,
she thought, with more imagination than her sisters, but Abu
Hikmat had promised her that as the eldest girl, he would
send the two culminating dresses of the marriage week, the
ones she would wear on Thursday and Friday, to Bethlehem
to have the heavy silver and gold embroidery added by the

celebrated seamstresses of the town, so that they would last forever and generations would be dazzled by his love for his daughter.

All this was talk. Buthaina sat in his lap and listened and tossed her hair back conceitedly. When she was just past her twelfth birthday he sat her one night opposite him, on the other side of the manqal, and told her, 'Tomorrow, my soul, you must be very good.'

'Shan't' she said, secure in her favoured niche, unassailable in her father's love and prosperity and favouritism.

'My nightingale has been chosen, it is my greatest joy and will be hers.' The word used, while it meant joy in normal usage, applied to a female meant marriage – the keenest irony in the language.

'No! Shan't!' But she felt excited. Attention would certainly be focused on her for the next few days. And she had said the right thing. It would have been shocking to wish for marriage. Her father hugged her and carried her to bed, promising her the full moon, honey and fresh pink pistachios if she behaved well the next day.

The women came the next morning. After a time Buthaina was pushed into the room with a tray of sweet coffee and cold water. She placed it on the round straw mat and handed the cups around, starting with the oldest woman present. There was silence until she had straightened up again and left the room.

Black Hajji kissed her and kept her in the kitchen until the delegation left. Then her father came in, picked her up so her eyes were level with his and smiled and smiled. 'My nightingale,' he kept on saying, 'Nightingale, nightingale.' Then he set her down and left the house.

She got what she wished. All attention was centred on her. Hajji was sent, on top of the crates of olives on top of the camel, with the cut and sewn dresses, one of striped velvet, one of heavy silk, to live in the Bethlehem workshop until the last incrustation had been whorled into the material. She wept as she left, and the camel-driver grinned and grinned and repeated, 'Your joy, Anissa Buthaina, may I return to see your joy.' Her stepmother sniffed and sniffed and repeated: 'One would think Abu Hikmat had no other daughters. I don't speak of sons, of course.' 'No, don't,' said Buthaina and saw the flash of triumph in her stepmother's eyes. The woman had never held much position in the house since the birth of her son had made it clear that he was no heir. She was polite to Buthaina and the littler girls, there was no affection on either side, nor between the father and his wife. It may have been a bleak existence but there was nothing to be said against her and she was treated with respect in the village. Whether this was enough, or whether she had once been the pampered nightingale of another home, was not known or thought of.

The women came again and this time Buthaina served them lemonade after the coffee and when the oldest of them took her hand she sank to her knees and kissed the stranger's fingers and held them to her forehead, keeping her eyes fixed on the ground.

'How pretty she is,' said the old woman. 'Abu Ramzi has been blessed.'

Then she and her two companions cross-examined Buthaina, beginning with the housekeeping. Could she cook yoghurt without it curdling? Or did she have to add starch? Did it always clabber first time or did she have to remake it? Did the parsley she sowed grow too profusely? (Parsley grows better under a headstrong woman's touch, and is an ominous sign for the groom.) How long did it take her to kill a chicken? How long since her first menstruation? How many days? Did her back ache at all? Her head? How far back could she bend her finger joints? It went on; Buthaina quite enjoyed herself. She thought the old women mad, but what difference did that make?

Then they sent her away and turned to the stepmother, who had been waiting.

That evening Buthaina asked her father about the most puzzling feature.

'Who is Abu Ramzi and why has he been blessed?'

'He is your joy and he is blessed in having you.'

'But why do they call him Abu Ramzi?'

The groom had a son, Ramzi, who was a few months older than Buthaina. And two little girls, who were much younger. His wife had died the year before and he had no time to look after the children and anyway, a man in the prime of life, impossible to live without a woman. No, Abu Hikmat didn't know exactly what his age was and hadn't asked – what for? His mother wouldn't remember and the man himself was unlikely to know. But not an old man, of course not, he was probably even younger than Abu Hikmat himself and the little gazelle couldn't say that that was old.

Buthaina began to howl. She was terrified, frozen to the depths of her shallow little heart. 'I won't. I shan't.' Until now this had always been enough to win her father round. She elaborated. 'Don't want husband. Don't don't.' It was funnier in Arabic. '*Joz biddish.*' But for the first time she didn't move her father. He set her down roughly on her feet and when she continued to whine he cuffed her.

So Buthaina, quite correctly, from then on associated married life with beatings and sorrow, which was perhaps as useful a dowry as any her father later gave her. Because of course he melted when she gave in and promised her that her headdress would be made up of gold coins, 'not a single silver piastre among them, my little bulbul. And your mother's *hijab.*' Which was engraved on beaten gold and strung on a long collar of seed pearls from the Gulf. The bride would outshine any of her predecessors in the village. He kept his promise, and after a moment's tremor she climbed up on to the camel, clinking with value, and giving a small smile through her tears as she touched her jewels.

But they weren't to be worn in everyday life, and this was hard. So much so that one wondered why her father had seen fit to marry her off to such a future, unless his second wife had had more influence over him than Buthaina ever suspected. She, who had never had to go to the spring for water, now found herself obliged to rise at four in the morning. She milked the sheep, prepared the *laban*, on alternate days made cheese or baked bread. It was then time to wake her stepson and give him his breakfast before he set out with the flock for the day's shepherding. Then it was her husband's turn. He ate and left for the fields. Then she woke her two stepdaughters, washed their faces, braided their hair, fed them, slapped them if they were dilatory, took them with her to the spring. She couldn't send them on their own because they were too small to watch their step, could easily fall in and drown, and she would be blamed if this were to happen. They were too small and frail to be of much help in carrying the water back.

On normal days, not counting the terrible ones of laundry, she went to fetch water six or seven times before the *zir*, the water jar in the courtyard, was full for the household needs. Then she prepared her husband's lunch and took it out to the fields with a pitcher of water, waited while he ate and drank and brought the empty pitcher back. Then she gave the little girls their midday meal and ate for the first time since she had woken. Then she cleaned the house, brought in the sleeping mats that had sunned all morning, hoed and weeded and picked in the vegetable garden, brought in the vegetables, washed, peeled, pared, hollowed and chopped them and made the evening meal. Her husband came home at dark and the food had to be served as soon as she had washed his hands and feet and he had stepped up on to the dais that served as living and sleeping quarters. She trimmed and lit the oil lamp, served the food, removed it and washed the tray and dishes, combed her husband's hair, or trimmed his beard or pared his toenails or whatever other physical attention he required of her that night. The young shepherd boy returned late and was fed, then she put the children to bed, checked that the poultry were locked up, the goats fed, watered and tethered, locked the windows and doors and, at about ten at night, fell down next to her sleeping husband. In the summer, when the days grew longer, she made jam and pickles and preserves. In the winter, if there was a free moment, she sewed, darned the family's clothes, the pillows and *lahhafs*. Her plump smooth hands grew gnarled and the joints swelled. Her cheeks fell in and lengthened.

The midwife miscalculated by about a month when the first baby was due, laughed at Buthaina and told her she was too impatient, like all of them. So Buthaina returned home and squatted on a heap of household cloths until the baby came. She cut the cord and bathed the two of them and oiled the product, swaddled it tightly and then lay down, leaving the tight little mummy in a reed cradle she had made the month before. She had prepared the evening meal before giving birth and when Abu Ramzi returned he sat down to it with the children, after greeting her as one does those who have returned from a journey: 'God be praised for your safety.' In some ways he was a decent man and he didn't blame her for the baby's sex, nor even make the traditional remark: 'A boy builds the house; a girl destroys it.' And when the little thing died after nineteen days he stroked Buthaina's weeping head and told her not to grieve, there would be many others and the important thing was that she was not sterile. The others also died, although each lived a little longer than its predecessor. When the third shrivelled away, almost eleven months after its birth, Buthaina asked her husband to take her to a doctor in Qalqilya. Abu Ramzi refused. 'Whoever dies, dies according to God's will,' he said. 'And who lives, does so with God's permission.'

When the magician spent a night in the village on his way to Qalqilya, the women sang his praises at the well until, without a word to her husband, Buthaina took her stepdaughters to watch the brief, perfunctory performance he gave in return for the night's hospitality, and kept her eyes fixed on his face throughout, never wavering away to note the tricks of his hands, not even gasping at his triumphs.

Tareq was so unnerved by this unaccustomed brazen stare that he performed better than he had intended, anxious to attract her eyes from his own. She was beautiful, but he had no wish for trouble of this kind in a small village; he wondered whether she might not be simple-minded. No respectable woman in her senses would make herself so conspicuous. When the performance ended, she walked up to him, holding the little girls' hands, through the noisy excited children begging for more, just one more dazzling trick.

'Lord,' she said, 'I beg you to help me.' Above the children's starling chatter she threw her sorrows at him too fast for refusal. First the little girl, then the second little girl, all of seven months at her burial, and then, ah! the little boy, at whose birth Abu Ramzi had put his hand on her sweaty tangled hair and told her, 'This house is yours, the fields are yours and all that graze on them; all yours,' and he had addresed her as Um Mohammad for eleven months. 'Ah!' she cried above the din. 'I have been cursed. Take the eye from me, I implore you.'

Buthaina was now past sixteen and hard work and grief had fined her down, given her an almost citified beauty more entrancing to a travelled man than the full-cheeked imperviousness that constituted village canons. She had had the wit to wear her gold *hijab*, half-peeping out of the slit in her fourth-ranking dress, so that the magician need have no fear of spending himself for no recompense. And, to do him credit, he was moved by her sorrow, common, widespread though it was and though he knew it was.

'All is from God,' he said as insurance, although he was fairly certain of the reasons for the deaths. 'Ask for His mercy and He will protect you.'

'Mayhetakecompassiononus,' she said crossly. 'The eye is from wickedness and not the province of God. I am not a foolish woman, lord, nor an unregarded one. When my son lives I shall own a flock of sheep, and I am not an ungrateful woman either.' She twitched the *hijab* in case her prudence had hidden it from his eyes as well as from those of the village gossips, and Tareq's face twitched in response, though from a longing to laugh out loud and not from greed, as she thought. She was a lovely thing, did she really think he wanted a sheep or two following him on his peregrinations? But he liked unbroken spirits, and they were rare among such young women, were more commonly to be found among the older women, who developed character as their beauty faded. 'Woman, tonight I have business and tomorrow I leave. If you wish to see me again you must come to the guesthouse at dawn.'

'I shall bring your breakfast.' She was quite brisk, there was no problem here, some woman had to do it.

'Then tonight you will clip your nails and your hair, just a sliver of each. Have you kept any of the cauls?'

'Yes.'

'Then place the parings in the caul and wrap it in a clean white cloth that has never been used, and place it under your husband's pillow to sleep on. Bring me the unopened package in the morning.'

Enthralled, Buthaina carried out his prescription and appeared glowing at dawn, with her laboratory samples hidden under the loaves of bread baked with such hope. The tray was heaped with enough for ten conjurors.

'It must be done fasting,' he said gravely, 'then I will eat.'

From under his robe he produced a small brightly polished brass bowl, incised with names and prayers inside and out. The flat everted rim bore the self-disculpating invocation 'In the name of God, the Merciful, the Compassionate'; from the centre of the little vessel rose a stem on which whirled a brass jointed fish with turquoises for eyes, surmounted by two short stalks each bearing a tiny, unarticulated fish that could be whirled around to point in any direction. Over the central fish a crude approximation of a bird, as whittled to its nature's essence as one of the great white symbols of hope that fly through Braque's studios, spread its wings.

'Take this and fill it with water from the spring, not from the well,' he ordered. 'And bring it back without spilling a single drop. Every particle of water that falls to the ground on your way back will destroy part of the protection against the eye.' Most women, confronted with the bowl, carried it as attentively towards the spring as though it were already full. Buthaina, though, grabbed it as casually as any sieve and ran off as fast as she could. She returned radiant. 'Not a single drop.'

Tareq's heart sank. He believed her; the thought also crossed his mind that if she were lying then she was on the watch and that too was unique: danger.

'Our lady,' he opened, without any religious connotation. He could hardly call her Um Anything since she wasn't and that was her problem. 'My lady' suggested that she was his grandmother, tactless and unsuitable. He felt no wish at all to call her his sister, nor was she old enough to be addressed as his maternal aunt. Her given name was of course out of the question and even were they to become lovers would remain so (but he would then call her the daughter of his paternal uncle) unless they were to fall into outer circles of hell and behave like the foreigners. 'Our lady' was blamelessly correct.

Sticking to the soothing conventions, he then asked her some simple questions that, relating as they did to the crudest basics of hygiene and physical aspects, would contain nothing but reassurance, familiarity, to any of 'our ladies', so quick to shy at the superficial, at the breaking of titular rules. Buthaina explained in detail when she, how Abu Ramzi, where, by what means, and how often, how soon after, how soon before, how she had kissed the rags hung on the carob tree as well, how – there was nothing to surprise or take aback in anything she said. Tareq nodded his head solemnly, approving as she went along.

When everything she could remember – and she could of

course remember everything – had been described in detail down to the last poultice, he brought the bowl back to the centre of her attention and gently added her body parings to the spring water, not disturbing the surface. Holding on to the abstract bird he twirled the three fish in different directions, for all the world like a child playing, while he murmured words in which 'God' and 'Iblis' and 'Son' came up out of the submerged incantation. Then he gave her some simple instructions, first about the act, then about feeding and resting herself – *not* Abu Ramzi, he repeated as her eyes grew larger – then about the care to be shown to the future infant at birth, then—

Buthaina was genuinely astonished. '*I* have to rest? Who runs the house? Abu Ramzi?' They both laughed, it was the first flicker of friendship. Tareq loved, admired, Miss Alice, but they didn't understand or share each other.

He went on, as lightly as he thought compatible with belief: '. . . and then wash it in warm water, no, don't trouble about the midwife, by now you know as much as her. Only take care to boil the water. . . .' Then he dropped the subject, made a final pass of hands over the still water in the gleaming yellow bowl and told her: 'Pick it up, and carry it home without spilling a single drop. Every drop of moisture that falls to earth is a year of your child's life, and who is to know how water is measured?'

She looked deeply impressed, awe-stricken.

'The very first night of the new moon – not the second, not the third when all can see it clearly: the first, place this,' he took a minute scrap of red linen out of his hand, a scrap folded like an envelope, 'without opening it before, and shake its contents into the water as soon as you can see the crescent reflected in the bowl. Then *leave it alone*, on the window sill or the roof or wherever you have placed the bowl. It must not be shaken or stirred until the full moon.' That gave scope for mistakes, there was nowhere in a village house where a brim-full vessel wouldn't be bumped into sooner or later, butted over by an animal or picked up inquisitively by a husband or child. 'The day the moon begins to lose his fullness, as he rises, throw the water over your left shoulder and say' and so on. He went on, at ease in the assurance that something would be forgotten, and at last waved her away.

117

'Pick up the bowl now, our lady, and do what I said.'

Instead she picked up his hand and kissed it and pressed into the fingers curling back with horror a gold *majidiya*. Tareq looked at it amazed. What he could not know was that her father loved her and had given her forty on her dowral headdress, nor that she had detached two to pay him but had decided, while carrying the bowl, to pay the second only when the future child reached his second birthday.

He returned the thin embossed coin. 'Keep it until the child celebrates his second year. Then I shall ask for payment.'

She took it and bowed, picked up the bowl and left, walking faster than he expected with it cupped in her hands. She didn't stumble before she disappeared.

He thought of her more than once during his stay in Qalqilya, which was large enough to boast a woman of no repute.

It was a large meeting, since the responsibility had to be spread as thin as human resources permitted. Whitehall would not complain of its own, but the press, the MPs, could never be entirely relied on. The absurd, the short-sighted irresponsibility, hypocrisy, of those who wanted the fruits of a policy while salving their conscience in yapping cries of outrage when they saw the pruned branches on the ground, irritated them all but no one spoke of it ever. They simply protected themselves in silence and this meeting was another manifestation of the bullet-proof administration.

'It should be Jaffa,' one of the younger District Commissioners had advanced. He was nervous that they might pick on his own area, notorious for trouble-making and unlikely to improve after lessons.

'It must be Jaffa. Everyone will understand the reasons and it's important that there should be no doubt if people are to learn.'

'And what are the reasons?' asked the Chief Secretary gently.

Several men began talking at once.

But there was little real argument about the choice. Jaffa was a symbol of trouble, it was where the General Strike had begun, its old city was a haunt of thieves and bandits (which was what the British called the people, maddened by a persecution they could not fathom into a despairing rebellion) and so lawless that the police feared to enter its crowded narrow alleys in which a man could easily attack them and melt back into the warren. Its notables and its press and intellectuals criticised the Mandate, often openly. At the same time, softened by the ease of life and the mild weather of the coast, by the easy fertility of the soil, the people of the town were less likely to over-react than those of harsher towns like Nablus or Hebron, although some of the men at the meeting suggested that it might be prudent to choose a town less visible to the outside world than Jaffa. There might be adverse publicity, there were always rivalries between the Powers. These arguments failed to win the day. The French were the only likely candidate for trouble-making, look at what they had tried to do, in Jaffa itself, when the British were first consolidating their hold in the country. But the French had their hands full with their own rebels now and were much too busy to trouble themselves with Palestine. And to cut the ground from under their or any other spitefully impelled foreign power's feet, the move would be presented as an act of town planning inspired by a wish to improve, almost to beautify the city. Men's instinct for games is as strong in politics or war as in hunting. The main pleasure comes from tying a hand behind one's back and then, with immense difficulty and ritual, achieving an end that, had it any real use at all, could have been reached quickly and efficiently in a moment without 'rules'. The difference comes from lack of need: the hungry man shoots his gazelle, the satiated one sends up his falcon and races after it for a thrill. The British were in Palestine because their army had entered it by force and defeated the army of its former rulers. When the inhabitants rose against them they imported more troops and fought the 'bandits' with greater force. There was nothing to prevent them from punishing Jaffa without a piece of paper to show that they were right, yet they would not move without one. Perhaps these papers are the difference between civilisation and savagery and fortunately they are not hard to come by: the ruling power writes its own as and when the need arises and abrogates those written by the vanquished. In this respect the British were no different from the Turks whom they had replaced. However, perhaps because they were less frank than the Turks, they were faced with a quandary.

The Order-in-Council which would allow them, as nearly as made no difference with an underdeveloped and undisputatious people ('Thank the Lord we're not dealing with the Jews,' murmured the Advocate-General, who for once was being more sincere than prudent), to do what they wanted was entitled Palestine (Defence). But how to justify what they intended to do in terms of defence of a country not apparently threatened by anything other than their own policy?

'You must be joking,' I exclaimed, but in politer, more circumlocutory terms, when Miss Alice explained this. I had got out to see her again and was anxious to return before the road was closed again for days, as it might well be. But still she couldn't be serious. Not that I knew what she was talking about. Not, for that matter, that I knew Jaffa, before, during or after its destruction. But still.

Laws, apparently, are laws, at least sometimes. After a subcommittee had been delegated to come up with an answer, after it had failed and recoalesced with its parent like an amoeba anxious at prospective future microscope slides, after much irritable coordination with the administration and recalcitrant town planners who forgot their racial loyalty in their professional support of the picturesque, a compromise was at last reached and the Royal Engineers, shedding little lustre on the monarch whose patronage they boasted, were called in. (As anyone who reads can see, I'm quoting Miss Alice yet again. She seemed more irritated by their title than by other people's decisions and gave me her word – the word of an Englishwoman – that after the event she never again said 'God Save the King' without remembering the devastation committed in HIM's name.)

What the committee, helped by Mr Kantrovitch, a lawyer whose services were lent by the Jewish Agency, decided upon was a town-planning scheme that would improve the insalubrity of life as it was lived. Death introduced the oxygen. Great swathes were to be cut in the alleys that kept out the sun, the oppressive heat, and the British. Air and light, and as a spin-off the West Kent Fusiliers, were to be admitted. And were.

Challis, for reasons of his own, found the way out. It read: 'The Government is about to initiate a scheme for opening up and improving the Old City of Jaffa by the construction of two roads, to the benefit both of that quarter and of the town as a whole.'

Generous ingliz! Benefiting people so mired in their backwardness that they didn't grasp their luck. The pamphlet, unsigned, untitled, continued: 'The first steps necessary will be the demolition and clearance of certain existing buildings, which are congested and insanitary, and advantage is being taken of the presence in Palestine of Royal Engineers to begin these operations.'

'For God's sake, Kit,' said Egerton. 'Who thought up this rigmarole? Did you initial it anywhere?'

'I wasn't even asked to observe,' said Kit crossly. 'Why? It's a town planning thing. We've nothing to do with it. They're full of longhaired chaps straight out of Hampstead.'

'Town planning! There are at least ten thousand people homeless as a result and the Jaffawis are giving a figure twice as much as that before they begin on the ones whose houses are cracked from ceiling to foundation, leave aside the windowless. What the devil do you mean by town planning?'

Kit moved things – mainly assorted flints – from one side of his table to another. 'They're going to get compensation.'

'*Kit*. I've got to write something about this for the rag. Have you been to see? Tell me something, for HE's sake. For God's sake. What compensation?'

Kit reshuffled. He found a paper and passed it silently to Egerton who read aloud: '"This preliminary work of demolition will be punctuated by frequent detonations and crashes of falling masonry and residents should not be surprised, misled, or alarmed when they hear these noises."'

'Misled is good,' said Egerton. 'I must use that.'

'Oh for God's sake stop being such a bore.'

Egerton went on reading.

'"Government" – that's you too, Kit, isn't it? – "intends to proceed with a scheme" (I like scheme, the *mot juste*) "to open roads and carry out improvements", um, um, yes. "This scheme" – they like the word too, do you notice? – "includes the demolishing of several houses" – *several*, for heavens' sake, what would they call it if it *were* in Hampstead? – "for which appropriate compensation will be paid.'' Appropriate to who, Kit? The Jewish Agency? They're trying to buy up cheap and having trouble?'

Kit threw his cushion at him, playfully. 'Stop it, you idiot. We'll quarrel if you go on like that.'

'Yes,' said Egerton, 'I think we might. Let me just read you the end, since you don't know what it's about. I'll leave out some fruity bits; but listen to the coda: "The law-abiding inhabitants of the old city will not be injured, but if any resistance takes place, the Military Forces will use force to carry out the work.'' You're absolved of one thing at any rate, I know you'd die rather than use force twice running like that. So you didn't write it. Approve now you've heard it? In particular the bit about law-abiding citizens not saying a word when their homes are blown up over their ears? Speak now, because I'm going to quote you for my own variety of rag, which I'm beginning to think is cleaner than yours.'

They quarrelled, unboyishly.

'But you musn't get angry with *me*,' said Miss Alice. 'It's not only that more than twenty years have passed: we really and truly didn't know what was happening until we heard the explosions and saw the people runing to the school. They were screaming.'

I was angry though, and there was no one else to take it out on.

Everyone was convinced that the school wouldn't be blown up because it belonged to the ingliz anyway. As it turned out they were right, and that insalubrious street at least wasn't beautified. They came streaming into the room where Miss Alice was giving a history class, carrying whatever they had snatched up in their panic. The most striking in memory was a woman carrying a repellent *cloisonné* vase stuffed with feathers from a peacock's tail.

'Bad luck,' said Miss Alice. 'And she was killed in Lydda in '48, which shows that there's something to these old superstitions, doesn't it? I doubt that one dies for lack of taste, otherwise as Shakespeare nearly said, who would be alive now?' Say it in her defence: when she spoke to me we had all grown so accustomed to Palestinians having their homes destroyed that it seemed a career rather than a fate and ten thousand, or double that number if – what a big if – they told the truth, was too piddling a total to worry about or to sympathise with. Nor had people like us dreamt in our worst insomniac small hours that such a career could embrace anyone. That instead of the peacock's tail one might be forced to choose between the Laurencin and the Janina brocade as one raced into the night before the same occupying armies, the same explosions. And the same incredulous sorrow facing the indifference of the safe.

Challis, though, was happy. When the lines had been drawn on the map he had been present by right of office. And when the map had reached his seat at the table for deletions, comments, realignment, he had added a squiggly connection to Um Tareq's house, slightly beyond the accepted border of the old city but sufficiently close to pass without comment. So her house was blown up too. Later it was classified as among those rickety structures incapable of resisting the hundreds of pounds of dynamite used all around. 'Which proves that it was unsafe to live in and that we did well to get the family out safe and sound before their house collapsed around their dirty ears and they sued the municipality.'

Abu Tareq was already dead, a stroke while humping wheat sacks. There were still six children in the house and Um Tareq, improvident to the last, herded them to the Rhodeses' without having saved so much as a pair of shoes for the winter.

Alice didn't know what to do about them. She asked the various Moslem charities in the town, but they seemed to have their hands full and to assume that any responsibility that fell on a Brit's shoulders could well be left there. No one would help her and Mr Rhodes complained, obliquely but persistently.

About ten days after the urban beautification Tareq arrived. He walked straight into the kitchen where his mother was helping prepare the evening meal and without a word of sympathy, commiseration, or greeting told her, 'Pack your things, get the children ready and come.'

Um Tareq began shrieking at him. 'What things? What have you ever given us? Do I have a son or am I deserted? All my things,' she corrected herself, 'all our things have been destroyed. By the ingliz, you hear? Your friends. What do you do about it? Nothing, nothing. Look at these orphans,' she dragged out one or two cowed siblings who lay to hand. 'Look at them! Fatherless, brotherless. Orphans, orphans.'

'I am here now,' said Tareq softly. 'Pack up the children if nothing else is left and come with me.'

She went on shrieking, drunk with relief and fear of leaving a known roof.

'Lady, lady, give me something to clothe my poor babes. They have nothing left, they – ' Tareq grabbed her roughly by the hand and, a brace of infants' hands in the other, began pulling them out of the kitchen.

'Tareq,' said Miss Alice, 'you haven't said a word to me.'

He looked over his shoulder and said, 'No. I have to go.'

'It's not my fault. You know I have nothing to do with government.'

He half turned. 'Nor do these children, but that didn't save them. Tell your friends in government that they did wrong and it will not be forgotten.' He nodded and left, his mother whining in his wake.

Miss Alice was very hurt and her soreness lasted, although she told herself that he had some justification. Challis, who stayed in Jaffa for some time to see if the urban improvements would smoke out, as he put it, some of the outlaws, came to dinner informally with her father and herself and no other guests. She told him of sheltering the family and how Tareq had swept them away, she didn't know where. Challis listened with interest. 'Won't be forgotten, eh? I should hope not. The sooner they learn their lesson the more peace we'll have. He's a trouble-maker, your pupil, you know.'

'I think he was just upset at seeing his family in such a state.'

'Perhaps,' said Challis and gave his unpleasant laugh.

The next day he joined the Ramleh Vale hunt for a run with the hounds and the local Englishmen remarked on his exceptionally good temper, even though the hunt ended with failure. 'Can't be helped,' he remarked to a junior colleague as they trotted back to the kennels. 'Have to put up with it from time to time, no use being impatient. And as the song points out, from a check to a view, eh, Edmonds? And we know what a view leads to.' He touched his horse's flanks and set it at a low hedge of prickly pears barring some farmer's field. As he sailed over – Challis was a graceless but efficient horseman – his voice rose in joy: '. . . from a view to a *death* in the m o o orning.'

His hunter's instincts often ran true, although for some time it did not seem so.

Egerton wrote his article and there were some questions asked in the metropolis, some kerfuffle, said Challis contemptuously, and a Visitor or two came out to see for themselves, after a decent lapse of time to show that Mandate policy was not at the mercy of any rag that chose to make a sensation. By then the papers had found other subjects, Palestine not enjoying the capacity to increase sales, and things went on as before, except in the destroyed homes.

Unfortunately the bandits also continued, apparently more galvanised into activity than terrorised by the punishment of Jaffa.

Buthaina did not report her consultation to Abu Ramzi but she took to giving heavier tasks to her stepdaughters, who were now quite old enough to handle them. After the sixth month she left the fetching and carrying of water entirely to them and she told her husband that she felt too ill to chop the firewood or to bring his midday meal to the scorching fields. He made the statutory grumbles to show authority and took his meal with him when he left the house. Buthaina, who had never felt better in her life, developed the habit of eating well and lying down in the hottest hours of the day, giving orders from her couch to the two little girls and watching their every sweep of broom. Her labour was the shortest and easiest yet, although the infant boy was the largest and heaviest she had produced. Abu Ramzi was by now so pessimistic about her progeny that he did not wish even to name the baby; Buthaina called him Saqr, because the day before his birth she had watched a falcon wheeling, rising and falling and rising again, all through the long afternoon gold on the fields. She knew he would live, there was none of the puny-limbed weakliness of her other children, and she began discreet enquiries into the magician's itinerary, setting Ramzi to work for her, since the shepherds covered large distances and met travellers who never entered the village. At last she learnt that although the benefactor's whereabouts were unknown, his family was in Jenin.

She told her husband that she wished to visit her father and show him his grandson. Seven years had passed since she had taken leave of him, sobbing through the jewels, and since then only messages, distorted by the multiple carriers, had passed between them. Saqr was bursting with health and deserved his name, a real little predator; nothing remained unbroken or untorn within his fat little grasp. Except his mother's heart, which he had made whole again. Let his grandfather see him, it would be a kindness and, for all one knew, lead to future good. Her father was still, by their standards, a rich man and this was his first grandchild. 'Fourth,' said Abu Ramzi with more accuracy than tact. She did not care, she knew the eye had been removed from her and her only anxiety was to pay the debt before the disappointed sorcerer restored it multiplied by his powers. A Westerner might smile at the situation, jump to the conclusion that a lovely young woman married to an older man was contriving a tritely obvious situation, magnetised by a good-looking star with the kind of gifts designed to appeal to her lack of schooling, like the as yet unheard of bobby-soxers who squealed at the sound of an untutored tenor bleating words of utter fatuity. In fact Buthaina never thought even unconsciously of such an explanation, but she knew that unpaid debts were the origin of most feuds and trouble and she had no intention of allowing one to threaten the adored chubbiness clutching at her dress. Nor was she as unhappy in her marriage as externals would suggest. The lack of a woman-servant was a perpetual gall, and so was the fact that there was no spring or even well within the close perimeter of her husband's land. Apart from these daily reminders of a fall from Eden she was contented enough. Her husband treated her better than an unproductive wife had a right to expect, only beat her when he had serious trouble on the land or in the village – she had been black and blue for days when the November rains failed three years earlier – but even then he only used his hand on her, never a stick or an agricultural implement.

Perhaps it's because men are such inarticulately clanking suits of armour, incapable of letting a wrist, a nape of neck, express their sorrow or weak chinks, that women always seem the put-upon suffering vessels, quite irrespective of the individual case. It can't be because men impose a greater physical strength, brute force having been since the dawn of time admired and praised and, most of all, *proved right* in history. Whether called a mandate or a *mission civilisatrice* or a massacre. There are other reasons for the cult of the suffering woman; whatever their grounds one's sympathies go, unwavering after quarter of a century, to the image of the little girl sobbing on the camel's hump, delivered helpless to the bestial old peasant. But the truth was that not only did Abu Ramzi never have a chance: he was a sad man from the start. He had loved his first wife from the time they had played together as children, betrothed at birth when a baby girl was born to his father's brother, he had mourned her irreconcilably when she died, and only the unpalatable truth that he could not work the land and also care for their small children had bowed him into a second marriage. Buthaina's beauty and dowry didn't corrupt him, she was too young, too alien to his nerves and muscles; sometimes he felt that he had acquired a third daughter when two had been more than enough and, irritated into a worse loneliness, he beat her out of despair, crying silently for his wife who rotted away in the earth and left him alone to be envied for his fortune. He never spoke of her to Buthaina, nor to his daughters; the furthest he went in revealing his wound was once when he rebuked Ramzi: 'Your mother would have been disappointed.' But neither the boy nor the other members of his new family understood how deep had been the accusation. He knew that Buthaina – he couldn't bring himself yet to call her Um Saqr even in slow heavy thought – was up to something. But he couldn't find the springy conceit, belief in self, to track it down. She was a little girl, she ran the house well and was no more exasperating than another little girl would have been in her place. If he had known another language he would have said, 'Let lying wives sleep.' He permitted her to visit her father. Arrangements were made, the most respectable transiter on his way to Nablus registered the human packages under his responsibility and Buthaina took Saqr to her father. Since she had seen him last the galaxies had wheeled around. She was strong and full-boned, mother of a son who was to live, and he, the father of it all, had sunk, complained, wept a little with rheum lingering in corners of shrivelled eyes, repeated the same questions four or five times in an hour, and worst of all said not a word of his will, although he gave Saqr a gold-scabbarded dagger from the Yemen.

Paying her debt was simpler than she thought.

After a week at his house she explained it. The doctor who had by his skill allowed Saqr to grow into what her father now watched every morning, late, when he rose, had to be rewarded. She would visit his wife in Jenin and return in the afternoon. Her father hardly paid attention, dangled his *masbaha* at the baby, murmured, 'Yes, yes, go when you will.' She did and for the first time in her life entirely by herself. Neither baby nor husband nor marriage cortège, she just moved through space, as she did through time, on her own.

Jenin was smaller in those days, but it was still a town and it proved harder to find the magician than she had expected. She didn't know his name, and was too well-trained to describe him in any way that would have led hearers to recognise him. 'The man who cured my baby' did not lead straight to his house and the fact that she repeatedly asked for his wife delayed her more. At last, almost noon, someone suggested that she visit Um Tareq. The mother of one seer might know the whereabouts of the wife of another.

Um Tareq was more than interested. With the cunning of the chicken-brained, she recognised immediately a search for her son. Buthaina had again worn her *hijab* and its value went straight to Um Tareq's liver and lights. 'Welcome, welcome, enter and wait for him, he will return immediately.'

Buthaina waited, politely parrying, sipping coffee and mulberry juice, for two hours. She knew as well as anyone that business was not for wives. Then Um Tareq let slip her relationship, unaware of the revelation. Buthaina thought again. She could not spend the night in a strange town, the afternoon was moving on, a mother had the right to learn what a wife could not. She explained her business.

'You may leave the payment with me', Um Tareq said graciously. 'It has reached its destination.'

Buthaina was not quite certain of this. She also wished to thank the enchanter herself, to assure him that his blessing would never be forgotten. She thought a little. There were two *majidiyas* wrapped in the same scrap of red cloth that had ensured her happiness wedged firmly between her milky brown breasts. If she handed them over, might there not be a temptation to keep one and give only the other? If she gave only one, how to separate them without her hostess, beady-eyed, seeing the manoeuvre in the small room?

'Aunt,' she said shyly, 'it will soon be dark, I never thought so much of the day would pass before I found you. I came to Jenin alone, I fear to return so late.'

'The roads are safe, the ingliz are everywhere. Watching for the young men, but they may as well protect a woman.'

'The ingliz!' cried Buthaina, and her horror was genuine. 'Maytheprotectorguardus! I've never seen them. Once they came to our village and someone told me and I went up to the roof of our house and looked: I think I saw a Hat moving along, perhaps not. But I cannot travel at night if the ingliz are on the road. My father would never permit it. Let me sleep here till dawn, with your permission.'

Um Tareq was caught, there was no way she could refuse a direct appeal, and one based on such well-founded fear. She grudgingly unrolled a *lahhaf* and put it out to air in the late sun while the two women helped each other prepare a meal. She still hoped that her son would not return before the rich woman left.

But he did, arriving after midnight and knocking softly on the barred little door, cursing his mother who slept so much sounder than any village spy, or the ingliz themselves, however far away they were meant to be. The children never woke. Buthaina did and lay for a minute or so, thinking that some overworked neighbour was already up to prepare the day's chores, racing against their accumulation in a hopeless attempt to have completed all work before the night returned. Tap tap tap, *tap* tap tap, it was some woman pounding the dried ropey roots with which to wash a carpet, she recognised the rhythm, the density. Then she realised it was very close to her bare feet, nearer than any conscientious neighbour had a right to be. Then she woke completely and understood her chance had come. Still covered by the bedding, she fished out the hot moist red envelope, well stewed by now, and holding it in her fist padded to the door.

She unbarred it as silently as she could and slipped out of

the opening crack to find no one there. Because Tareq, when he didn't hear his mother's thumping steps, the bang as she thudded down from the sleeping dais, the complaints as she woodenly unlatched to grumble at him and his late hours, had understood immediately that he was trapped. The informers had lost their awe of him, the soldiers were within his home. He lay immobile, sheltering in the little earthen trench that led water, rain or soapy, away from the threshold, his white keffiya scrunched under his brown cloak to avoid reflection, and waited for the shouts and orders. The sight of a woman, her head veil slipping off her hair, silhouetted against the brilliant starred sky, baffled him as much as his non-appearance did Buthaina. She looked around the sky, he squinted, at toe-level, at the embroideries of her hem. As she began to retreat he lunged and caught her ankles, bringing her down fast enough to stop a scream. Then he felt upwards, over soft mounds that Um Tareq could not claim, to her cold cheeks. He neither recognised nor thought of – remembered – the weeping childless wife but he recognised a mistake and got up, leaving her terrorised on the ground. Instead of getting up at once and explaining, she began scrabbling feverishly in the soft dewy earth. Quite silently.

'What are you doing in my house?'

'I've lost them, I've lost them.' She swept her palms round and round, feeling the earth.

Debts of honour have to be paid quickly. Buthaina wasn't thinking so much of the value of the *majidiyas*, which she was able to replace, as of the renewed journeys back and forth and the extra debt of hospitality which might have to be added. And of appearing in the doctor's eyes as inefficient, incompetent, a hen scratching in dry dust for a mislaid egg.

If she had been a weaker woman she would have wept. As it was she cursed. Tareq, for once, was mystified by another person. Intrigued. He couldn't bear this feverish fumbling at the earth without an explanation and pulled her to her feet, 'What are you doing here?'

Then he began to laugh, still keeping the sound too low to wake ill-wishing ears.

'We'll find the coins tomorrow,' he whispered. 'Come inside, sleep. I will wake early and find them. No one will visit this house before I rise.'

They went back into the house and this time Tareq lay at the threshold and Buthaina slept on the platform, shovelling the children's bodies over to make room. He rose at dawn and found the red envelope immediately, opened it and looked, assessed the thin gold discs within, put them in his pocket and returned to lie down until his mother woke him, nudging his body with an astonished foot.

After they had eaten he walked his patient to the town square and saw her, with personal recommendations of safety, into her cart. She thanked him, formally, on the way, told him the baby's name, asked whether she could in future give birth without anxiety. He assured her that she could.

So she returned safely, her duty done and an impression left behind. And a reputation. An informer told his officer that the magician now brought women to his mother's house, shamelessly. And married women, according to the mother's boasting. They already knew that he was inclined to play, but this was the first time he had gone so far. And it was in the same week, two days afterwards, that he had made a dangerous speech.

'We've got him in sight now.' Challis restacked the papers with delight.

'I wouldn't cheat her if I were you,' Egerton told Kit. 'She's more serious than your strings of little Cookies.'

'But I'm *not*. She's so beautiful. She shines. It's such a relief, every time I see her again I give a great sigh, honestly. The boredom of this life. And I used to think it had a glamour. Look at this: "The Hon. Phyllida Merrillee will be arriving P & O September sixth"; you know I rushed to *Debretts* because it's such a pretty name, do admit – and guess, just guess, Francis, how old the Hon. Phyllida is?'

'Not a day under fifty, if you sound so disappointed. What did you expect? The pretty ones are always penniless daughters of missionaries.'

'I love her, she's so beautiful. But I simply don't believe that. Someone must have a pretty daughter, somewhere. And the odds prove that she must be young at some time or other, so why not in my time?'

'How much do you owe, Kit?'

'No more than lots of others. Don't be such a prig, mentor mine. I don't drink and I hardly gamble, but if things go on as they are I won't even be able to hunt, so don't put on that pained look. I know what my income is and I know enough not to exceed it by a guinea but it's a long tiring haul uphill and what on earth for? Everyone expects me to do my duty and it's a bloody sight more expensive than my income allows.'

'You are so beautiful,' and he sighed with longing. Their relationship now allowed him to run a finger round the curve of her cheek: Kit had been cleverer than many acquaintances would have thought. He had reached this stage without ever saying a word, a phrase, that would have compromised him in less flushed ears, while the warmth of his words had hoisted him to a sunny slope of confidence, filled with flowering alpines. He was in fact on his way to collect the Honourable Phyllida, and had arrived the day before to collect a little love en route.

Alice told him of whatever had happened to her since his last visit, mentioned her nagging worry over Tareq, burbled, fed him, waved him goodbye as he left for the port. He had told her of the Hon. Phyllida and her age, although he hadn't mentioned how he knew this, and she took it for granted that his work entailed tediously polite welcomes. Alice was not, then or after the fact, a jealous woman.

But in this case she made a mistake. In the Hon. Phyllida's train came Lady Camilla, young, presentable if one had no eye for structure, the daughter of one of the richest titles outside the Catholic hierarchy. And a second daughter, which made her the more available. Had Kit ever thought of it, he would have realised from the start that the higher he flew the lower down the string of siblings he could aspire to or attain. He hadn't, but now that he did, he accepted the fact. And his bride to be was the easier to get since she was followed by three other sisters, adding to their father's worries and rendering him more malleable by the year. Any one of them off his hands was a problem the less, and their ambitions dwindled as they grew out of nursery ignorance into grasping the facts of social life. Farren, who had complained of never coming up against the right age of suitability, had at last fallen on his feet. Lady Camilla was the most sensible – the least impractical – of her nursery and she saw at once that he had a career of his own, laid down in the right lines, and abundantly open to improvement by her satisfied/relieved father and sole brother. He was sufficiently close to her own background never to offend her friends and sufficiently beneath her to feel a silent gratitude for the rest of their married life. She swooped.

'I didn't hesitate for a moment. I knew,' Kit told SHE triumphantly. SHE told HE and they agreed that this showed their perspicacity in selecting or at any rate keeping Kit on as ADC even when he had gaffed. They congratulated him and gave a well-chosen little dinner to confirm the engagement before Lady Camilla sailed again. Kit didn't tell Alice a word. She went on thinking, in a blindly presbyterian sort of way, that they were involved together in some livelong adventure of the spirit and flesh. But as she was a discreet woman no one else knew of it and so no friends came forward to point out her mistake. Egerton had outraged his own reticence of nature too often in his working career to feel any interest in opening private people's eyes, and he had, at any rate, taken himself off to the Lebanon in search of a story.

Although the contiguous hills and coasts of Lebanon and Palestine merged indistinguishably into each other and accents, food and customs resembled each other in the fields and orchards stretching on either side of the newly drawn border, there were differences. The first was recognised by Egerton's little hired Austin gratefully soaring over the smooth straight road which proclaimed its Frenchness with every tree shading the travellers' tired eyes. Egerton, who had done the road before, waited, refusing leathery eggs and brown slivers of floury matter in Palestine, standing hungry at Naqura to stare down the sheer limestone cliff into the churning waves, turned an intense blue-green turquoise by the erosion of chalk, while his papers were processed slowly and ungraciously by the Palestine side and then wittily and fast by the Lebanon side. As soon as he had crossed he turned left off the road and sat under a pergola of dried banana leaves, with the sea, now shallow and tame, frilling at his feet, and ate a grilled fish straight from the nets, with sharp triangles of fried bread and wedges of lemon and a bottle of iced araq to help down the salads of green thyme and marjoram, the fresh radishes, the whole pleasure of table as understood by Arabs and French, but of which the Balfour Declaration had deprived a people, before depriving them of home, work, hope and, ultimately, life itself. It is a noteworthy aspect of English puritanism that it thinks the softer things of life are bound to corrupt others, but never itself.

Another difference came from religion. The paradox is that the Holy Land was less obsessed by this form of human difference than its neighbour, known for its ease and luxury, purple living, for millennia. The various Christian sects in Palestine fought each other with gusto, watched jealously over their privileges as custodians of this, that or the other grotto or hill or curtain or window, but these battles were less than internecine in significance. Even the question of who was to wash the tiny pane of glass fixed immovably by some antique fool into the wall above the Grotto of the birth of the Prince of Peace led to the Crimean War, since the window itself (giving on to no view, admitting no air) 'belonged' to a sect protected by one European power, while to wash it they were obliged to place the stepladder on a piece of flooring 'belonging' to another power, thus ineluctably leading to the death of thousands in yet another country – even then the question had little effect on the lives of the people of Palestine, who for the most part paid no attention to the war, even when they had heard of it. Metropolitans, archbishops, cardinals and archimandrites might battle each other, but together they formed such a tiny percentage of the population that their disputes hardly rated a paragraph in the local press, devoted to matters of acute public interest such as the level of the water table or the olive harvest.

Things were different across the border, even though this frontier was a brand-new one, agreed upon not by the inhabitants of the respective 'countries', who had lived together in a generally acceptable state of muddle, feuds, local rivalries solved by elders and betters, for three thousand years, but by the powers whose running of their own countries was to be no example of shining concord illuminating the century. One power was Catholic, although it denied this at home; the other wasn't quite sure but assumed responsibility for whatever came first to hand. In their skirmishes for supremacy over other people's property both seized on local wishes and sharpened them to use as daggers in their own struggle. And left their lethal impedimenta on the ground when they finally went away.

Lebanon was different. There was no majority so secure in its tolerant observance of minuscule sects as to ignore their protests. Every sect felt threatened, and sometimes was, by another. They all spoke, publicly, of their respect for other monotheisms; they all refused to give an inch. And concurrently, they all tried to browbeat their internal schismatics into toeing the line. Lebanon was the joy of students of comparative religions and the despair of anyone else.

Except journalists. The lazy ones explained to their editors that it was all too futile, too mediaeval, feudal, backward, incredible to be taken seriously. The ones inclined to reflection, study, of their ostensible field of work, were sucked in by a world, a star, that reflected a light on their own past as well as on a future that the contented sheep did not care to envisage. Most foreign editors reacted fast and pulled out such Cassandras. What they called, in the fullness of their summer hay, a world war – meaning the world that they knew, which was smaller than the Arabian peninsula – had tried their readers and worn them down. Circulation rose with free offers of happiness, not with prognostications. Egerton was luckier than most in that his paper didn't think anyone read foreign dispatches anyway, so it hardly mattered what he wrote. It was just an alibi, might come in useful at some time or other, might not; made no difference anyway and cost less than the set of encyclopaedias they were offering to any reader who could remember the name of his own monarch.

The story that had brought Egerton north wasn't one with which he expected to make a headline, but a background, five-thousand-worder page three that could be filed, sliced, and used on an empty day, under a variety of subheadings – 'Religion, lingering on of', 'Arab world, backwardness of',

'Superstitions, worldwide manifestations of'. The assistant foreign editor not being a fool, he was as likely to pigeonhole it under 'Fleshpots, our correspondent's longings for', and indeed Egerton was sick of Jerusalem and the dry manias of all who lived there and their intensities and irritabilities and the sky that seared the eyeballs with its white light all day long and showered one with falling stars through the vivid night to remind any who was likely to forget that worlds fall out of existence without a whisper. He longed to sit in the hot damp mossiness of a bar on the sea in his sweaty sticky shirt, looking at the promise of coolness, the white icing on the mountain looming over the bay. To unwind, to be reminded of the infinite corruptibility of man, of the possibility of buying anything with a small creased piece of paper, grease rubbed into its folds. Of the ease with which life could be got through, from birth to death, if one threw concepts of honour, belief, dignity, into the garbage-sodden bay with the shells of the sea urchins, scooped out with a special silver spoon, but without a plate, since the sea lay all around.

The story wasn't new. A man had claimed to be different from other men. What man with a gram of spice to him hasn't done the same? The villages in which he had made this assertion had interpreted it, as they always had, in the way, the channel, in which their minds habitually ran. In other traditions they might have acclaimed or hounded him as a painter or poet. Or mathematician or philosopher. Or sociologist. All depended on time or place. In his context the claim was a simple one. He was a god, possessed of powers – just like the District Commissioner – that were neither apprehended nor analysed by the herd.

Egerton didn't make the future comparison, but the one with the past. In the steps of another came the new man, Man. It didn't matter whether one believed in his claims or not, it was a story, and a pleasant one to follow up. He stayed in the new hotel, cubic, squatly hideous and extremely comfortable, and sent off his letters of introduction to assorted grandees of the stagnant little town. Hospitality was quicker in response and far more lavish than in the dour highlands of Jerusalem and in less than a week he knew 'everyone' and their foibles and knaveries, and the striking beauty of their women. Lebanon posed a major genetic mystery: how could such startling loveliness give birth, generation after generation, to such hideous little men and yet again and again reproduce beauty in the women? However, the frog-princes were rich enough to buy whatever beauty they wanted and no one seemed to mind the incongruity except some of the younger French officers, who did their best to improve the strain.

Higher-up French officials did not, however, show much enthusiasm for Egerton's presence. Evidently he was there to spy out the land for his masters and would cover his real purpose by writing ignorant and hostile stories for his paper. The only 'story' possible was a comparison between the British and French methods of running a colony and the French way was too civilisedly subtle to be grasped by the British. 'Your roads are so good,' Egerton repeated defensively. 'I hardly mention the food since it would be sacrilege to compare the tables of Beirut with what we get in Jerusalem.' This always won a smile of satisfaction, but suspicion remained and was justified to the extent that Egerton would certainly tell what he learned.

He did some tourism and spoke of it enthusiastically after each day's outing. At the end of the week he announced that he was leaving, asked for and got an introduction to the archaeological mission based in Tyre.

There he was treated with the supreme lack of interest that the profession shows towards laymen and after they had showed him round their work they left him to come and go, only directing him not to miss Eshmun if he wished to write about Phoenicia. Egerton lazed around for a day or two: swimming over the sunken columns of the antique city; walking round the Turkish one with its narrow whitewashed alleys and blue doors and windows showing that Greece had left some influence as well as the narrow causeway; sitting in little cafés brushing off the flies. Two days were enough for all the inhabitants to have got used to the new foreigner, and because grass is always greener in another species of Mandate than one's own grievously parched variety, they welcomed him for the same reason as the Sûreté had cold-shouldered him: he wasn't French. On the third day he felt that his welcome in the café where he daily ate a midday fish was warm enough to chat to the proprietor over the tric-trac and coffee.

No, the man had not heard any stories. Anything like that was almost bound to take place in the hills, people there were backward and credulous and easily taken in by claims that a sophisticated city such as Tyre would laugh to scorn. He tilted his chair back and hailed the other clients as though they were separated from him by a mile of choppy sea. No, they all agreed, no such story. They asked Egerton some sensible questions of fact, which he couldn't answer.

'If this man came from Galilee, then why should he cross at the coast?' asked one. 'He would only have trouble at Naqura.' Everyone agreed.

'And why bother to come down from the hills? He would go straight across and find himself welcomed by those mountain ignoramuses without any trouble of frontiers or papers or police.'

'There was that wedding,' a small man with a rubbery face and an aura of brownness remembered. 'A really big wedding. Abu Rabie was asked to go to Ibl Saqi a week before to start slaughtering and skinning the sheep. And I heard he took all his womenfolk with him to help with the cooking and they were *paid*. With *money*,' he added, to bolster the wedding's unusual magnificence. 'If anyone invited your magician it would have been then.'

Other men had heard of the wedding and there was some discussion, centreing on what it had cost. One young fool chipped in with the price of a rutl of rice, suggesting that 'at least 2 would be needed for the stuffed sheep, and as they had ten sheep that would mean. . . .' He was shouted down with such contempt that he was never heard of again that afternoon. 'A feast like that and they would only use 20 rutls of rice? You think they are skinflints? At least 5 rutls per sheep, at least. *You* wouldn't know, you haven't married on so much as a goose yet.' 'And they used fresh pistachios with the nuts on the rice, Abu Rabie told me there was a sackful brought from Aleppo.' The list lengthened. Kubbi cost money, not only the richest cut of lamb but the payment for the women who pounded all day. And the sweetmeats and the incense. And the sugared almonds for the guests to take home. They had a lovely time, it was more interesting than the wedding itself, although the political implications of that were not neglected entirely. It was said the girl was lovely, so lovely that the difference in rank had been quite forgotten. The real question was: how had the groom discovered this beauty? And did it prove his flamy initiative or that his great family was petering out in feeble-souled heirs who were blinded by a pretty cheek and ready to sell their name for a year or two of fleshy bliss? The young fool, who often dreamt of that bliss, longed to defend it but didn't dare. Egerton said nothing at all and registered names and places. Three weeks ago, and in the mountain balcony that jutted over Palestine, covered with goatpaths like a creeper that neither British nor French could check: if the magician had entered anywhere, if there were a magician, this was where he would have entered.

The next day Egerton pointed his car's stubby nose up the steep road. He might have lazed in the capital, but social life offers names if not substance, and for a journalist if for no one else the one leads to the other. The mountain he was headed for was not so backward as to be deprived of great names, and these names spent enough time in the capital to be encountered as a matter of course. They spent, indeed, little time in the places that gave them their importance and led to their inclusion at the silky orangey-red dinner tables, glowing under the coast's sybaritism. Because these places of origin were pretty bleak even compared to Jerusalem or Damascus. A castle – 'Come and stay with me in my castle' – sounds splendid; but a castle is built of imperfectly morticed stone, cannot possibly be heated, is always erected on the peak overlooking the potential attackers, which means it isn't a snug little thing huddling into the mountainside for protection against the winter, is always owned by men who spend so much on armed guards that they can hardly afford to place a pane of glass in the dark stairwell, let alone generalised heating, and who have to entertain so many of the potential attackers so often that the only furniture consists of two or three hundred rickety frayed straw chairs and the same number of coffee cups, while the dream of a single deeply comfy arm-chair remains beyond the means of an amir. Seven or eight generations of this led sons to tatty nightclubs called things like 'Gloria' or 'Athena' where even if the curtains were ploughed with dust they were still made of a warming velvet that kept the chill out in winter and the mosquitoes in in the summer. Egerton had met them at these places, the unique version of champagne served there had led them to write out directives, remembering in sluggish veins the attitudes of a thousand years of ancestors; Egerton had nothing to worry about, unknown little upstart from the northern swamps whose parents 'lived' in a cubicle smaller than the bedroom of an amir's groom's assistant, and that only for the last fifty years or so – after the end of time. But an upstart backed by a gun, or a gunboat. As his own language had defined it, began by defining it: 'Terror: (1) Government by intimidation.' As though there had ever been another system, except during the collapse of strong central kings, or administrations. Even Egerton, disabused though he was, thought of it as a strong government, needed to restore order to those who inexplicably had loosed their grasp.

So he held, in the apology for a glove compartment, papers from the preceding aeons that passed him on as a successor, without thinking of what it implied for his own land's future. Just that they would ease him on his immediate way, as they did.

The balcony of Lebanon is precisely that, jutting out onto a not very wide view over the plains that lie immediately underneath. Any man of sense would assume that what lay there, at the feet of here, would, in the event of threat or dispute or faction, be hopelessly endangered.

'You see, Ajaltoun bey,' the mukhtar said, doubly triumphant, having got his tongue round such a funny name and turned it into euphonious familiarity, 'they are mad. We shall *sweep* down and then, like a thick broom, *out*. Not,' he added politely (to his own history? to what was to follow? out of simple well-fed tolerance?), 'that they worry us. They are welcome. But they are so arrogant. Lord Ajaltoun, we welcome everyone. Let them live with us and we will live with them.' As he had been accommodating the French and, sometimes, when they inched over the League of Nations borders, the British, quite successfully for over a decade, as his father had accommodated the Turks and, for a brief spell, the British, French, Austrians, Prussians and Russians and then, all of a sudden, the Turks again, and as he was still alive, he felt with some reason that he was talking sense. He was, at the time of his speech of welcome, accommodating the rather timid Zionists too. But they didn't worry him since they repeatedly told him that they too were fleeing from the terror of the *franj* and returning to where they had always felt themselves safest.

Egerton introduced the subject of the wedding.

A triumph. Nothing had gone wrong. The mukhtar wasn't sure why not, but the fact was that it had all gone smoothly.

Had there been entertainment? Yes, of course. It had been an important wedding. Not every day that a Shehab condescended.

Yes, but significant entertainment?

Naturally, a Shehab wedding would have a quality that others didn't, wouldn't it?

In what way would this entrancement be different?

Well, just *better*. As the bey would know. Quality was all.

And how to ensure better quality?

The bey was joking. You simply paid more, then the quality was better. Was the land of the ingliz different? Surely all the world was the same: you got the quality you paid for. Or not?

Egerton's problem was that he couldn't really gauge, or find out how others gauged, the quality of a sorcerer. Nor did he want to suggest that he believed in such a quality, because however airy he might appear he still at the last stuck to a national solidarity, a racial solidarity that presented a solid front to the outsider.

He did think, though, that if his quarry were to be found anywhere, this wedding would be the likeliest place. The café's patrons assured him he would be welcome, all the more since he wasn't French, and the owner sent children scurrying through Tyre to find and arrange for transport and guides.

The next day it had been organised, payment agreed upon, strings of connections established. And the following dawn Mehdi appeared at the archaeologists' house by the wide curved bay and helped Egerton pack the stuff into his little Austin. Mehdi was eighteen or nineteen, with a sweet rather stupid face and black hair that fell as soft and straight as a

Chinaman's into his long dark eyes. He was from Ibl Saqi, wished to return for a few days and his transport was his payment. In return he would sponsor the visitor, vouch for him as an intimate of Samaki's, and probably offer him shelter during his stay. The importance of this role silenced him so utterly that he could not bring himself to give directions to the amir of the machine and they spent a fair amount of time trying to find the mountain road. A road which showed a decent sense of shame in concealing itself. As they scraped over hummocks of clay to fall into potholes, or veered sideways into the mountainside to avoid the *bosta*, the high-built bus apparently made of tin sheets coloured red and green, soldered onto an apology for brakes and engine, which carried the post to remote villages, Egerton looked forward more and more to the stage he had dreaded while still secure on the coast, when they would transfer to animals for the really difficult stretch. It could only be better than the unending succession of hairpin after hairpin, so that even French enthusiasm for signposting the dangers ahead gave up after a dozen Zs had been placed on top of each other and left the rest to the driver's imagination or sense of consecutive logic. They went up sheer mountain-sides with the Austin whining and then, more frightening, sheer down the other side with the Austin galloping, until they at last crossed a narrow single-track bridge spanning a gorge and far beneath a foaming deep green torrent. Senegalese soldiers stopped them to examine their papers and note their names, slowly and with labour, in a large open folio spattered by rainbow drops. Here Egerton looked back and saw, away to the west, a glint of metallic water winking up at him to demonstrate that their apparently senseless switchback ride had carried them up hundreds of metres, out of the steamy ease of the coast. They drove on, skirting the looming shadow of immense quarried stones. 'The fortress,' said Mehdi who had recovered his powers of speech. Egerton longed to stop and climb, the view from there must embrace all of Palestine, it had to be Crusader, it had to control the lands stretching below. But he said nothing, this was the kind of wish that led all around, from Senegalese to guides, to suspect the foreigner. And the French would at once assume that he was spying out the land for a future war.

On and on, through bands of mist that drifted across the road and cooled the boiling car, past mountain-sides streaked with a soft golden light singing of dead ambition and futility, onto a plateau planted with fruit trees, cultivated in recognisably human furrows. A straggle of buildings centred on a large white rectangular arched house with a flat roof, dogs barking, donkeys braying, women screaming, proclaimed farmhouse. This was the staging post and although Egerton, when he had heard the distance in kilometres that separated it from Tyre, had protested against any need to spend the night there, he was now crippled and strained, wrenched by the unending drive and longed to lie down. He had been told the distance as an eagle flies.

The next day they switched. The Austin was stowed away, Egerton picked a small bay mare with a blaze and a lock of coarse black hair falling across her wide eyes just as Mehdi's did. Mehdi took a dunder-headed roan, with shoulders that stood so badly as to suggest a swayback, and selected two geldings to carry their luggage which Egerton thought of as packhorses. Mehdi had offered him one, a grey, to ride, but Egerton liked the looks of the little mare, spirited and sensitive. They left, as always, at dawn, picking their way carefully down another valley path into the night's mists. But this time they really did go down, and down. And down till the sun shone out in a heat unknown on the mountainside and they were walking soberly through the gorge of some unnamed stream, the golden face of one side of the cliffs rising high above and filled with small furry animals scampering in and out of little holes, clinging to the sheerness. Egerton could have sworn they were almost back at sea level, although the limpid stream glinting shallowly over friable purple and orange rocks should have told him better. They rode in single file, the packhorses between them, until the sun had crossed the gorge and lit the other face. Mehdi stopped the caravan at a small pool, hobbled the horses and scooped up some tiny blue-marked turtles that fitted the palm of his hand, then grilled them in their sweet little shells for their meal. 'Now we must watch for the tigers,' he told Egerton after eating, having repacked the flaps of bread and kicked the embers into the pellucid water.

'They can't tell meat from fish, they love anything that we

grill, they may come.' Egerton laughed. The comfort of lying in the baking cleft, of ceasing to ride on and on, the pleasure of the place, intense and pure with its sun and clear water and little beasts scampering, or paddling here and there to be used by the lords of creation, the smell of hyssop and round-leaved thyme, the deep deep silence and the frilling snorts of the horses, had washed through and through his fatigue and boredom and loneliness. In another place he would have visited a nightclub in the hope of finding this intoxication welling up, slowly but from some source so deep as to be ungraspable; in this place he didn't understand its emollience but he had no wish to move, ever, from where he was. He didn't mind talk of tigers, it was a verbal spice to be added, and if it suited the guide then let him rattle off traveller's tales.

He remounted the bay heavily, a slumping in the saddle that didn't come only from the araq he had drunk with the turtle meat. With or without an angel Eden must be left behind; the flaming sword is time, the setting of the sun, the chill of the western sky. They went on, climbing again. The araq drained out of his bones, his guide was no companion, the sun grew cool and the light dull. Egerton plodded on, the reins trailing on his exhausted mare's neck. Then something skittered across the pathless field: a leaf, a coney, a field-mouse? He never saw. The mare threw up her head, plunged it down again, the reins tangled in her forelegs and the bridle snapped. She stretched out her neck and galloped, Egerton clinging round her neck, flat and leaning forward.

'Don't gallop on stony ground,' yelled Mehdi.

Egerton had no breath to answer, but rage filled him. Couldn't Mehdi see? Did he think that Egerton looked as though he were enjoying himself? That Englishmen had no idea of how to ride? He kept both arms clasped round the mare's neck as they raced past an open-mouthed guide, silenced by the folly. Egerton's eyes were fixed on the ground, he saw every stone set in the earth flash past, sharp and killing. As soon as they grew less he would throw himself off, he knew that nothing would stop the mare's panic flight but a crash, although he kept on reassuring her in a whoa-ing rumble. The terrain was too dangerous, it frightened her more with every averted danger. Ahead he saw the rim of the plateau. It might stop her, or not. But the ground was still as stony, if not worse, he dared not throw himself on to it. They reached the edge, the mare plunged her forelegs into the soft earth crumbling down the slope, tried to swerve and crashed down on her side. Even though Egerton had slipped the stirrups off some way back he was caught half under her. The mare scrambled to her feet and stood quiet, panting. Mehdi ran up and tried to pull Egerton up. He was winded and remained curled up, then felt an agonizing pain and gasped with it.

'You must get up,' the boy said again. 'We can't spend the night here, the tigers will attack.' He tugged at Egerton's arm and the pain stabbed again. This time he thought he knew what it was. A broken rib, or two. Nothing else could be so painful to every breath, but it wasn't as serious as he had feared.

'Don't pull, I'll get up by myself.' He rolled on to hands and knees and slowly got up, yelping once or twice as the pain lanced. 'I can't get on a horse.'

Mehdi shouted with terror. 'You must. I'll put the bags on top of each other and you stand on them and mount.'

'Mehdi, there are no tigers here, there haven't been for thousands of years.'

'Then what eats the village goats? And what do the men shoot? I've seen the carcasses myself.'

Egerton shook his head. 'The best I can do is walk. And very slowly. And it's growing dark, can we reach a village in less than an hour? I'm not going to walk round the mountain at night.'

'On horseback it will take about an hour.' That meant at least two. Or more.

'I'll spend the night here, in the morning I'll feel stronger.'

Mehdi kicked at a stone and kicked again. His people were right when they said it was best to avoid foreigners, they led to trouble. Nothing would make him spend a night in tiger-ridden territory, but if the visitor were attacked in the night he would never be forgiven his desertion.

'Then I shall go without the baggage and with only one horse, and fetch men to carry you.'

Egerton didn't care for this at all. He knew there were no tigers in South Lebanon but there were certainly wolves and jackals and probably hyenas. And there was a Syrian bear, he knew, though whether it came as far south as this he didn't.

He wanted to lie down and sleep while Mehdi kept a fire going and watched through the night.

'You'll have to take two horses at least, in case there are none at the village. Or three, since you'll have to guide the men back. And no one will come with you until it's light.'

But Mehdi refused to take a second horse, saying it would only slow him down, and refused to stay. He did lead Egerton back to a shallow cave they had passed, which Egerton hadn't seen in his manic flight past, and settled him there, propped up on the saddlebags, with a stock of branches to keep the small fire going for a couple of hours.

'Don't go to sleep,' he told him as a farewell.

Egerton couldn't. The pain didn't bother him as long as he neither moved nor took too deep a breath, although it sliced him in half every time he gingerly added to the fire. But the blackness beyond the fire, and the sharp inexplicable noises that broke the silence as deep as the dark, and the horses' restless movements, soon wore away his assurance of being all right until help returned. He would have liked a drink but the thought of the pain of turning round and digging through the saddlebags to find the araq flask was stronger. He tried to write an article in his mind, some jokey feature on 'Phoenician nights' or 'Thirty miles from Tyre, Lost in the Past' that would appeal with a mixture of topical misadventure and dangers and a sprinkling of classical quotations to a more literary type of publication than his own; but the fire hypnotised him and he drifted into a night's day-dreaming until one of the horses – he couldn't see which – squealed and plunged at its tether, breaking the rope but apparently not going far. Nothing followed this but the memory of an ivory at Tyre, carved with the vividly observed scene of a large cat – tiger or leopard? female anyway – scrunching the cringing haunches of a horse whose rider, twisting supple in the saddle, tried to spear the predator. Squeaking like a bat, he awkwardly shoved another branch on to the fire. There was certainly not enough wood for the night and he doubted that the supply would last for the promised two hours. It had not occurred to him to look at his watch when Mehdi left and he now thought it must have stopped when he fell and then started again much later: it said only 8 p.m., which he knew to be impossible. It was the hour of the wolf – or the tiger – when the futile scrabbling of one's activities and lovelessness unreel repeatedly to screen the hopeless waste of a life. The horses whinnied and shifted, he heard something else moving in the black. No cat would make such a noise. It *was* a bear, one of those dusty moth-eaten animals travelling fairs dragged around with them in the muggy heat of the coast and forced to dance by prodding them with pointed sticks. They looked pitiful and sad, he had wished them free and was now to get his wish. Gasping with pain, he stood up, holding a burning branch in front of him.

A man appeared in the firelight and said softly, 'Peace. I have come to help you.' It was the Tarshiha entertainer; as he recognised him he also understood that this was the magician he had been looking for.

'You look well enough: the boy said your bones were broken.'

The tone of voice was more sympathetic than the words.

'I think it's only here.' Egerton couldn't remember the Arabic for ribs. The man knelt by him and felt his side with his fingertips, kneading very gently, When Egerton yelped he sat back on his heels and said, 'Certainly, a rib or two. Let me just see if there's anything else.'

There didn't seem to be and he sat back after his examination and threw another branch on the fire.

'Go to sleep, it will make you stronger for the ride. I will keep watch.'

'Why not start now? It must be nearly dawn?'

He still feared some wild animal, something. The pain would be no better for an hour of rest. It would be no better when they arrived in some god-forsaken village or cluster of lumpish huts, for that matter. He was ready to howl.

'It is nowhere near the dawn and I will not move until light. Sleep a little, you will feel stronger when you wake.'

And he did, in spite of his resentment at the imbecility of fate.

When he woke the fire was out and its embers kicked aside. The horses were saddled and the Tarshiha man was tugging at the bedding that had made his pillow. Without thinking, he got up. A stab of pain in his side, but bearable enough, he made no sound as he stood on two feet.

'I do feel better.'

'Good. Don't bend down and don't pick anything up.'

He finished packing the horses and then turned to Egerton, holding his linked hands slotted together by the mare's flank.

'Put your foot in my hands.'

For a second, less than that, Egerton hesitated. Fear of that involuntary pain, distrust of the mount. Loss of face was stronger and he did what he was told. The two hands, as solid as a mounting block but springier, hoisted him into the saddle. A memory of pain.

The magician mounted his own horse, gathered Egerton's reins over the mare's head and held them loosely in his hand. 'There is nothing to fear, she is exhausted.'

They rode off side by side, picking their way carefully down the loose scree, until they reached another narrow wadi, this one without a stream, when Egerton's reins were casually placed back in his hand and he didn't have the nerve to protest. Up another mountain path, winding round the steepness in the deep shadow of the western flank, the horses plodding wearily, snuffling a little. Out into the blaze of heat where the sun had struck an hour before and the hyssop, the wild sorrel and the finches were all expressing their selves in scent and song, then back into the pre-dawn shadow and the path was transformed into a wide muddy lane, a street sided by houses that showed in their construction where the stones had gone. Low and hostile, one-storey if not half a storey, beetling out at the outside world from their huddle in the lee of the mountain. A pile of rough stones, shoved into walls as they came to hand and plastered with mud, thatched with thorns and more mud.

'We have arrived,' said the magician generously. 'Ibl Saqi.'

Egerton thought of the stories he had been told, of the miraculous man, of the fabulous wedding, the feast, and laughed until a twinge stopped him.

They stopped at a house like all the others. A very old man, or a man too quickly pickled by time, hobbled out bent in two and helped them to dismount, unload, enter his domain. Mehdi was fast asleep inside on the living platform, but he woke and welcomed Egerton.

'I knew you were safe, otherwise I could not have closed my eyes. I shall order some tea.'

Which they drank. Mehdi, after the right sort of time had

elapsed, told Egerton how happy he was to see that the accident had not after all been serious. And Egerton, about to snap back sharply, understood that he had ridden up a steep slope on horseback feeling a perfectly bearable ache that did not prevent him right at that moment from stretching out his arm to have his cup filled again. A bruised feeling: certainly not a broken rib. He said nothing, but raised his cup to the saviour.

'The wedding festivities were over two weeks ago. Of course they never know anything in the towns. Still, wait another day or two to let your wounds heal completely. The air is healthy.'

A whole day and night, of nothing but boredom, had passed. Mehdi had disappeared, visiting cousins. Egerton and the magician sat on the platform with a cold smoky narguileh between them. Conversation was as ashy.

Then, in the well-being that one always feels after the cessation of acute pain, Egerton said rawly, 'You know, the reason I wanted to make this trip wasn't the wedding at all. It was because I had been told a miracle worker, a magic-weaver, was to attend.'

Tareq smiled. 'In these villages, anyone who has read a week-old newspaper is a seer.'

'No, but they said there was a man who did much more than that. Who found the lost. Healed the sick. Cured the . . .' and then he felt his intestines drop limply away from their moorings as he thought of his ribs. He stopped talking and stared at the wall opposite, which bore a commercially calligraphed injunction, no doubt Qoranic: 'Patience.'

'You weren't here to report on me to the British police?'

Egerton pulled his eyes away. He had been about to think something of importance. Patience: the root letters were the same as the word for prickly pears, though the diacritics were different. Arabic was such an enchained language, each link slipping through the next, that one was forced, whatever one's inclination, into the poet's musing on origins of meaning. Patience was as thorny to bear superficially and as sweet and juice-running as the fruit of the cactus? As good a guard against the attacks of the external? Or had he simply confused a hard S with a soft one? Sometimes when he thought of the language, so alien to his others, he was tempted to spend the rest of his working life evolving a mode of thought so different to his classically scholastic training that all fundaments would be undermined. But these moments passed as marginally as they came and left nothing behind.

'Why on earth should I report you to our police? Have you murdered someone?'

'You think that the only reason for us to be hunted?'

He shook himself back into a properly alert sense.

'You must have done something. The law exists for all, it's the one thing we have done, you know that.'

Tareq reached for the narguileh and fiddled. When it was alight he drew on it in a properly theatrical manner, saying nothing while the water bubbled and gurgled and he frowned at the pipe to show proper concentration on the real mechanics of living.

Egerton persisted. 'Tell me if it's not true. I can write anything I like.'

'Really? Or do you just think I'll believe you?'

One can tell a journalist anything, however insulting, without ruffling him if he needs your story, even merely as a footnote. Except for one thing: that he may not be allowed to write the truth as he sees it, believes it. Egerton went whiter than with the pain of broken ribs and realised the truth of the saying: impossible to treat an Arab as a friend, he always overstepped the mark. He pulled his feet back and remembered that even if he got up there was nowhere he could storm out to from here; insults had to be swallowed until the morning. Tareq did not apologise: he began to talk easily. It was a description, not a defence.

A month or two after Buthaina had paid her debt, he had passed near her village and, remembering the story, had decided to go there for the night's hospitality, guaranteed by his success. But at the entrance to the village he saw people, mainly women and very small children, too young to be at work in the fields, milling around, scattering like ants. An old man passed him, lurching on his trotting donkey which was covered by a bunch of tiny babies, clinging like grapes to an uncertain stem whipped by the dusty wind. Behind them ran a middle-aged woman, clutching two squawking hens under one arm while with the other hand she dragged, half-running, half-scraping on the ground, two older infants who were howling with terror. A large frying pan and a tin charcoal-firer clashed together on her back, strung round her neck over a *lahhaf* and a round straw mat. Tareq looked at them amazed but they passed him without a word of courtesy. They were followed by a flock of sheep and goats, indiscriminately mixed, and lolloping too fast for their udders, driven by a fat sweating man in the uniform of the Palestine Police, who rolled his eyes at Tareq and went on, 'rr'ing at the flock as he panted. A small lorry, with two young men hanging on dangerously to the flapping unsecured tailgate, shot past him, flouring him with dust, swerved through the panic-stricken flock (the policeman had dived into the ditch just in time) and disappeared, driving much too fast, round the bend in the lane. They were the only men of fieldworthy age that Tareq saw, outside those wearing khaki or navy, during that hysterical hour. He went on into the village where he was stopped immediately by a soldier, searched, and asked for his papers. As he showed them an old woman, without her head veil, her stringy grey hair appearing in public for the first time since she was a matted little imp, flung herself at the soldier's feet and rubbed her forehead over his boots, shrieking incomprehensibly even to Tareq. The soldier spoke not a word of the language anyway. He looked awkward and thrust the papers back at Tareq without more questions. Tareq left the old woman grovelling, all self-respect driven out by necessity, and went into the village centre. Here a few soldiers were grouped together round a pink lieutenant who was reading out from a piece of paper to a man who could only be the mukhtar. Whatever it was about, all Tareq heard was the mukhtar's reply: 'But sir, she was a government teacher, it isn't possible. Sir, she is retired, she is *old*. She didn't marry because she wanted to teach. She has no children. No other property. What will become of her?' The officer turned his back on the mukhtar and said something in English to the soldiers. Women were screaming all around. A furry baby donkey clattered through the little square, followed by a tiny child shrieking hoarsely at it. The pi dogs barked and barked and dust was everywhere, scuffed up by the purposeless, restless villagers. The soldiers saluted and moved away towards a house set back from the lane, leaving two of their men behind, holding in leash two police dogs. They kicked

the door open and went inside. The old woman, still bab-
bling, started to follow them but the mukhtar caught her arm
and pulled her back to the square, where some village women
surrounded her and led her away, scrabbling distractedly at
her pathetic, shaming hair. The soldiers came out of the
house and went back to the officer, who held the piece of
paper up in one hand, said something shortly in English,
which a police inspector had begun to translate into Hebrew-
accented Arabic when the hand flashed down, a soldier
pressed a plunger, and the house collapsed in a pile of rubble.

'It was so silent,' said Tareq. 'There must have been an
explosion of course but all I heard was this extraordinary
silence for a second or two. The shrieking, the arguments, the
barking, even the birds, everything had stopped. Then it all
began again and the dust drifted around and got into our
mouths and nostrils.'

He pushed through the crowd and went to look for his
debtor. A child pointed to the lane leading to her house and he
went on until the village petered out and the green large-
leaved herbs growing around lemon trees showed her bound-
ary. Buthaina was sitting on the *mastaba* outside the front
door, under the vine, suckling a son old enough to know
better. She couldn't bear to wean him. Her head-covering
had slipped back and her glossy hair showed, reminded him
of the grey-streaked dishonoured old teacher grovelling over
the dusty clumsy boots of the English soldier. As he came up
she hurriedly re-covered herself, made herself fit to be seen.
But she made no attempt to hide the feeding breast, exposed
from the root and with the milky-frothing nipple showing
more and more as the child grew sated and blew bubbles.
There was nothing forbidden, no erotic connotation, in such
a sight. But all the same, it was a lovely gland and she was
more beautiful with happiness than before. Unfilial thoughts
rose in him.

'Your presence lights us. Look at your success.' She drew
the child away with a little plop and tucked her breast back
through the nursing slit in her dress. 'Abu Ramzi is still in the
fields, but honour us.' This meant he could not budge from
the *mastaba* until the man returned, although she would now
disappear into the house to make coffee and fruit juice and ply
him at regular intervals until it was possible to return to the

kitchen and begin the immense unending meal of gratitude. He sat down, swaying his masbaha at the child, but she did not move. She asked after his health. After his mother's health. She replied. Yes, thank the Lord, they were in good health. The little one he could see for himself. Yes, and Abu Ramzi too. Yes, a good season, blessings on His Name. Yes, the olive crop showed signs of compensating for the year before. Yes, it had rained in time. Yes – and large tears rolled over her curved honey cheeks and dribbled down her neck into the round embroidery over her collarbones. Saqr went on grabbing at the beads, nothing serious could be wrong. The warm salty water went on flowing and Tareq stared down the lane at the village behind them, listening to the noise and the yells. He could hardly ask what was wrong.

'You see, Egerton thought, ever after, that this was the give-away. You know better than I do that journalists really aren't writers *manqués* at all, as the majority of people think, but detectives, spies of the heart, the soul, always watching for the chink in the underground armour, always ready to swoop on the weakness, the little furry snout poking rashly through the grass, twitching, betraying itself. That's why you like your hawk so much, isn't it? Because it's always on the alert?' She gave me another cup of tea and said, 'Not about things that really matter – you're going to over-run the curfew if you don't watch out – but about their *stories*, God help us!'

She was perfectly right and I drank the tea fast and said goodbye. At the door she added: 'After that one little sentence Egerton never believed in his otherness again. Forgot the oddities, forgot even the pain of his own ribs; just decided that had the man been, well, anything unusual, then he would have known at once why the girl was crying. I expect his feeling for her had probably swamped his gifts and he had just fallen into the calfish idiocy of anyone in love. Think of all the newspaper tycoons who make the silliest of miscalculations in that state, that's what I told Egerton; but he paid no attention, perhaps he wanted a purity that he had thrown away in his own life, at least that's what I think now. I could be as wrong as he was.'

Churned by the weeping, Tareq did ask. She immediately invited him to enter the house, as though she had been waiting.

The vernacular alters with climate, altitude, not according to the fantasy lines that Mark Sykes and Georges Picot laid down in the hallucination of empire. The house that Tareq entered, breaking all rules save those of the Mandate (but decency, convention and their opposites have never applied to the rule of terror, arbitrary force, the advent of violence in traditional society), was so similar to the one in which he sat describing his intrusion, pulling more and more strongly at the water-filtered nicotine, that Egerton saw the image printed, inflicted, on every household god around them. Ibl Saqi was built, externally, of lumps of stone and mud, its roof was not a perfect dome, nor was the stone hewn and abraded to turn gold ochre with the days of the sun, nor was the ceiling a perfectly arched vault that led thought to follow smoke to the centre of the firmament. But inside all was as it should be. The small entrance zigzag so that even were the door left negligently open no one could peer into privacy, the sloping, tiled squares before every room where shoes were sloughed with the mud and fatigue of the external day, the blissful reassurance of stepping up into intimacy, in bare or stock-inged feet, into the clean patterned space of domestic life, scrubbed and sluiced daily, the copper and brass shining like sun and moon, the carpets reminding one during the fearful flickering candle night of the elaborate, formal patterns of the garden's day; the solid wall of patterned silos, sculpted and curving and carved – more reassuring to those clinging to the rim of physical life than any book-lined wall in the cities of richer coasts – scented with barley and Persian rice and the pale gold of crushed wheat, all ready to pour down as soon as the painted bung was solemnly pulled out over the scoured red copper *tisht*; the great oil jar whose comforting smell re-minded the household all through the winter of the spring on the narrow terraced fields, with cyclamen sprouting from every laborious dry-stone wall and the babies rubbing their cheeks purple and red with anemones, the—

Tareq bent his head under the lintel, looked and forgot to slip off his sandals. It took some time to sort out. The main reason was that the cotton stuffing of the slashed bedding lay everywhere; even when soaked with the contents of the smashed olive jar, the white or grey fluff covered the floor. The silos were split, butt-thudded open, and the grain had disintegrated into a mash that lay soaking, sodden, on the carpets and clothing, inextricable, however devoted the washing. The pathetic contents of the *sini* cupboard – the few bits of china that every woman treasured in her home, kept out of harm's way in the specially carved niche – lay in a small heap, jumbled with the broken pane of flimsy glass that had been installed to protect them. A thick muddy river of lentils and beans and coffee, carried on the year's crop of olive oil, lapped at his toes which squelched in it. He bent down and picked up a disintegrating Qoran that came apart in his hands, reeking of kerosene. He dropped it back, onto the twisted (hammered with rifle butt) copper saucepans, wedged by the force of the blows one onto another. He picked up a rag to wipe his feet before retreating and saw it was densely encrusted, striped. It was Buthaina's very best dress, the one she had worn on the Friday of her wedding week. It was, anyway, too soaked in destruction to serve any more. Leaving the print of his toes marked in oil on the smashed mosaic he returned to the terrace. Buthaina sat in the same position, looking at the child playing in the dust. At least it was dry and didn't reek of oil.

'Abu Ramzi is with the brothers?' he asked.

'Abu Ramzi? Oh no.' She began to laugh and then immediately to wail, keening. He hit her, a full buffet on the round cheek and she stopped at once and said nothing, staring ahead. There was no way that the lost stores could be replaced until after the following season: they were insurance, life, for the winter months.

'But what did you do? You must have done something for them to come to your house.'

'It was a mistake. They were looking for Mahmoud Sheib. He has the last house on the road, like ours. But it was the other direction, on the western side.'

'And so?'

'When they found out it was too late. They left here and went and did the same to his house.'

'They'll help you?'

'No, they told me it was a mistake. The Jewish Inspector came back. He's a policeman. Not in the army. He told me Abu Ramzi can return, they have nothing against him. "You can send for him," he said. "He can return in safety." Return to what? How shall we live? They stole my jewellery. It was in the *sini* cupboard.'

She bent over double and began keening again but this time Tareq didn't hit her. He paid no attention and thought. Then he decided.

'I'll stay here tonight and help Abu Ramzi. We'll clean away the dirt. Tomorrow I'll take you to my mother, she has a house with two rooms, you can stay there and help her until we see what we can do. I have friends, I will ask them to help.' He was thinking of Miss Alice: she knew the English, they were her own, their sins were hers too. And she was brave.

'The dirt?' Buthaina had heard nothing else. 'The dirt is my life. Our lives.' She slid off the stone bench and crouched on all fours on the ground, beating at it with her fists. 'My dowry. Everything my father gave me so that I would marry an old man.' She thumped at the earth and her hair slipped, swung out from under her veil and beat too. In spite of its sleek thickness Tareq was reminded of the old woman, scrabbling in the dust at the feet of a red-faced man the age of her grandson. He knelt down and hoisted the girl to her feet. A hot smell of milky nipples and wheat and olive oil and terror rushed out from the nursing vents. He went on holding her when she had stood up again, breathing the smell, looking at her half-uncovered hair. Then he dropped her round elbows and stepped back, looking behind him. But there was no one.

In the event, there wasn't much Alice could do. It turned out that Buthaina was not the only innocent in the story. The old schoolteacher had also had her house dynamited by mistake. The dogs had pointed at it, but for the wrong reasons. The man whom the British were hunting appeared in Damascus and gave his own version of the story, citing enough concrete details to show that he had done the deed. The old woman was as innocent as she had claimed, but her house was a ruin all the same. Fortunately she died of pneumonia that winter and the burden of supporting her was lifted from the village.

Miss Alice did talk to Kit, quite indignantly. She asked him to use his influence to push an inquiry. Kit was in rather a hurry but indulgent.

'My sweet, these people lie as you and I breathe. They have no concept of honour. If we looked into every complaint there'd be no time for anything else.'

Presently he said, 'But Alice, don't forget that one of us was killed. *Murdered*. That can't just be overlooked, you know. Police do make mistakes, everywhere in the world. We're a jolly sight better than the French are, across the way, and I think people should try and remember that and put up with ordinary human error.' Then he said, 'Yes, well, I've got to run now. The governor's giving this deadly do. Nothing but your Arabs there, you'll be pleased to hear, so I expect I'll hear a lot more of the same.' And left, after a kiss on the cheek almost as chaste as that of any village intruder.

She was too undermined by a sense of soreness even to tell Tareq that she had tried. So he assumed that she hadn't and confided in her no more.

Um Tareq was at first quite pleased to receive guests. She remembered the gold *hijab* and the *majidiya*, she thought they were distinguished people, the kind who employed her son. Tareq warned Buthaina.

'Tell my mother nothing except that you are fleeing the British. Nothing else at all. And take care not to mention your losses.'

Buthaina understood perfectly. She told her stepdaughters and her little son to keep silent: there was danger. Ramzi had refused to accompany them, saying that a good shepherd could always find new flocks and that he had no intention of having a second stepmother telling him to take his shoes off. He said he would stay in the village and camp in their reeking home, although Buthaina suspected that he was in fact ready to join the brothers and that the calamity had pushed him into decision.

But although Tareq asked Abu Ramzi for discretion, in terms redolent of higher secrets, dark man-to-man business, it was useless. Abu Ramzi knew that had he only been at home when the contingent came he would have saved his house. He would have taken the officer aside and proved the error before it had been committed.

' "Coronel" – you understand,' he explained to Um Tareq, who was fascinated as never before, 'he probably wasn't a coronel at all, but the ingliz like to be called that, more than by the names of their sons. If they ever have any, that is.'

'Why shouldn't they?' asked Um Tareq, who genuinely wanted to know. 'Are they made differently?'

'No, but – ' here even Abu Ramzi hesistated. She was a woman of respectable years who by now certainly knew everything there was to know. That wasn't what gave him pause: a grandmother! Life held no secrets and the skin was far too toughened to blush. But he didn't as a matter of fact know enough about the ingliz, although he suspected. 'Even when they do have a son they prefer to be called coronel,' he said with authority. 'They are very different from human-kind, everyone knows that. So I would have addressed him as he liked, and explained. "Coronel, you do not know the east from the west," I would have started.'

'And this would please him?' There was no irony in her tone, only anxiety to acquire knowledge against an uncertain future.

'Not immediately, perhaps, no,' he conceded. 'But I would have gone on at once: "The man you want, the criminal, the mischief-maker, the man who says openly that the ingliz should leave us in peace, lives in the *other* lane leading out of the village, like ours, but on the *other* side." Then he would have been very pleased because they like to be called these names and I was giving him correct information which is more than that fool, that chicken-brained woman thought of doing although she is the mother of my son and in charge of my house and then he would have decorated me and made me a *ghaffir* and later I would have been mukhtar instead of which we are destroyed, ruined, thrown on the mercy of kind strangers and—'

Um Tareq had stopped listening. She had learnt two facts of importance. Tautology: all facts are important, come in useful, are better than a couple of chickens because they need little feeding and can lay fresh eggs after years have passed. She had learnt that her son had deceived her, used her. These people were neither rich nor influential, yet she had to feed them. Why? Perfectly clear. She re-ran the memory of Tareq returning flushed and glowing from his trip to Nablus. He had been pretending to be shining with the success of his performance, but that had been the night he had fished this incompetent pauper's wife out of some ditch and insisted she sleep in the house, next to his respectable father's wife. As a result she was the mother of a son, yes, but this old fool couldn't see a watermelon even if it split open before his nose. She said nothing but yes and no, absently, while he went on confiding until the child and his mother returned from their walk with firewood and food. And she said nothing all evening except, 'Please, take a little more of this, and this, and add some *laban*, or I shall think I have lost my touch.'

The next morning she slipped off and went to the grocer to ask for matches. Tareq would have been surprised at her capacity for deductive thinking. It went roughly like this: Now that the brothers are creating trouble for them everywhere, the ingliz need, must have, spies everywhere. Who is it here? The mukhtar, of course, by his function. Yes, but just because of that there were things that people hid or tried to hide from the mukhtar. Making one of those lateral leaps of imagination which in a happier country would have turned her into a successful entrepreneur, Um Tareq decided that the ingliz needed a man who saw everyone all the time, at times when they needed him more than he needed them. That was certainly not the imam either. The midwife? Possible, but restricted by nature. The teacher? Definitely not. So she threw the house's matches into the well and went to buy another handful. Neither rashly nor unthinkingly: O, how wrong Tareq was about his dam. She waited until there was no other customer before the shelf of wood which separated the grocer from his supplicants and then transacted her open business. One of the few necessities not fabricated at home were matches, she had nothing to fear.

'I've got him in sight now!' Challis picked his nose with as much abandon as another man might have carolled. He nearly ate the snot, he was so happy. 'A view! A view!' Two of them. The girl and her dubiously-born son were a minor possibility, useful as a back-up, like the death-watch beetle that gnawed its way, ticking as implacably as a metronome in memoriam through the furniture of the Jerusalem homes that resolutely ignored it as though it were a senile member of the family farting in front of guests. The major, the A-major theme, was

159

that Tareq had apparently lost his self-control after the devastation of the village. He had left his light of love and gone to Jenin, and there, in a town known to support the brothers, had incited the populace.

'You will all lose your homes,' he told the gaping audience which for some time went on hoping to see what they had all heard about, the hat turn into a keffiya, and felt rather disappointed with what they were getting instead.

'You will lose your fields and even the wells' – everyone shifted incredulously here – 'and you will never be able to rebuild them. You will be driven out. Unless you stand up now and defend yourselves even the names of your homes will vanish from the face of the earth.'

This was too extreme. The audience didn't care for it at all and Challis' network of informers was supplemented by a surge of unpaid volunteers, shocked to the core by such raving.

'He said we would be driven out,' an outraged baker told a tolerant assistant inspector who had been listening all morning to protests. 'He said that justice would cease and we would crawl over the face of the earth as far as our strength could carry us. And then be killed. He shouldn't be allowed to say things like that. Lock him up. You locked up Bassim when he drove his cousin's cart into the ditch and that was a mistake and it cost two goats to get him out. Bassim wasn't mad, just a little excited. Where is your justice? I shall begin to think he's right if you don't do something before the children begin arguing back at us.'

'He said the name of our villages would be wiped out of memory and that even the cemeteries would vanish. He is quite mad. People can't play with the forces of the jinn and not be affected. Stop him ever coming back to us. The trouble I've had with the children since that night. Stop him. Send him to Nablus, they're more used to madmen.'

'He said we are being played with. That the world is a lie. That we will live to see even the fields taken from us. And the trees. He said he was prophesying. My son *contradicted* me this morning. He suggested I was *wrong*. Are we living in this world or in chaos? Where is the government?'

'Sir, I have worked in the water office for fifteen years. Every day I check the tap in the square. And the level in the wells. In ten years I shall have a pension from the ingliz Sultan. I am not nobody. I tell you I cannot wait ten years while madmen are permitted to say what they like. The Turks were better.'

'A view! A view!'

Then Um Tareq came and the first warrant was torn up and another, for *atteinte aux moeurs*, written out.

'Much much better, boys. No one, nothing, not a single effendi lawyer, will defend him over this.'

No one had ever seen Challis in a better mood at the Sporting Club.

But Tareq had gone. The French were not over-careful about some stretches of their frontier. The British said that the French didn't choose to be, but, said the French, the frontier could be policed on both sides, so why blame them for allowing the quarry, which wasn't even their own, to slip through?

'But what *did* you do? I haven't quite understood.' Egerton was genuinely puzzled.

Tareq looked, rather slyly, down the sides of his nose.

'Nothing, I talked to them.'

'Why was Challis so excited?'

'I talked too truthfully.'

It wasn't – still isn't – easy to belong to a conquering people. Some sort of a bill has to be paid. Egerton's situation, independent-minded journalist belonging to the occupiers' race, was much the same as that of anyone living (but not residing) in a country whose taxes he doesn't pay. Providing that he doesn't overstep the limit, of time in the case of fiscality, of emotion in the days of occupation, all may be well. Involvement with the people he lived among was as fatal to Egerton as staying another week to spend Christmas with one's beloved would be today for the supertaxed. And, like the prudent rich, he never actually faced, let alone spoke aloud, the real causes for evasion.

'I wish I could be here. How I envy you, all being together. If only I didn't have to.'

Egerton didn't really understand and he decided that there

were too many inexplicables, too many loose ends to risk a story that seemed so incomprehensible.

So in the event, he wrote nothing, although he did send his paper a series of pieces comparing the two approaches to governing the Arabs, some of which showed the British in a better light than the French. These were published.

A minor possibility but serviceable. Challis set out on a little inspection trip, which as it happened included Anabta. He arrived there an hour before sunset and was duly offered lodging. After a meal whose lavishness was calibrated to balance the extent of damage in the village, discussions opened with the coffee. Abu Ramzi had fled, the man whose house had been the original aim was in the Moscobiya, the old teacher was a woman and would therefore have been ineligible even if she hadn't had a stroke the day after her house was demolished which had deprived her of the minimal prestige that someone of her sex, position and lack of family bucklers could ever hope for. So the men present were all able to speak with the weight of innocence, disinterest. Challis, who expected this, didn't mind at all. He listened and nodded and waited out the long silences and registered the omissions, louder than what was actually said. It was evident that in this region the brothers exercised greater striking power than the administration and that faced by a choice between alien power and son of the land, the sweet nourishing pith of life and harvest would not go to the first if it were weaker. He said little, although when the men rose politely to allow him some hours of sleep, he told the mukhtar that he would, himself personally, look into the question of admitting the old schoolteacher to some suitable hospice in Nablus, even though her pension might have to be increased to cover this. Although no delighted response was made he continued, scratching his neck reddened by the day of driving through the baking dusty roads, to explain that he would like, the following morning, to see for himself the consequences of the raid that his hosts had mentioned. He would like to visit the ruined homes.

'No one is living in them,' said the mukhtar. 'Except for the shepherd boy when he returns with the flocks, and he comes and goes without telling me.'

'Nevertheless, I should like to inspect them.'

So he did, blinking his stubby eyelashes at the remains without a word nor a twinge. These sort of events were the ineluctable consequence of a policy, and Challis was neither too weak in will nor in character to refuse to stomach what he earned his living by implementing. Force makes the world go round and those who resent the particular variety applied to them would do well to gauge their respective strengths before risking the happiness of the weak as well as their own lives. These people had not done so: the British would remind them of certain truths. The weak, who of course suffer most, would be the first to rebel against the bill. Then Challis would point out, when the High Commissioner was asked for some background stuff to feed the Colonial Secretary during question time, that the British had done hardly anything, it was their very own people who had risen, in a frenzy of love of law, against the brothers, as they liked to be called: in fact a bunch of little thugs who thought that resentment at the blowing up of the homes of one or two traitors (disloyal to the Crown) would be sufficient to wipe out the local implantation of an Empire that had kept millions on millions of black and brown and white serving the pleasures of the British people. Shopgirls wanted to buy lipstick, their parents wanted to keep pigeons and go to a pub and have a few days off once a year at the seaside, a bet on a game of darts, their young men were looking at small cars with new surmise. Everything has to be paid for, and a small island with neither mineral wealth nor a devotion to a work ethic has to turn to violence to acquire a standard of living that can otherwise only be based on a continent's resources or a frank acceptance of the helot substratum. Challis, whose parents had been only too close to the slave plantation themselves, was perfectly honest about the aims of his country as well as of his own. He wasted no belief on muzzy hypocrisies such as great games or little men's burdens, which gave him his unshakeable strength. Of course what these pathetic villagers called the brothers would turn against the conqueror, quite natural. No one really *wanted* to be a slave, or perhaps (Challis thought hard about his job) many didn't mind being slaves and some even wanted it, but some did not and these last were impelled by the sort of devotion to an abstract cause, a work ethic, whose lack made their enslavement so necessary to their rulers. Intelligent though he was, able to grasp the bone under the flabby muscle run to fat, Challis wasn't by the standards of either Britain or Palestine what one could call a well-read man and he didn't know the lines about the Maxim gun, although he lived them and worked well according to that principle. So he did well, succeeded, rose in his job, slept soundly and expected, rightly, to retire with honour after a career spent in furthering his nation's appetites.

The next morning he visited the devastated homes, and he wasn't undermined in the least by the inspection of the rubble of lives, some of it so misdirected. Mistakes were always made; he reminded the mukhtar that only a week before the brothers had shot a man in mid-market, thinking, wrongly, that he was his collaborating (loyal to the Crown) brother. The man was dead although he had been loyal to his country, and his children were now orphans.

'Yes, we are living in terrible times,' said the mukhtar.

After the inspection Challis enquired, and was told where Abu Ramzi had taken refuge from his era.

The next day he went to Jenin. Here there was a certain amount of immediate work, since the town was large enough to include a barracks as well as a police station and its market gave an excuse for a great deal of movement on the part of young men unknown to the informers. He didn't visit Um Tareq for two days, during which he had seen so many other people that hostile inquisitiveness in his visit was dulled. She told him enough to be useful.

Tareq was near Tyrz when a small, rather spotty man came to see him in public for a cure for his bed-wetting child.

The other people present, disgusted by the details, soon left. The spotty man talked to the magician in private and two days later Tareq crossed over at the Naqura post and returned to Palestine, taking the main road direct to Jerusalem.

The pockmarked man had transmitted his message well and truly; there was no need to spell out the choice a second time. Not that Challis felt any queasy shrinking at speaking his actions; he left that sort of half-virginity, desperate clutchings at torn fringes of a tattered self-respect to the Kits of this world. Why they needed it, how they could be taken in by their own self-deception, was beyond him. It explained why they could deceive no one else, having blinkered themselves so effectively. Excavating his ear and gazing contentedly at the neat wedge of marmalade wax that lay under his fingernail, he began to explain the situation to Tareq again. To be cut off at the mention of Buthaina.

'I have heard it, I will do as you wish. I shall stop speaking to the people and' – he couldn't for the life of his honour prevent a smile showing in his eyes – 'I shall stop changing hats into keffiyas.'

'On the contrary, I wish you to speak to the people more than ever before. And to perform tricks.'

Tareq looked around, but there was no window at all in the room, no sky to gaze at for a moment, although in this little Kremlin trees grew around the onion domes and soughed through the days and nights, their resinous scent filling the cells, seeping through the wooden stalls that the British had installed to divide their prisoners from the comfort of seeing each other, while they could still hear every hoarse spirit's surrender, every scream and sob. In this room, there were solid walls and the sounds didn't seep through, unless Challis chose to open the door, polishing his thin-rimmed spectacles as he did so, to remind the detainee that the eyes of the British were as keen as the pain they knew how to inflict with their talons, that the empire stretched everywhere, was omnipotent, unmoved by the anguish of those who were disloyal. Now he did open the door, and left it gaping, so that the life and agony of the place trickled, gushed in and formed the sort of background hubbub that makes large foodless parties so good a venue for private exchange.

Against the noises off he explained, reading from a memorandum on his table, lying to the left of his wife's photograph, what he wanted done, and where. At the end he peeled off a copy and gave it to the magician.

'Keep it, to remind you.'

Then he escorted him courteously to the door, handed him over to a guide dressed in navy-blue worsted whose face shone, under the navy helmet with its polished steel spike, with a worried longing to do well, who convoyed Tareq to the main gate of the building and clanged it to in his back.

. . .

'*Ya ta rubinni amma ta taliqni*.' The Arab soul is over-recep-
tive to natty rhymes, opens to them as, say, the French one
does to a flash of wit, or the English to a stray limping mon-
grel, the Italian to a legato stretch of song. 'Either you take me
to the feast of Nebi Rubin – rubinnate me – or you divorce
me.' The Prophet Reuben had chosen his burial place on
the banks of a small stream that trickled through the high
sand dunes bordering the sea just south of Jaffa. His feast
sensibly fell in the worst month of summer when the
humidity brought to shore by the southerly winds was driven
back by the cooler foothills and returned to lie like a miasma
on the houses of the city. Every woman wanted to take her
children to the dunes, swept fresh by sea air, and most of them
did. A temporary town sprang up every summer and lasted a
month, with tents as homes, as suqs, as cafés and play-
grounds. Fairs revolved, with little tin boats swinging on
dangerous rusted cables, sheep roasted, multi-coloured paper
windmills were sold everywhere, and pink spun sugar clouds.
Women swept out the sand floor of their festive homes,
sprinkled some clean sand to restore the diminished level and,
giggling, went to spend morning and afternoon on social calls,
sitting on low straw-plaited stools with their toes wiggling in
the hot white sand, fanning themselves with split grass axe-
shaped fans. They were free: the children were rolling in the
undertow, shrieking and gulping, while a few young men took
it in turn to guard the notorious currents of that shore. It was
a picnic, a holiday from solid houses, from polishing and
scouring, beating carpets, recarding mattresses. The wild
pleasure of living in a tent, with only the bare necessities, with
the stars and sun visible in every corner and the breeze
whistling through the sharp tough grass. 'We're living like
real Arabs,' they told each other and giggled again with the
thrill, the memory, that some old *hakawati* would recall
almost nightly, of the caliphs in their desert tents, fleeing the
stone chains of the city to live on an air untainted by living, an
air that smelt of nothing but the zest of breathing.

Um Tareq had asked for money and Challis had given it.
She returned to her home town and for the first time in her life

166

took a tent at Nebi Rubin. Buthaina and Saqr came with her, but after a week of it Abu Ramzi left and returned to the mountains. He had never lived on the coast, suspected it of every plague and sin, couldn't sleep in a tent for the singing and the tambourines and clay drums that thrummed and the camel bells ringing tin-tin-tin through the day and night.

'And your son? He's too grand to return to Jaffa?' the women asked maliciously. 'Is there a magic greater than the *biyyara*? Is the almond sweeter than the orange?' They looked sideways at Buthaina but said nothing about her, inspecting Saqr closely and arguing among themselves about his features.

One night she took him to hear the *hakawati*. The old man sat on a little hillock of a dune with the children and as many adults at his feet in a crescent. He had a petulant, self-indulgent face, the deep wrinkles that weakness causes under his shabby tarbush. Nor was he particularly good at his art, although his audience, enthralled, could not judge. The long story rambled on, one myth confused with another and cancelling them both into pointlessness. The warrior, whose courage had been overlooked, and who should have revealed his quality in the epic battle, accompanied by the names and genealogies of all his victims, turned instead into the mad lover, deceived by his tribe, undone by his loss, and yet – more confusion – turning back into the warrior and changing all his attributes again so that the chant ended with a marmalade of all the ingredients present on the battlefield: the wicked amir; the triumphant warrior, dying in his capacity as lover while enduring as conqueror of the faithless; the beloved at the same time weeping and suicidal and exultant, ready for the apotheosis; the traitor slain; the invader repelled; and the roc sweeping down to save the warrior from his enemies, simultaneously defeated and omni-potent. The audience loved it, there was a response to every emotion vibrating in their irrational little souls, they went home deeply satisfied. Saqr played for days at being the roc, sweeping down when all seemed lost to restore justice to the stricken hero.

Um Tareq took her guests to visit Miss Alice. Who received them kindly and gave the little boy sweets to take away with him, but without much warmth. Her coolness stopped Um Tareq's mouth, spoilt her plan, silenced her insinuations. She never found out whether the child reminded the Englishwoman of another boy, and left offended by the withdrawal of a friendship that had never existed except in her runny gossip. For once Miss Alice had been too preoccupied with her own feelings. The day before, Mr Rhodes had said from behind the week-old paper, 'Young Farren's done rather well for himself, I see. A duke's daughter, no less.'

'Show me.'

She read the announcement and returned the paper.

'He'll do well in life, I think. He's alert and he knows what he wants.'

'Yes.'

She waited for a letter of explanation, of something, even regret, but it did not come.

Since the general strike Jaffa had lost much of its importance. Most ships now docked at Haifa, or even at the new jetties the Zionists had hurriedly thrown up just north of the Arab city to take advantage of the immobilised port. British officials avoided the city if they could and ADCs met guests of importance at the Lydda junction. So there was no need for Kit to think up any excuses, the Revolt had provided him with one. But Egerton came, curious to see the tented city on the beach. He called on the Rhodeses, and stayed to lunch.

'Great feather in Farren's cap, eh?' said Mr Rhodes. 'Done well for himself.'

'Yes, I expect so.'

Egerton had met Lady Camilla, she was attractive to look at and listen to, there was no vulgar comfort to offer his hostess who was anyway unlikely to be consoled by her lover accepting ugliness of spirit or body for the sake of money and social position. She asked about his trip to Lebanon and he described Beirut and the antics of the French and the yellow-washed houses set in their moist lush gardens, the new excavations at Byblos and the rubble of Tyre but he didn't refer at all to the magician, any more than to Kit.

A month after his return to Palestine Challis had come up to him at a Jerusalem party.

'I've been wanting to see you.'

'I was travelling. Lebanon and then Egypt.'

'I know, I know. We do read the papers. Come and sit in our host's study, too much squalling around here.'

Apparently Challis wanted to congratulate him on his articles on Lebanon and then, more understandably, pump him about what the French thought they were up to and how they thought of going about it. He knew a fair amount and seemed to have good sources of information as to the proclivities of the native politicians. Egerton said as much.

'Well, they come here for a month or so in the summer you know, or their wives do – the ones who can't afford Paris, I mean; but one can learn quite a bit from them all the same. It all adds up.'

Challis was at his best when working kept his mind off personal malice; Egerton found him more companionable than ever before and felt mildly irritated when his hostess shrieked into the room that she simply wouldn't have two naughty men sitting in a huddle talking shop when there were so many charming ladies just longing to dance.

As they moved into the blare of the two-step Challis said, 'Oh, by the way, you remember that magician of yours? The one you were so excited about in Tarshiha?'

'Yes?'

'My men tell me he's performing round here nowadays. If you feel like seeing him again I can find out where he'll be in the next couple of days. It might be amusing.'

'All right.'

An assistant rang the next day to say that Challis bey was going to Silwan on Tuesday to see the magician and would collect Egerton en route if the time suited him.

As soon as the chairs had been fetched for them and the bowing and scraping had subsided Tareq stepped onto the earth terrace just above them and began his act. First he asked the audience for a glass of water. There was some scuffling at the edges of the crowd, then a dripping glass was handed to him and he held it up high so that all could see it was plain water. To make quite certain he pointed out the fact. He turned his back on them and chanted some gibberish, his head bowed down between hunched shoulders, his elbows jerking a little in the full sleeves. Then he turned to face the spectators and held up the glass, now full of a liquid that was magenta. This, if not the high spot of the performance, set the general level. Egerton watched incredulously as one clumsy trick followed the next. The man hardly seemed to wish to deceive the audience, so awkwardly did the egg get transferred from his wrist to his ear, so creased and bundly was the scarf he finally managed to extract from thin air. The children squealed but most of the adult men drifted away, smiling tolerantly. A few girls stayed at the edge of the crowd, gazing at Tareq. In the few months since the Lebanon meeting he had put on weight, his face was puffy and his eyes looked smaller under the bloated flesh. Even his eyelids looked heavier, there was a droop at the corners that gave him a look of unreliable cunning. In the flaring lights hung from the olive trees his skin shone with grease.

The last flabby sleight of hand produced a Union Jack, which Challis loudly applauded, smiling around as the village imitated him. The conjuror bowed and made a heavy little speech, thanking the beys for attending his humble performance, and remained where he stood until the two men had risen and gone into the guest-house for a last cup of coffee. He did not join them and had vanished when they left the village.

'And these are the people you think are ready for independence!' Challis said in the car.

'You've said that before and I've answered you too.'

'They're pathetic. And that man is no good. Did you see the way he ogled the girls? There'll be trouble over that one of these days.'

'Something's gone wrong with him, certainly. He's not at all the same as before. He looks ill.'

Challis snorted. 'Fleshpots, that's all. They all go to pieces when anyone pays a bit of attention to them. No character.'

It wasn't clear whether he meant conjurors or the people of Palestine.

The latter, however, seemed able to do without self-indulgence for the time being. The revolt spread. The ragged handful of peasants who had begun with rusty muskets and a complete ignorance of military tactics, let alone strategy, lurking in the caves and ancient cisterns and silos cut deep into the living rock all over the hillsides, emerging for a fleeting hit-and-run operation of significance to no one except the local papers, grew in strength. Recruits joined them from the cities, educated boys vanished for a few days and returned smiling and brown, to look conceitedly at their parents and hint at epic deeds. The British imported soldiers and then more. Their chief function was patrolling, and dynamiting houses in whichever village lay nearest the last raid.

'Sooner or later they'll see sense. The bandits can't protect the villages, never will be able to. Nor the harvest stores. When the villagers have lost enough food they'll stop giving any away. They're all bone-stupid of course but they'll come to their senses one of these days.'

Yet they didn't seem to. The more they suffered, the stronger the brigands seemed to grow.

'Don't you think there's a danger that men who have lost their livelihood might think their only alternative was to pick up a gun and fight back?'

'Where's the sense in that? They'll lose their lives on top of everything else.'

'A man might be so maddened by rage that he wouldn't care if he could get his own back first.'

'Well, there's no question of his doing *that*. They're a nuisance, I grant you that, but I can assure you, Egerton, the British Empire isn't going to be defeated by a bunch of illiterate peasants. This is off the record of course, but we're getting reinforcements next month from Iraq and India. If we have to we'll fill this bloody country so chock full of infantry that there won't be standing room left for those thugs.'

'Well . . . yes . . . but what happens after that? How will we pick up the pieces? I've been travelling round a bit, there's a lot of ill-feeling already.'

'Who cares?' said the Secretariat man, who knew that he could censor anything he didn't like in the final article. 'We've promised to put the Jews in and put them in we shall. Anyone who doesn't like it can lump it. Why don't they all go to Syria? They're getting most of their guns from there already. Let them go there, with their guns too, and let's see how much the French welcome them *then*.'

'They say we're giving guns to the Jews ourselves. Training them to fight the Arabs for us.'

'I really couldn't say, old chap. I'm nothing to do with the military side, as you know. And they're not likely to tell you, one way or another, and I shouldn't let you publish it even if they did. And now, if you'll excuse me, I'll get back to running this country, badly as you think I'm doing. Are you going to the garden party this afternoon? See you there then.'

The new regiments arrived but the troubles stayed. Cement cylinders, rather like inflated grey pillar-boxes, were erected all over the golden hills, to keep the Tommies safe. Barbed wire began uncoiling through the landscape and round key buildings in the towns. Kilometres of the still untarnished stuff were soon being offered for sale by the ironmongers of Syria and Lebanon. After the third troop train had been derailed all trains slowed their speed to accommodate their armed lookouts' eyes and everyone grumbled that it took longer to get around the country than in the days of the Turks. Rates and taxes were raised, municipal and department of education budgets cut back and the funds saved transferred to the defence budget. The grumbling increased and some went so far as to say that in the end the only difference between the Turks and the British would prove to be that the Turks hadn't allowed thousands of foreign Communists into the country. The troubles continued and grew worse and so did the reprisals. Leading politicians and notables took public stands, some for, some against, the revolt. The British arrested and deported the first, built up the second. Internecine warfare began. The Rhodeses ordered pairs of narrow-slitted steel shutters for their two bedrooms. Mr Rhodes wanted iron bars installed over the sugar tracery of the terrace arches, but Miss Alice won and they continued to sit on in the evenings, though without a lamp. Too slowly to be perceptible something was seeping out of their lives. Sometimes during those darkened evenings, in spite of her resolution, Miss Alice fell into the repeated groove of old conversations, trying to unpick the warp, the knot that should have warned her in time. One conversation returned again and again. Kit had been in Jaffa for official business and his day and dinner taken up with spin-offs. He had slid out from under the Bishop's dinner, explaining that he had promised 'to keep his ear to the ground' and to report back to HE on what non-officials were thinking. The Bishop, reminded of this quotidian intimacy with the master of all their days, had been rather impressed. Flushed with this triumph, and probably with one of another kind which she didn't tell me about, Kit had boasted of his cleverness.

'O you are a cheat,' she cried. But of course she was delighted.

Even for the upright curfews are a weariness. Jaffa was not a city where people were accustomed to move much after dark but the fact that one couldn't even if one wanted to had its effect. Not even the neighbours dropped in after the half-wit of Suq al-Bilbaisi wandered a house or two away from his immemorial stamping-ground and was shot through the lungs by a nervous eighteen-year-old boy fresh from Devon to whom he seemed the image of a wild Arab, ready without reason to wage war on civilisation and the rule of law. This murder, though it shook the general public to their roots, was perhaps the cleverest use of force the British could have manifested.

'They have no mercy at all,' the women agreed at home.

'There will come among you a people so pitiless that not even the beggar, the orphan, is safe from their savagery. Woe to those among whom men without compassion are let loose. Bow your heads: let the blind fury pass.'

As a result everyone stayed at home and support for the brothers fell away.

So Miss Alice felt safe in organising a picnic for her pupils, in spite of some prudent remonstrances from first her Yaffawi colleagues, uncertain as to how far this would compromise them, and then from her father. The colleagues were as frightened of losing their jobs at a time of widespread unemployment as of being shot by their compatriots, and it would have been a poor imperialism that hadn't trained its daughters to override that sort of cringing, however fond of the children of their foreign policies they might have grown. And once he learnt that the Palestinian teachers had (reluctantly, but he didn't know that) agreed to the project and would be there themselves to provide primary targets for nationalist bullets, Mr Rhodes dropped his objections, only too happy not to argue as long as he wasn't forced to go along himself. Miss Alice was only defeated on the matter of site.

173

She longed to take the children, peaky and lacking in chlorophyll, to the banana-leaved jungle of Jreishi, where the Awja stopped its frenzied zigzagging and broadened into a placid wide river mouth flowing past the millstones, as old as the Arab Conquest, that gave the place its name, and where foolish little skiffs skimmed around like mosquitoes, anxious to be hired by people as silly as their shallow pretensions to a secure life and to be rowed down by singing, ululating featherheads who invariably had a tambourine or a lute among them, and who made music at the tops of voices and handclaps, waving good-naturedly at all the other little scuts, all of the loads smiling so widely that one would have thought they had been saving up for all the winter months and were now determined to spend their balance of happiness in one day of the sun striking through the juicy leaves onto the dappled flowing water that, in spite of its stillness, ran under the smooth surface as fast as death to the unseen sea that lay behind the last cunning twist of the perverse river. Palestine! When I read your name, mentioned in the secure editorials of the retired robbers as a synonym for criminality, I think, for no reason, of that old schoolteacher and the cracked sepia photographs she showed me of the picnics she gave the living dead.

Not on that specific occasion. They all wanted, as always, to go to the *biyyara*. This meant harder work for her, the servants had to be sent out early in the morning with the trays of cooked and raw dishes, to sweep the earth flat under the orange trees, dig pits, get the charcoal going, grill the lamb and pounded meat and chicks split flat. It hardly mattered whether the food was well-spiced or not: everything was eaten round the well, with its tender little frogs leaping glistening onto the rim and then falling backwards in alarm, in an overpowering heaviness of orange blossoms, immense, waxy, a scented presence of reality confirmed by the unripe hard green fruit, carrying the promise of the mature orange season, its sense of adult reality, of the future syrupy cauldrons, to be stirred and stirred and stirred, congealing lumps scraped off ornate tiles on a floor still solid under unmarred brown feet, the noisy chirping children dodging under an arm to lick the huge copper ladle, the eternity of the seasons that had not yet learnt enough of the pallid empire. Syllables of security, demolished like the thick stone walls that created the feeling.

They were still sitting, chewing, absent-mindedly by now, when Tareq appeared, striding across the shallow canals that carried water to the roots of every cherished tree. Miss Alice was doubly pleased to see him.

'Come and eat and then tell them a story. They'll be wrecking the irrigation system soon.'

He dropped down heavily beside her and then she saw the change in him.

'Tareq, aren't you well?'

She called on the servants for coffee and water, but the servants took their time. They had served their neighbours' children all through the hot morning, for the sake of the lady; now they were resting. Tareq knew how to make his own coffee and if he had forgotten he could fetch his mother to do it. She earned less money than the Rhodeses' servants, not to say none at all.

In this they were behind events.

I say events, but I mean a war, civil or of independence. The word 'events' is just a translation of what we nowadays modestly call, or what our papers call, '*les événements*', meaning such bloody warring that it is almost impossible for me to reach Miss Alice, living twenty-five kilometres away, and pointless even if I do, my paper having dropped not only the idea of a series on life a generation earlier, but also the ambition of appearing daily six days of the week. If I still wish to finish the story, it is because there is nothing else to do at present, rather than to earn a bonus. And there is a twisted comfort in recording *their* pathetic amateurish attempts at a war, where a revolver counted as artillery, or a shabbily tinned car as a tank. It makes us feel that progress has taken place in every field.

'It was just as frightening to be killed by a pistol as by a mortar,' she said, 'and one was just as dead.'

'I expect people felt like that about bows and arrows,' I said smugly.

'I expect they did, and they were right. You're not more dead because you're blown apart by a bomb rather than shot through the eye by an arrow.'

'Shell-shock?'

'Knife-shock was probably just as bad. Anyway, why argue about it? Whatever is used at the time is the worst weapon imaginable and frightens people out of their wits. It doesn't make them happier to be told that their children, if they survive to have any, will face something unimaginably nastier.'

'I'd better go now. Just time to get home before curfew.'

'If you'd like to spend the night I can give you a toothbrush. We can sit up and talk and you can finish your research in one go, instead of driving backwards and forwards.'

I felt the parasitic fear of all interviewers, that if one once let go the subject might slide out from under, for ever, and one would be left with the incompleted story gathering silverfish in the files, unusable but too interesting to be scrapped. It's a pang that impels journalists to exert whatever magnetism they possess on people they will never see again while they later flop at home, like the great blue jellyfish inflated into perfect curves, invisibly ballooning in their element and ending in a gelatinous pale puddle on the beach. I accepted the invitation, after a token excuse that the hawk had to be fed.

'It won't die in a night, and if what you said about the cockroaches climbing up through the drainpipes is true it'll scour your flat for you.'

As it turned out the curfew was extended for all the following day and the night after, the 'events' having taken a noticeable turn for the worse, so I learnt more than I had bargained for and the hawk did survive. It savaged the curtains though, probably after moths.

Tareq didn't tell her all of it but enough. The rest she learnt.

Life, the keeping of, had never been far enough above the danger line for Palestinians to feel secure if the rains were late or the Turks cut down the olive trees to fuel troop trains or – a twentieth-century innovation – there were a general strike that went on and on without evoking any reaction from the rulers. The British made speeches about their empire being a greater Moslem power than any khalifate in history, but they were not immediately subject to the pressure of Moslems dying, starving under their aegis, as all other khulafa had been. Neither Whitehall nor Whitechapel cared if Khirbet al Beida were swept by famine, and in this respect the British were immune from their policies' consequences and the countryfolk were lost. They had always fallen into debt before every harvest, now there was no hope of their climbing out again. Their grey rulers spoke at length of peasant problems and then accentuated them. Interest on seed, on onion sets, on fodder, passed the 100% mark and went on increasing. Men fed their children in May the grain that should have been sown in November and hoped that after the rains something might save them. But nothing did. Land had always been the core of life's meaning. Sex or gold or power were what people in colder countries killed for, worked for, dreamed of, perhaps because in those places the city has taken the place of the village. But from all the shores of the Mediterranean radiated a single passion. Northern hinterlands had checked and opposed the industrial city to this monomania, but to the east of the sea (to its south the desert was a more effective check than an alternative ambition) it ran wild across plateaux and deserts until it reached the ocean and faced again a people it had fled from in the centre. The earth was not for sale. At best, or worst, a man exchanged it for his soul's salvation and then his enraged family, unable to break the pious endowment which placed what Latin jurisprudence so accurately termed its dead hand on fertility, still benefited through eternity from the reflected glow of a name warmed by a sun that would never fail. Or families fought over the scrap of untilled rocky unproductive soil, carrying their battle with the banners of the earth flying undirtied through successive conquests, régimes, changes of pashas and *qaimaqams* until at last the strong inheritor sallied out from the *serai*, waving the parchment that gave him full rights to a few square metres—rights that also enjoined him to accord the female descendants of the original, forgotten, owner the fruits of half a tree on this patch, and quarter of the harvest of a tree on another and, and—because on these pieces of paper, so lusted after, two things were always recorded. The number of olive trees, even if there were only one and that barren, and the passage, presence, potential or actual, of water. A well, a cistern, the flow of a spring and whether it gushed in summer as well as winter, the presence of a dry clayed irrigation canal implying some antique right, all were recorded and added to the price. Just as in other countries the use of central heating or air-conditioning affects the rent, without according possession. To own an olive tree! It is the one point on which Arabs agree with Greeks, though why it should give a deeper pleasure than to own an oak or a beech or even a walnut or plum isn't understood. But it is real, and not to be surrendered.

So the man who possessed the treasure of land didn't give it up easily, nor did he forget it because pieces of paper had changed hands. If he had to sell, and by had to I mean for the potbellies of children too young to work even by the standards of that time – or of this time, the Israelis showing themselves no more hesitant than any of their predecessors in employing children under ten, provided they accept wages conforming to their age – then he sold to a neighbour, a relation, the friends of a neighbour or relation, it being understood that when he had earned enough money to buy his patrimony back his physical presence would constitute a sufficiently menacing form of blackmail to undo his misfortune. Anyone who has attempted to refuse this selling back to the millennial owner by pleading improvements, annexes or whatever, will know what a Mediterranean village can threaten. The grey-eyed straight-browed frown has been inherited with other more frightening attributes from the goddess.

So Um Tareq proved invaluable. It wasn't only that she was known, a native, but that she was known to be helpless. A widow, her father dead, no brothers, her sons either compromised or living abroad. Not even a maternal uncle. There was no potential threat when the land was to be clawed back from her pieces of legal flimsy. No one asked how she had acquired such ready wealth. Everyone sold, grinning at her folly, her inability to bargain. Not that they asked much more than the going rate, one or two percent at most, but she paid it. It never occurred to the slyest among them that she was acting for the Zionists. In its connotation of land-agent the word *simsar* came in the end to mean traitor in the Palestinian vocabulary; or Judas, selling the land for coin being worse than selling

178

one's god, who by his nature could not be bartered if he were truly divine. But while ignorance lasted she bought and bought and villagers wise in the ways of their life screwed up their faces and nudged and insinuated that her son must have political aims, like beasts, in view.

But he did not even suspect what his mother was doing. Buthaina had returned to the sodden gritty ruin of her home and was earning a little money to buy food by embroidery. Abu Ramzi borrowed more from the itinerant money-lender. Ramzi had disappeared and there was no income to be expected from him in future. On the contrary, he would return one night to ask for contributions, as they knew. The two stepdaughters had both reached marriageable age and there was no remote hope of endowing them; they would have to accept whatever was offered. Buthaina's father had died just before the house was destroyed so he had not made good her losses as she was sure he would have done, and her sisters kept everything for their own families, sending her only a Qoran to replace the one reduced to purée. Tareq brought it to her. He had guessed her expectations and passed by Qalqilya, hoping to bring her some material comfort. 'Yes, we heard,' her elder brother-in-law told him. 'These are terrible times for everyone. I owe seven pounds myself and I've taken the eldest out of school, although I always planned that he should stay and take his certificate. But I need help now, perhaps the younger one will manage to finish his studies later on if things improve. Tell the woman I am sorry for her but we sold all my mother's jewellery last year when Subhi lost his job.'

Tareq, looking round the clean shining house with its re-tinned copper and new glistening straw mats, gleaned from the year's good harvest, murmured some hallowed periphrases on compassion, charitable duties to female dependants.

'She is not a widow.'

'No, but the man is not a young one and his own son has gone.'

'And is that my fault? They are all fools. They bring trouble on us and then we have to support them? Let them stay at home and save their families from ruin, instead of coming in the night to ask us for help. Do they think they are going to defeat the ingliz? I tell you, all they are doing is escaping from work, playing at Antar, and we have to pay for their fantasies, their laziness. I tell you, two of the pounds I owe are—' He stopped short. It was very dangerous to admit to giving to the outlaws. There were consequences, as serious at least as what had happened to Buthaina, who was innocent of this.

'Here, take this to her. She loved her father, I send it as a memory. Tell her I can do nothing more this year, next summer we'll see how things are going.'

The Qoran, had any of them known it, was more valuable than all their houses put together. Fathers and grandfathers had treated it with care, and in the slit flap of the calf cover lay a letter from Khalid ibn al Walid, or thumbed by him over a Byzantine scribe's calligraphy, praising a warrior ancestor who had not yet been seduced by the grey-green leaf turning silver in the sedentary breeze. The inheritors acknowledged its worth by keeping it loosely wrapped in one of the plum velvet squares, embossed with silver thread, in which ladies used to wrap their towels, copper soap-dish, emery file, pumice stone and essence of oils, placing the plush, oddly bulging bundle on the head of a serving-girl who led the way on Thursdays to the public baths, while decent men turned their eyes aside lest even the passing thought of nakedness should affect the procession. With the collapse of the empire and the subsequent leaking of civilisation into taps, these cloths had flooded an ignorant market and were sold for the price of a kilo of the eggplant which so often tinged their pile. A generation or more too late to be of any use to her, Buthaina could have exchanged the covering alone of the Book for enough grain to sow all their fields, with an ass thrown in to plough them and carry the harvest to market.

Tareq thought about the gift he was carrying to her. The shoddy games he was now playing with villagers still brought in as much reward as the truth the ingliz had forbidden him to tell: he thought of adding a thin gold coin to the envelope within the Book. But if the truth came out? If she were to express too much gratitude to her brother-in-law? And he, irritated by the evident irony, were to lash out? At best Tareq would never be able to see her again; it was more likely that Abu Ramzi or her family would avenge the insult by killing first her and then himself. So he handed over the bundle and watched her as she roughly threw open the thick velvet square and riffled through the eleventh-century illuminated pages, tearing some in her anxiety. Her eyebrows met over her nose, the classical double-crescent of undivided beauty.

'The Book? Is this a joke?'

'I told him yours had been destroyed by the soldiers. He sent this in memory of your father's love.'

'Maygodhavemercyonhissoul. What kind of a messenger are you? Did you tell him the soldiers destroyed my *house*? The oil jar? My dresses? The *sini* cabinet? Did you tell him they stole my gold? All my dowry? That I am now a woman without a dowry? That I can never leave Abu Ramzi whatever he does? Even my wedding-chest? Even my copper? That I own *nothing*? I am a woman without standing. Without anything? Why don't you answer? What did you tell him? Am I to roam the roads of this world with a *Qoran*? Is that what stands between me and a second wife? Have I a brother or not? Am I an *orphan*?' Her voice rose to a shriek at the end of every question.

'Um Saqr—'

'And then Um Godonlyknowswhat. If my brother doesn't protect me, why should my son? Supposing it's a girl? Then what do I do? Feed her the bookblessedbeitsname?' He looked at her, squatting on the earth floor with her dress pulled in a tent over her knees and she stood up over him at once. 'Yes, look! Look. Men have to look to see, but we see without an eye.'

He got up himself. Why feel so sad? All over the country . . . She was luckier than many. . . . But angrier at her fate. No one could do anything effective about it, he didn't even feel that he should, let alone that he could.

'Um Saqr. . . .'

But neither Miss Alice nor Egerton could ever tell me what he said to her then. It didn't matter to them either, the words of an illiterate village woman, whom they probably thought of as dirty – shuddering in some racist recess of the soul, where other people's habits are too alien to be accepted or thought through. Everyone feels the same. 'They don't scrub their floors nor hose them down,' an appalled woman told me a generation later. 'They nail their carpet to the floor and then they leave it there, and they never wash what is underneath. Children of the forbidden!' Her eyes grew rounder and bigger as I told her that I had once lived in a city where all the women did just that, where the police came round if one hung the carpets and bedding out to beat them, because sunning them was against the law. 'And you lived there long? How could you breathe in that filth?'

All over the country men were being arrested. It was time to finish, once and for all, with the minor irritant that this tiny backward people constituted in the great oiled differential of empire. A decree was proclaimed, enforced by its proclaimers, the troubles were to be ended by *iradé*, pretence of democracy suspended until all had returned to order, when the same humbug could be prated about all over again and self-congratulatory speeches could be editorialised upon without contradiction from the news reports.

'He thinks he can defy us? That cheap little tuppeny pierhead conjuror? Take our support and cheat us with impunity? What does he think? That we'll deport him to the Seychelles? I'll hang him higher than Haman.'

'That was a Jew, Reginald, wrong quote.'

'He won't know the difference by the time I've finished with him. The treacherous little snake. I've always said you can't trust one of them. Bowing and scraping and then the knife in the back. Fools into the bargain. No one will lift a finger to save him when they hear the truth. I've got him just where I want him.'

'Don't you wish you had the Husseinis in the same place?'

'Yes, but I don't, more's the pity. It would save a lot of trouble.'

One of his strengths was that even in a rage he could pull back from the brink, and now he did. And stood a jovial round at the bar before people could begin saying that his job was stronger than he was.

After a fair amount of drinks he returned to the Moscobiya to order the arrest.

. . .

Accounts of what had happened in Qalqilya were neither clear nor concordant, the chief police spy not having bothered to attend the performance himself, and his informers' reports being diametrically opposed. When their superior, baffled by their stories, sent men to gather general gossip he grew more alarmed. No two people had seen the same performance, except right at the end, when everyone (except one of the informers who had gone home to bed and subsequently lost a pleasant little stipend) saw exactly the same sight and heard the same words. A sleek, glossy roan in splendid condition materialised out of nowhere behind the conjuror, who turned and grasped her rope halter, leaping onto her bare back and riding her without apparent effort as she curvetted and tried to rear. Looking like the archetypal dream of the collective Arab unconscious, he raised his forearm, which some but not all gaping spectators said carried a curved silver sword, and cried out words which the policemen before Challis agreed were blasphemy as well as public disloyalty to the Crown. The mare then gathered her well-fed hocks beneath her, took a flying jump through the scattering audience, which in some cases fell flat on its face to make her path easier, and raced out of the market-place, into invisibility as far as the CID could find out.

'Incitement to rebellion in a time of revolt: no question about that.' Challis' overhanging eave of an upper lip rippled with pleasure. 'And blasphemy is a capital crime too.' He repolished his spectacles that had misted up for the nth time with happiness sweating out of the ginger pores.

'I don't think we need to bother HE with that aspect,' said Kit uneasily. 'When I got your note I asked Cairo for some advice.' He pulled out a file from an unusually work-laden desk. 'I won't bother you with all the details but the gist seems to be that since the man is a Sunni and since they don't recognise incarnation then he can't be held to have blasphemed.'

'Whatever do you mean? It's precisely because they don't accept it that he has blasphemed. Only God can be God. He's claiming more than their prophet ever did.'

'Well, I gather that that's just why they don't take it seriously.' Kit riffled through the file. 'After we got the experts' report from Cairo we asked the locals, off the record

183

of course, what their opinion was. They seem to think that he must have gone a little, a little, well that just making the claim shows he should be pitied. We really did go into it a bit, Challis, and they all just smiled when we put it to them. I don't know, I don't think we should push it too far. There may be something we've overlooked, but really, I don't advise following it up on these lines and I'll have to tell HE that.'

'You'll tell him nothing at all,' said Challis contemptuously. 'This is a matter of security, not of precedence at ladies' dinner tables. *I'll* tell him what the CID think, that's what we're here for. The man has been a public nuisance for years and now he's a public danger. We've known all along and now we have the proof.'

'I was at that garden party too,' said Kit, 'I'm not arguing about his nuisance value. But let's not make fools of ourselves when we can do the same thing intelligently. I repeat, we really did go round town asking for opinions on this and they're more likely to be the true ones because we're not paying for them. Paid informers often say what they think their cash source wants to hear.'

'The men you'd ask would say what they think – and they're as wrong in this as in everything else – that HE would like to hear.'

'Well, I don't know as much about these things as you do, of course. But I feel they're not all in league with each other to that extent. You know the old shaikh on the corner of the Street of the Christians? The one who's never come to any do?'

'The roof-garden? The scroll from Saladin giving his family the right to preach on the night of power?'

'That's the one.'

'It's a fake: he only uses it to get a bribe from the Mufti to relinquish his heritage.'

'I wouldn't know about that: our men say that he's getting old and he admires the Mufti but you're probably right. Still, he carries weight.'

'And he says?'

'Well, he was quite roundabout.'

'I'll bet he was. Did your man offer him a substantial enough quid pro quo?'

'No, I don't think he did.' Kit's "man" had been the Mayor of Jerusalem, a close friend if one takes into account the unchanging fact that power distorts, corrupts friendship at its heart as much as the imbalance of sexual longing. 'The occasion didn't arise.'

Challis gave his celebrated giggle.

'No, really. Our "man" was a friend of the shaikh's. They like each other.'

'And the result?'

'Well,' said Kit uncomfortably. 'I learnt a lot about what they believe in. Did you know they think we're childish to need saints? They think it shows a nanny complex?'

'God help us! Are you comparing this charlatan to a saint?'

'They think that any intermediary between one's self and the hope of God shows a fundamental weakness.' He shuffled the papers again, not to read them but to row himself back into whatever conviction had been blown into him and was now leaking out again. 'The old shaikh said that if we were so worried about a village sorcerer's claims it showed we didn't trust our own beliefs. He wanted to know' – even Kit hesitated here – 'or he said he wanted to know, in what way Issa's magic was more valuable, that we went on believing in it for two thousand years, and killed a thousand times two thousand men for not believing it. Were we frightened of history repeating itself?'

'If you want to listen to this rubbish I don't.' Challis turned back at the door. 'This isn't the country for you, Farren. I'm not sure it's the empire for you, but that's your business, not mine. But don't put spokes in my wheels because that *is* my business and I'll see you get run over if you do.'

He wasn't a man to have doubts; he tackled HE.

Who hummed.

'Tricky business, this, Challis. They're all buzzing around as it is. Anything to do with security, you know I don't hesitate. But sometimes it's difficult enough to draw the line even there. This business about the houses.' He stopped talking for a perceptible moment, a couple of seconds or less. 'I'm not saying anything against it, but' – he paused again, safe in the knowledge that he was the one man in Palestine whom Challis could not interrupt.

'I don't disagree with it, but, but suppose a mistake were

made? It's really tricky, you know better than I do. Supposing the wrong house were demolished? I had a delegation to
see me the other day. Couldn't refuse them. No no.' He lifted
his hand, anticipating Challis' objection. 'Not owners of
houses. I would never agree to see them. They can go to you if
they have proof of something going wrong. This lot were too
high up.'

'We look into things quite carefully, sir.'

'Of course you do. I wouldn't dream of questioning your
judgement. But—'

There was another fraction of a silence.

Neither mentioned the possibility of yet another Royal
Commission. Both thought of it. It would come out, heralded
by shawms and trumpets; its members would ask appointed
representatives why the people whom the British had appointed them to represent objected to being deprived of their
homes, lands and jobs. The representative would try to
explain why in as modern, as westernised a manner as
possible; the Royal Commission would take notes and then
put it to the Jewish Agency that perhaps a little accommo-
dation, gentlemen, a little patience, try and see the other chap's
point of view. The Jewish Agency would then send Dr
Weizmann back to Britain, since he was a British, not a
Palestinian, citizen, to dine with every Zionist in Whitehall
(not few on the ground). The White Paper would then
disappear into oblivion. In spite of what had become yet
another British tradition, as hallowed by practice as Rouge
Dragon's title, the men on the frontiers did not greatly care
for Royal Commissions and did what they could to avert
them.

'You know, Challis, if I were you I'd drop it. You know
more about it than I do, goes without saying, but I can't help
feeling that it might be wiser to overlook the whole thing.
Make the man look foolish by ignoring him. Village charlatan, beneath our dignity, that sort of attitude.'

Challis' spectacles glinted at the governor of Palestine.

'If you say so, of course, sir. We'll wash our hands of it.'

HE laughed, quite loudly. 'There's never been a man in
this post since Storrs who hasn't thought of that one. Doesn't
worry me at all. Fact. The man got bad publicity, came up
against the Zionists of his time, poor chap. If you ask me the

real story was probably utterly different.'

'Um,' said Challis, who for once was really shocked.

'That's that then, we'll forget about the whole thing. Let the man gambol on his camel round the whole Middle East if it gives him any pleasure.'

'Sir.'

But as he rose to leave, some god of the secret police inspired him.

'There's the morals business as well. They take that sort of thing so seriously. It leads to trouble, feuds, counter-feuds. Never stops. Gives the local men so much trouble.'

HE fell. 'What morals?'

Challis told him at some length.

'That's something else altogether. If you're certain of the facts then there's no question. Man must be tried. But it must be certain. We don't want the wilder fringes saying that we rigged a woman because we couldn't touch him over other things.'

'There's no doubt of it. His own mother will be a Crown witness.'

'His real mother or a second wife?'

'No, she's his blood-mother. He forced her to take in his woman. She feels the disgrace.'

'I don't want to hear the details,' said HE with distaste. 'The same sort of thing goes on all over the world; one's better out of it. I remember when I was cramming French in Caen there was something of the sort in a village on the coast. The locals talked about nothing else for a month, even in the dairy.' He thought back for a moment. 'Especially in the dairy, as a matter of fact. There were some repellent details that seemed to appeal to the milkmaids. Professionally. I don't know, Challis. Perhaps we'd do better to let this whole business drop. Not really our level, you know.'

'I'll go through the dossier myself,' promised Challis, as though he hadn't already done so for month after baited month. 'And report back, if you like, sir.'

'Yes, do that, would you? Don't bother to report back of course. Trust your judgment. But read through the whole blasted thing before you give an order.'

'I won't fail to do so,' said Challis.

The warrant was issued first thing the following morning.

If the proverb is right and haste is a gift of the devil, he did not this time look after his own. The warrant was useless. Tareq had vanished, and not even the spies in South Lebanon reported a scent. No one dared tell Abu Ramzi that his wife's name was sinfully linked with another man's, perhaps because Buthaina frightened them. Nothing happened at all and Challis had to stop asking when it was going to. But there *was* another Royal Commission, whose members were so perturbed by what they learnt that, beyond the worst fears of the government of Palestine, a whole bunch of Arabs were invited to London to speak of their grievances and document, if they could, their apprehension. This was the first time that the empire had invited its subjects not only to complain, but to do so in the metropolis, and budgetary work ceased in departments of the marches. Some weeks before the conference was due to begin the order went out: not a single house was to be demolished until after the talks had ended.

'And how do we keep order, Captain effendi?'

'I'm waiting to hear myself.'

'They are walking openly in the streets of Hebron. They say that they have obliged Londra to think again.'

Until now the sergeant had always used epithets. Thieving, outlawed, son of. . . . If he, at his age and rank, was now calling them 'they', by the time the conference assembled he would be using 'brothers', a term hitherto punishable by demotion to the ranks.

Captain effendi was far behind events. They were walking the streets of the Old City where the sale of manqals had tripled. Tinsmiths were clanging on extra large ones, to roast the lamb of joy. The antique worship of victory swept through the country; those who had hesitated for too long took a handful of coins from under the patterned tile and contributed to the cause that had won. In every small village mosque the Friday sermon resounded with new texts. The exiled delegates were swept into a sultan's yacht and sailed in triumph from their desert island.

Tareq crossed the frontiers again, left the dead cities of the north where he had been skulking and returned. There were no more glasses of crimson madder water, there were no more performances of any kind. He simply stood on a platform of sorts, either an earth terrace or a construction of wooden crates, and addressed his audience with words. A few times, as a concession, he did something that helped his petitioners. Water seeped back into a well that had gone dry; the threat of locusts was averted at the last moment and the clicking brown cloud chittered out to sea before a branch had been stripped.

'Cunning sort of humbug, isn't he? We haven't quite worked out yet how he rigs his game. Pity they all seem to benefit the largest amount of people possible.'

'Seem? I wouldn't have thought that anyone at all would mind about the locusts going.'

'No, that's right. That particular sham did please everyone for miles around. The well business rather annoyed the man who had hired a tanker to sell water to the village at a fairish price.'

'Was he a local?'

'No.'

'Yes, well, the question is: how the devil do we go about it?'

'Blasphemy seems out. We can hardly get more excited about it than the turbans, and they keep on saying that they can do nothing until the Mufti rules on it and he can't do that until we let him return and—'

'I know, I know. It's not for us, who have impiously deprived them of their spiritual pastor and master, to natter about a village quack. I've got all the reports here, thank you very much, Miles. Other thoughts?'

'I don't quite see why we should take that lying down.' Green had been newly recruited to the giddy level of off-the-record seminars in his boss's home, hoped to show he deserved the promotion.

'It's just because the top medicine man is out of commission that it's our duty to hold the fort in his place. *In loco necro?*' He shut up. Miles had been longer in the job, and was less enthusiastic about it.

'Yes, but what I was leading to is why have we dropped the women business? I thought that was all tied up? I mean, there was a woman to testify about at least one incident. And there were a lot of other little coneys we could pull out of our own hat. The Mufti won't be able to defend anyone on that side, surely? Has it been stopped?'

'No,' said Challis, 'but we'd rather keep it in reserve until we're certain we can't get the man on cleaner things. The woman side means a lot of trouble and it tends to ripple out, they've all got sisters and aunts and daughters who are married to men we know and brothers and uncles and whatever and that means endless palaver.'

On the whole, though, Challis was fairly content with the results of his seminar. It was more of an alibi than a brains trust, and he had no intention of announcing his plans to them, but still, it was running in the direction he had hoped for, and the proceedings were being dutifully recorded by the stenographer for the file. His sister Lucy's maid had already submitted her testimony for inclusion, but that too would not be mentioned here.

There was no longer any question about incitement to riot, disloyalty. Everywhere the man went now he made speeches attacking the British. He supported the rebel gangs openly, saying that without them the ingliz would have stolen the land from its owners and given it to the Jews. It was thanks to the gangs that the recognised leaders of the Palestinians had been released from their captivity and brought in triumph to speak to the rulers of London, thanks to their resistance, their bravery against enormous odds. It was the duty of every village to do what it could to support the struggle, to furnish food and horses and donkeys and clothing warm enough for the icy caves where the dedicated slept, sacrificing everything that made life tolerable for the sake of the future. Any man who refused to help, however poor, was collaborating with the British, whether he knew it or not.

This was more than enough, under the emergency laws which the British had decreed and which in effect suspended every law that protected individual rights, to arrest the mountebank a dozen times over, and send him to rot, forgotten and untried in the parched camp at Sarafand, or the dank cells of the Ottoman prisons of Beersheba or Nablus.

'Still, if we can, better to use the blasphemy charge.'

'More leeway from the public?'

'Fleet Street certainly, no doubt about that. The papers won't even bother to pick it up, no one's interested in what the allahs get up to among themselves. It'll do us no harm here either. All our pigeon-toed little effendis will be frightened out of their money-loving wits by the thought of a jihad.'

'Won't be much trouble about proving it, that I can

promise,' said Green. He pushed forward a reasonably plump file full of declarations, many of them attested to by village scribes or mukhtars, to the effect that the testifier had with his own ears heard the man say, before an audience assembled on the night of such and such, that he was – but here there were slight difficulties. Either the witness was a good Sunni who knew that other sects were heresy, in which case he stated that the claim was to the hidden imamate, or he was a good Sunni who had heard that the claim was to being Pythagoras metempsychosed, or he was the same and advanced the names of Jesus' great-grandchild or the return of Jacob according to whether he was convinced respectively of the fierily theological convictions of the Christians or the Jews, or he was a Druse, in which case he had heard Tareq lay claim to quite other hallowed beliefs. No witness was a Jew or a Christian, partly because Challis felt it was better to keep things where they belonged, and indeed he dropped the Druse witnesses quite soon, finding that they tended to swear to what they thought he wanted. Not that he minded this, but their opinions on the subject did not often precisely coincide with his own.

So that after Challis had sifted through the painstaking collation, which would have won its compiler a Nobel prize for religious anthropology in the distant future when such a subject became popular (only to happen after most of its human goldmine had ceased to believe), discarding the useless, the hostile, or the potential land-mines, there was less than he had hoped for. He balanced the now rather thin file on the palm of his hand.

'I don't know. I think we need a little more. There doesn't seem to be enough outrage here.'

'Outrage?'

'I may be wrong and I don't mean you haven't done a splendid job. But in my experience judges go for a sort of *cumulative* effect: dozens of people saying in rather simple terms just the same sort of thing so it piles up and he reads through it and says, "Just so, they all feel the same way so it's true." Even if he doesn't think it's true he makes allowances for them being simple people who don't talk the same way. Or think. Then he decides that if thirty or forty people think one-thirtieth or one-fortieth of what he himself might think in the same circs, then, added up, he's got a serious complaint made by a valid witness.'

'Thirty or forty.' Green sounded depressed.

'I may be quite wrong of course. Some people think that one or two witnesses are quite enough provided the intensity of their testimony is convincing. Intelligent witnesses though, that's the trouble. Then the judge says to himself, "Why, they're people just like me" (doesn't mean that of course, means people whom people like him meet and pretend to find equal) "and therefore in this benighted spot they must be right." I don't agree with this myself; give me the bulging court-room with village packed on village to swear to the same shock, but it's a theory.' He paused. 'The trouble is, we don't seem to have that either. Nothing specially striking in any of these. Or have I overlooked something?'

'No,' said Green and he got up, tidied the edges of the papers that overlapped the deflated file and put it under his arm. 'I've understood it for the first time and now that I see what's needed I'm sure I can find it.'

'Splendid.'

This time round the midwife came of her own accord.

'I can manage,' said Um Saqr. 'I know what I have to do.'

But Abu Ramzi, who was being broken away from his earth, and had taken to sitting in the courtyard, insisted. Buthaina accepted, grudgingly, the help she could do without. As she had feared, the baby was a girl.

'Destruction of the home,' said the midwife, enchanted.

'She will learn how to rebuild it.' Snappy, sweaty-haired, the mother who had survived the destruction of her own, without any help from husband or baby son, only wanted the useless fingers out of her privacy.

After the forty days' lying-in she told her husband the wish that he had to grant.

'We can leave his circumcision for a time yet, he's still too young.'

'No, now.'

He had to grant the mother of a new baby her wish, and did.

Buthaina's younger brother-in-law Adel had lived in at-Tor ever since he found a job as servant to one of the ingliz. They went to him. A pleasant house, built of stone, a little too square – the masons who knew how to construct a dome were now too busy with the public buildings to lend their unpaid services to family. There was a good view, overlooking the Old City and the Haram from the eastern side, and the jumbled cries of children, mad old ancestors, dogs and donkeys rose every morning with the early sun to their terrace.

To help her hostess Buthaina went to market every day. It was a local one, in the valley below them. She carried up the food, breathing out loud. Saqr trotted next to her, holding on to the side of her thick indigo calico dress, his hands growing faintly blue.

It was Ramadan and they were all fasting, which meant that more food than usual was needed for the night's meals. Abu Ramzi grumbled that he was spending more on sweetmeats for the host's children than he would have done for all their normal food at home. And the ceremony meant endless expense. The whole village intended to come and they all said they were used to expensive Jerusalem trays. Buthaina and Saqr and their hostess scrabbled up the flaking limestone path, the dust flying on to the grease paper over the judge's mouthfuls, the palace bread, the puce and yellow honeycombs teased out of dough and filled with syrup.

Buthaina had bought them on credit, but she didn't say so when they reached the house, hot and shiny.

'Have you let him know the woman is in Jerusalem?'

'Yes. We used three different men. He certainly knows.'

'Has he been to see her?'

'Not as far as we know.'

'Good,' said Challis, ticking off some note that in fact had nothing to do with his snare. 'Then he's waiting for the circumcision. Thinks we won't notice him among the crowd. I'll go along myself, just to make sure.'

'Must you?'

'Perhaps not. Just as well to be certain.'

Like all good hunters, he carried the outline of his quarry

imprinted on his brain's eye. So that when the image overlapped, bled onto the dappled shifting shape, lurking camouflaged among the breezy leaves, over the clouded sands three metres under the surface it triggered the forefinger without a millisecond's hesitation. That is all that hunting means: carrying the unmarred shape in the forefront of one's mind incessantly at the dinner table, at the film, distractedly moving the steering wheel too late so that the peaceable think of you as clumsy, vague, absent-minded. But their aim seldom fails the obsessed as soon as they return to the longed-for element. Challis saw him at once. Dressed in western clothes, a tarbush squarely on a changed head. Dark glasses. The caricature of an effendi. Policemen didn't look at him twice.

'That's him. When they all start you-youing, pull him in quietly.'

When Saqr arrived, perched all by himself on the camel's pinnacle, his feet insecurely clinging to a thin plywood crate that said Carr's Biscuits, his face screwed up with terror at the figure with a knife, the women all ululated to drown his future howls. The police detached their man without trouble.

'You've done very well,' said Challis, back at his Moscobiya desk. 'I congratulate you. I'll see him tomorrow, it's late now.'

'The charge? Sir?'

'Tomorrow. There's no hurry.'

The next day, some time after lunch (his lunch, not Tareq's), Challis looked at a by now rather battered conjuror.

'Didn't you agree to work for us?'

Tareq mumbled something that Challis chose to find incomprehensible. This was not difficult, since the man's front teeth had gone and his mouth looked like an overripe pulpy water-melon.

'It's no longer relevant, as it happens. We're not over-choosy, but there are things that we do draw the line at.'

There was a dribbling silence.

'You'll be pleased to hear that we shall try you immediately. None of what you called' – he looked down at his notes – 'the forgotten dead in the garbage pits of the Moscobiya. You won't be forgotten, at any rate.'

Tareq with an effort spat some of the pink spittle out on to his knee.

'But there's just one thing I want to tell you. Pay it more attention than you did before. If there's one word, not even a word, if there's one silence that suggests to *anyone*, and I mean anyone among your filthy hangers-on, that suggests anything at all that I don't like, then after you're hanged that woman goes into the Moscobiya and stays there until her own son will have nothing to do with her. I'm sure you know what I mean and you know now that I always keep my promises.' He took off his spectacles and smiled at the man. 'You've often complained that the British don't: now you see one who does. Pleased?'

Tareq rose to his feet and fell forward over the desk, gobs of mucus and saliva swinging out of his orifices onto the neat papers. He made a sound whose intonations suggested a phrase with meaning.

Challis had already rung his bell and two police guards were at the door.

'Just remember: I do keep my word.' He took out a large whitish handkerchief and fastidiously mopped up the slime on his desk. 'Take him away now.'

The trial did not open immediately because the police dentist needed time for the torn gums to hold teeth even temporarily and the bruises showed on the fallen-in cheeks for several days.

'Doesn't matter all that much,' Challis told Green. 'They all gossip about the goings-on here anyway and it's not a bad thing to give them something to chew on. Frightens them back into the straight and narrow.'

He had been in a radiant mood since the arrest.

'Something not to chew on,' said Green hopefully. Challis laughed out loud.

When it did take place, the trial was speedy and straightforward. There was no question about either charge; the one of incitement to rebellion took major place and led without difficulty to the death sentence, the emergency decrees being admirably worded on this point. The only question arose over its execution. The prisoner not being in the best of health, the choice lay in sending him, suitably guarded, to a hospital to be cured, at which time he would then be released from the security ward and driven to prison to await hanging, or alternatively in hanging him while ill.

The Chief Justice discussed the matter for some time at some length with HE.

'No, sorry sir, I simply don't see the sense in it.' Challis was in danger of slipping back into the cold rages that had once controlled him. 'It means a lot of trouble, letting the local rags have time to think up objections, demonstrations round the country and for all we know in Egypt too, and then they'll send some of their bloody mixed court lawyers, all Greeks and Jews, over here with appeals and stays of execution and heaven knows what else and then Nablus will riot and Hebron will follow suit to show Nablus they're not the only troublemakers and it will go on and on and the end result will be the same but with much more ill-will and trouble. Much better to get it over with as quickly as possible. Even the wizard understands that: didn't trouble to appeal. He knows he hasn't a hope in the end.'

'Seems a bit cruel, though? A sick man? He's not such a threat to us, when all's said and done.'

Challis rubbed his forehead. 'The law's the law, surely. Not a question of a threat? And I think on the whole they'd consider it crueller to keep him, fatten him up as it were, just to get him in shape for the last day. They're very childish in that, don't understand justice and never beating anyone in anger.'

He won.

Then a new problem arose. The date of the execution had been announced and published in the gazette when Farren asked for an appointment 'on behalf of the High Commissioner'. Challis threw himself back in his chair and sighed out loud and said, 'Oh no, not more of this,' for the benefit of his secretary. He expected another suggestion of tactful clemency, but it wasn't.

'HE wants to know whether you've chosen the date to make a deliberate point.'

'The date?' Challis looked at his desk diary.

'There's been a delegation – no, no, not to stop the thing, just to postpone it for a week or so.'

'They haven't managed to drum up enough support yet?'

'No, really. It's just that it seems a bit tactless, rubbing it in.'

'I don't understand what you're getting at.' He looked at the diary again, but it was still blank.

'Well, end of Ramadan. . . . As they said, it was bad enough hanging a man during the holy month, but this is either the last night or the first of the Feast. We won't know till the Azhar says and they feel we might be embarrassed to have to postpone it at the eleventh hour.'

'Why should we postpone?'

'Oh come on, Challis, we can't hang someone on Good Friday. You know that.'

'It's not Good Friday.'

'We wouldn't do it on Yom Kippur either,' said Kit angrily. 'And as you know, we are mandated to treat all religions equally. No one is ever hanged during Ramadan and it will upset people quite unnecessarily.'

'Are you certain? The man committed blasphemy. He's claimed something that no good Moslem can possibly accept. It might make a point to finish with him at a time when believers are exempt.'

That same evening Kit was invited to a party. He usually was, but this time the hostess was an Arab: one of the rare examples of the capital who mixed races at her parties. At the spread of food, heaping an admirably eclectic mixture of tehina salads, smoked fish and roast beef on to his art deco plate, Kit found himself next to a local architect, doing the same.

'Farren!' He sounded as though they had met by chance in the Bering Straits. 'Good to see you here. I've been meaning to congratulate you – given up the fight at last.' He was a Magdalen man too, and, Kit sometimes (not often) thought, chafed at some incompatibility in his own Jerusalem coupled with a reluctance to become too involved with the occupiers. 'Come and sit with me – I don't know a soul here. Except that one,' he twitched over his shoulder, 'and she's so cross about her dining room that I've been avoiding her ever since the masons finished.'

They found a mixture of seats, the architect squatting on a leather square and looking at Kit's salmon, on a level with his lips. 'A word to the wise: don't do it.'

'What? The fish?'

'Don't hang the man. You'll have nothing but trouble.'

Kit really didn't understand. Their conversations until then had been about Auden and Eric Gill.

'You know what I think of politics. A subject for those who can't master anything useful. All the same, better drop this man. He's not worth the trouble. He may be a charlatan, but he's convinced the peasants.'

'But why should you care?'

The architect scooped up some eggplant and pomegranate seeds in a little envelope of bread, carefully stamped the mound with a sprig of parsley and swallowed the letter. As he munched, his eyes slid past Kit's and looked at the hall, full of mainly English people, some of them in uniform, all with a heaped plate in one hand and a glass defensively clutched in the other. When he had finished his substantial mouthful he looked, this time directly, back at Kit.

'I'm not completely in favour of it, but there could be worse worlds than this.'

'Whatever do you mean?'

'Something much worse could follow. No, no,' he said impatiently as he guessed what Kit was going to say. 'It's not so much a cheap juggler, it's a whole attitude. You all think you'll never have to pay for anything. You'll just go away and do it somewhere else. But I think that the whole thing might come to a stop with a crash and everyone will be much worse off, and you should listen to me because I'm not in the least interested in what all those fools call politics, so I'm more likely to be right.'

'Yes, all right. But I don't quite see what you mean.'

'Leave silly little things alone, they'll be forgotten in a year's time.'

'Wa'el,' said Kit, growing pale, 'have you been got at to get at me?' He didn't believe it: a man who had been with him at university wouldn't forget their friendship and betray; but then he had heard so often that one had to be on one's guard, 'they' were all on the watch, one had to be alert, there could be no trust between the two races.

Unluckily Wa'el is a difficult name to pronounce correctly, and Kit, like so many Englishmen, produced an approximation of 'wail'. His fellow student had accepted this, without pleasure, while he was in England, but it jarred once he was back at home. 'Farren' could also be mispronounced in Arabic, in which case it became 'two mice', but neither in Cambridge nor in Jerusalem had he ever been so careless. Nor was he pleased at charges of treachery. He put his plate down, hard, on the shining marble floor, where it neatly cracked in two, got up and left the house.

'These Arabs,' said his Arab hostess a little later. 'No sense of obligation. They break my china and leave without saying goodbye because they're too ashamed to admit it.'

Wa'el, though, had enjoyed Cambridge and genuinely liked the friends he had made there; he had wanted to pass an amicable warning to Kit about how strongly feelings were running in Jerusalem over this ridiculous business. In spite of despising politics, he knew from family experience that much trouble could be averted by casual remarks in public meetings, and that this was the main reason sensible men attended otherwise futile gatherings. But now he decided the English did not share a civilised tradition and he never again spoke to Kit of subjects other than polo or the latest dances.

Those who interested themselves in public affairs, however, were not so aloof; Ramadan is a month when tempers always run high, are easily exacerbated. Lack of sleep, hunger and upset digestions regularly lead to trouble, even in good times. This year there was a slump, growing unemployment, a deep turgid fear of the threatened future. And the acknowledged leaders were in prison or deported or escaped into exile. Their substitutes appealed to the Chief Secretary. Something was in the air, Jerusalem's narrow streets were seething with newcomers arrived from the hill areas – Jenin, Qalqilya, Nablus – where trouble was endemic. The notables dreaded the thought of a spark igniting a fire they would be unable to control. The Chief Secretary did not share their fears.

'We have seventeen battalions here now,' he reminded them gently. 'That's a very substantial number of well-trained and disciplined men, gentlemen. This is a tiny country, at least by our army's standards. If we can control a sub-continent without difficulty I doubt that a handful of ill-equipped untrained brigands can make much trouble for an army using all the most modern resources. They have neither planes nor tanks, you know, and now that Teggart's Wall has been completed they won't be able to get so much as a rifle from our allies up north.'

The delegation gazed dumbly at its feet. Not one of them was ignorant of the fate of the Wall: strung across the porous frontiers of Syria and Lebanon, its last posts were still being hammered in at one end when kilometres of brand new barbed wire from the other were being offered at reduced prices in the suqs of Beirut and Damascus. Nor were they much impressed by the effectiveness of the concrete pillboxes called Teggart's Forts. These, although less architecturally impressive than Crusader castles, and far less dominantly sited, suffered from the same drawback as their ancestors: designed as impregnable, easily defensible carapaces for the tender flesh of the rulers, they drew their effectiveness from their sealed surfaces, broken only by thin slits from which a man could certainly fire, had he only been able to see what was going on around him. Did the Chief Secretary believe his own words? It hardly mattered, since they had no intention of arguing with him. All he meant was that the revolt would continue and the armoured might of the army and air force would also continue to strike at available targets, which were invariably civilian. This was a war waged with the bodies of peasants: when enough of their blood had been spilt the rebels would give up, out of compunction. The delegation was partly impelled by pity, sorrow for what it knew of the sufferings in the countryside, but also by fear that the rebels would prove obstinate and, maddened by what was happening in anonymous, unimportant little villages, might carry the war to the cities. This was why they appealed to the Chief Secretary. Jerusalem of course would never be bombed, but they weren't all from Jerusalem.

They had agreed among themselves that a Christian delegate should make the part of their appeal based on the religious facet of the cutting diamond they had been contemplating for days. The Latins had refused to attend and no one had even considered asking the Anglicans. A minor power-struggle had taken place between the Orthodox and the Armenians, but precedence was easily surrendered in such a disagreeable task as this and the representative of St James ceded his claim with grace. His suppleness would win him a far pleasanter duty the next time round; he sent his private secretary to represent him, kept to his bed by a nasty chill. So the Rumi bishop patted his bun firmly into place and addressed the Chief Secretary in his deep warm rumble, the timbre of which, steering between the frivolous rr-ing of Parisians and the querulous huskiness of Attic, still evokes in its secure throaty dark treacle the security of the one church, there on this land for as long as a church has existed, whose children absorb the thick incense from birth, together with a sophisticated acceptance of all ways and means, learning indirectly that all comes and goes and excitement belongs to the temporary, while the origin remains, bowing like a reed, digesting the indigestible, observing with tolerance the gold sovereign conversion, never spelling anything out, never committing itself to opinions that might be raised against it a few hundred years on, always there, unthreatened by conquest or its children's emigration. Olive tree, deeper rooted, more fruitful and enduring than the fragile cedar whose own sons eradicated it from the face of the earth, selling it to the Israelites as timber before they chopped it down for souvenirs, than the palm of the oasis or the death tree of the Latins.

His theme was a simple one: 'Forgiveness. The church enjoins us to forgive. It is the great step forward from the Old Testament. . . .' He went on gently for some time; he had often been told his voice was the most irresistible in Jerusalem. 'Ramadan is a holy month,' he evoked its sanctity briefly; 'even the worst kind of murderer is not executed at this time, and in a city holier than the month. And as I understand,' he wound up briskly and to the practical point, 'this man is not accused of any death.'

'Directly, no.' They all registered the lack of preamble, of the conventional flowers of pleasure at meeting so agreeably in the dusty wastes of the morning's duties. 'But what he has said in public has led to many deaths, and troubles of every kind. The Administration considers that his responsibility is all the greater.'

Not a word about the timing of the execution, either.

The younger, second-ranking shaikh rearranged his robes over his knees. 'Excellency, I may have been misinformed. All that I heard was that he told villagers not to sell their land, to show vigilance against the aims of the Zionists. He seems to be a man of no importance, a conjuror. He was upset by some personal story and began making claims that no man of sense would listen to. God often touches people, for reasons that no man can fathom. We have not attacked him for sacrilege, he is not a threat.'

The Chief Secretary in fact did not know the details of an affair far below his level of concern. The rank of his petitioners had forced him to receive them but the briefing that his assistant had received from the CID and then further condensed before placing it on his desk marked 'immediate' the morning of the appointment had become even briefer and showed no reason why a raggle-taggle galla-galla man should cause this concern. Or take up his time. Many of the prelates facing him were not above supporting the disturbances secretly. It was no accident that the Orthodox Church had survived intact, steering through the reefs of so many antagonisms as expertly as the celebrated Jaffa boatmen, for whom, he knew, a special epithet existed, lauding their giant skills against only too natural odds, commemorating their victories, daily repeated, against the currents, shoals, and the tide race that again and again tried to smash their rowing boats against the sunken rocks with the irresistible undertow of the so-called port whose name meant beauty. No sensible man would have done it twice. As for those who had made their living through the centuries from such folly, he had once asked, in all sense, 'But why is it the port? Haifa, Acre, are the only possibles. Why the worst stretch of the coast? Even Gaza would have been preferable, although. . . .' The answer, as so often with the Arabs, was laziness. Laziness over the immediate, that is, whose ultimate consequences required endless work, effort, danger. The stretch of coast where Andromeda had been delivered from the dragon reefs abutted on the citrus groves that from the fifteenth century had supplied the courts of Europe with the *shammuti*, prized above all oranges for its flavour, its juiciness that survived to reach the courts of Henry VIII undesiccated within the tough rind. Orange growers were willing to plant, graft, irrigate, pluck and pack the golden apples, even to pick off the parasitic greenstick insect that swallowed the buds every morning at dawn; but the thought of building a road to Haifa and shipping the fruit from there, for it perhaps to take the name of its sterile rival, wasn't considered for a moment. Jaffa oranges were shipped from Jaffa, and the city's boatmen simply had to learn unusual skills and slide their heavily laden barges over reefs that no sensible surf-rider would have approached with a board.

The Chief Secretary felt a longing to say to them, at last snapping the lunging-rein that chafed them more the older they grew: 'Gentlemen, a *little* commonsense. All this talk of religion, of traditions, folklore, harvest dances, whatever you call it, enough, enough. There is a real life and it matters. More than anything else, as you all very well know when you sack your wives for not having remembered the cummin. I know we're not meant to mention such vulgarities when we're between ourselves, but has it ever occurred to you, dear gents and shaikhs and beatitudes, that in the eyes of the empire you are rather like the ladies who serve your meals and apologise if they're not quite what you hoped for? Do you ever forgive them if there aren't chickpeas in the *mughrabiya*? Or if you find a cockroach's stewed wings, still neatly folded, in the same? Or in another dish where the rice has to be dark brown with spices? Would *you* forgive? Break open the insect's abdomen and swallow the germinating grubs? So why should we?'

He adumbrated some of this, more delicately. The answer came back from the second shaikh, goaded beyond what he had ever thought he might have to endure. 'Because you never paid the dowry.' And encouraged, if one must tell the whole truth, by the silent impetus, beaming from both eyes, of his supervisor who, in the Mufti's absence, ruled the world.

'What dowry?'

The delegation had made no difference. Tareq was duly hanged on the appointed date. This turned out to fall on the opening of the Feast of Sacrifice, when sheep were slaughtered in the city to commemorate Isaac's escape from the same fate and his father's stoic unswerving love of God. Challis took his oath that the Azhar had moved the eyelash crescent a day forward, simply to spite the British, but it made no difference to justice.

Green was deputed to witness the execution and he arrived at the jail half an hour before it was due. It was a beautiful morning, he stood under the clean washed sky chatting to the prison officials who had come to receive him in the hot early sun. The prison governor looked at his watch.

'Last rites taking longer than usual; we'll give him another five minutes, then I think we should go in. It doesn't do to delay the business, makes the other prisoners more restive than they already are.'

But as he spoke the gate opened and the shaikh came out. He was very pale and he passed the British without a greeting, giving them a look of black hatred.

'Pherh! He looks as though we were responsible.'

'He seems upset,' said the governor. 'He's not usually like that.'

'The shaikh's shaken,' said Green, and tittered.

They went in.

Tareq entered the vaulted room walking as firmly as though his hands had been free and not handcuffed behind his back. When he reached the scaffold, prison guards strapped his arms tightly while the governor read him the death warrant: Tareq watched him throughout, smiling slightly. His face had grown thinner after the questioning and his eyes were again the huge luminous stars of his youth. Then they were hidden by the coarse black cloth hood that the guards pulled down over his face, sparing the witnesses the sight of what they were to witness. He was placed on the trap and his ankles bound together. The trap was sprung and everyone then waited until the prison doctor could declare the man dead. In this case it took twenty-eight minutes for his heart to stop beating. The governor then invited Green to join him for breakfast.

'You may think you won't be able to eat, but you'll find the reverse is true.'

And he was quite right.

Um Tareq had attended neither the trial nor the execution, but she sent her son Yusuf to Jerusalem to represent her. He went to see Buthaina, who offered him a roof in at-Tor until the time came for him to claim the body.

'Um Tareq is too ill with grief; she felt it would only harm him to see her sorrow. I shall do what is necesary.'

'Yes.'

While he waited Buthaina showed him endless generosity, hospitality. Yusuf deserved his name of *ashawiss*, which Jaffa boatmen have won by their courage and strength against their treacherous sea: he was stocky, sturdy, a brown open face with merry little eyes and a great ruddy moustache spraying over his mouth. He knew everything about his sea and nothing of anything else; the iron malice of Jerusalem took him aback.

'I should have foundered without you, sister.'

She accompanied him on his errands, helped him with the formalities, signed for the prison visit. He came out bewildered.

'He thinks that they will not kill him. He told me it was all a masquerade and at the last they will spirit him away.'

'Did he say why?'

'He told me there was nothing to fear, there is a debt owing.'

Buthaina went on kneading dough and said nothing. She had learnt that Yusuf liked a womanly woman, also that she enjoyed playing any part, even the one that had bored her since her marriage. She lowered her eyes when he arrived and set to tasks that she generally avoided. Above all he enjoyed the making of bread, so she made more and more and sometimes sent the surplus to neighbours with a graceful phrase. She had not yet approached a mention of her aim.

The day before the one set for the execution a bomb exploded in the vegetable market in Jaffa. It went off early in the morning, when most housewives were milling round the stalls, squeezing the fruits before buying, accompanied by those of their children who were too young or too poor to go to school. The news reached at-Tor in the evening, after the train from the coast had disembarked its passengers. In a way this was lucky: had Yusuf heard it earlier he would have started for home, leaving his brother to lie on a slab. As it was, he wanted to take the early morning bus. His wife went to market every day at that hour, with two of his babies. There was no other way of finding out whether she had escaped, since the British had forbidden toll calls of any kind, in the hope of making life harder for the outlaws.

'I must go, sister.' Tears welled silently out of the corners of his eyes. 'They say more than thirty children are dead.'

The 'bomb' had been an oil drum, packed tight with old bits and pieces of rusty iron scrap and nails and explosives, rolled into the centre of the market-place from a lorry which the authorities never traced, enough for every Arab to know its origin. There was a British officer training the extremist Zionists, who until his advent had never done this sort of thing. thing.

Buthaina had to think quickly. She was almost certain that Yusuf would have done what she wanted, that she had kneaded him into a perfect state of pliability ready to rise with the slightest breath of heat. If he were to agree, then she was beyond criticism; if not, then her plan would be almost impossible. Would it be better to let him go and ask him to delegate his powers to her? Would he? A woman was not an honourable substitute. She was gambling on uncertainties in both cases and having to think faster than she liked about the odds.

'If God wills,' she began reluctantly, fencing as she could.

Whether God was on her side or not, her brother-in-law walked in.

Yusuf grabbed him, embraced him hard against his iron boatman's shoulders, kissed him three times and now at last wept openly in loud sobs. Adel thrummed him hard between the shoulder blades, as though he were a drum in need of re-stretching. The men sat down and she brought them coffee while they discussed the tragedy. Then they agreed on what was to be done. Yusuf perfunctorily raised the dangling triangle of her sleeve, held it to forehead and lips. 'You will explain what needs to be done, I leave it in your hands, my sister.'

'Yes, I will.'

So, after Yusuf had left and his brother, hanged in spite of his expectations, had been thrown on the slab with his face too purply congested to be recognised, Buthaina organised the necessary convoy. She brought a shroud with her and wrapped the indecent flesh before they shovelled it into the back of the small pick-up. Adel's function was to hire the

206

transport, the driver, and a third man to help them with the task. Yusuf had already given them the notarised procuration deputing them to remove the corpse in the absence of family. It was almost noon when they left Jerusalem.

In the late afternoon Adel said to his sister-in-law, whom he politely separated from the alien driver in the front seat: 'The later we leave the crossing the better. We had better stop soon and ask for shelter before the frontier.'

So they turned off the coast road where the British were powerful and the Zionists growing stronger and drove into the hills. They stopped at the first largish village they came to, which happened to be Tarshiha, and asked for a night's shelter. As they did not mention the corpse they received it without trouble and sat out in the fine night on the terrace where Egerton had once thought he had seen something strange. They did not qualify for meat, not even a stringy hen, but were happy dipping their bread into lentils and eggplant. More villagers came to see them than had approached on the night of the ingliz and they had more trouble explaining their errand, which Buthaina had not thought out before.

'Tyre,' she hissed at Adel, 'the sick uncle in Tyre.'

He was awkward about it, which helped immeasurably. Every villager knew what sort of illness drove a man to hospital across the border: it was called Sten, and the less asked the better for the asker. The rest of the evening was spent in discussing soap and matches, the rising price of.

They rose early, gratefully accepted some coffee and bread, truthfully gave the names of their villages for future hospitality and drove down the road as though they were going to the coast. This was only to spare the villagers lying: the night before they had been told, quite casually after they mentioned hospitals in Tyre, of more than one unpatrolled but serviceable track across the frontier. Once Tarshiha was unable to see them they doubled back and took the one that served their purpose beyond their hopes.

The fortress was a ruin, even then. But in those days it still towered grimly over two brand new frontiers. Not just a hearth for the beacons to be transmitted from north to the last south, but a real castle, almost the equal of the black grimness nearly two hundred miles to its north. Icy green water rushed through the gorge so far below that the welcome sound could not be heard; on two other sides the escarpment sloped down so abruptly that later generations of travellers would find no new pleasure in their airborne view of the mythic plain. From here the sea was tame, flat. The van was a tough little machine but incapable of this. They pulled out the long bundle and began to climb, slipping and scrabbling on the loose-stoned path. It took a long time and the sun grew hotter.

'Forbidden,' muttered the driver. 'He should have been buried before sunset yesterday. This is cursed.'

Buthaina, who was holding up the side where the head should be, turned and looked at him. They went on climbing; presently Adel, inspired, said, 'It would be worse if we were to return. We wouldn't be able to bury him until the third day.'

'Forbidden.' But after that he said nothing else and climbed.

When at last they reached the outer enceinte of the castle they dropped the bundle on the stony ground and sat down, sweating and panting. Some brief rain had touched this mountain and tender green shoots showed among the grey rocks. A few of those touching autumn crocuses had shot up, a mauvey pink, in succulent little clumps, quite leafless and apparently baseless. An eagle sailed not far above them on air-currents thrown up by the massive building.

After they had rested they explored. It was quite easy. There was a large vaulted room with thick squat pillars whose masonry showed. The living rock formed the hind wall. The two men used the broad-bladed hoes that they had brought and after a time the hole was deep enough–the earth was surprisingly soft in this place – to be certain jackals would not scent it. After they had buried it they covered it with stones, some incised with characters, that Buthaina had hunted out and set one of them upright at the head, hammering it into the earth with the butts of their implements. Buthaina then gave her brother Tareq's turban and he wound the material round the standing stone and knotted it firmly so that the first storm wouldn't blow it away.

'In the name of God, the merciful, the forgiving.' Then they went away.

'Thank the Lord we've finished with that little headache,' said Challis, at about the time the illicit party were supping at Tarshiha.

'I suppose so, but the trouble is nationalism is an incurable disease.' Egerton bought a new round of drinks to save his popularity.

Commonsense won over every passionate instinct and I let the hawk go. The 'events' had now grown so overwhelming that we were kept under total curfew for five consecutive days without food or water. And although I had tried hard to tame him by taking him to the office every day, scrunched up in a brown paper bag, and talking to him for the prescribed four hours to accustom him to my voice, he was as wild as ever. And bigger and hungrier and more imperious. No one came to see me any more, even when the shooting allowed; the flat reeked of regurgitated raw meat and droppings and angry feathers. Only the thought of future liberties persuaded Nicholas to drive me as far from the city as we could then go, all frontiers being closed against our little war.

'I wouldn't mind a picnic: we'll go early and after that folly of yours is well rid of we'll relax.'

Another long golden day. The moment we left the city's outskirts, then so sharply defined, our spirits lifted. The sea stretched on one side pale and tame, on the left the deep blue mountains rose clear after the muzziness of the summer heat, every house and pine picked out. Nicholas began singing, 'Where did you go? Where did love go?' He knew most of Um Kulthum's songs.

Along the coast road, dodging the crazy drivers, re-seeing the local landmarks that the events had made us forget, the round house, as mad as any lorry driver, the lovely arches that rose above the roadside pottery, the banana and orange groves as the south approached. 'You told me we should never part: where are you? Where is love? Where is my life?' He was in such a good temper that I let the hawk's angry little eyes out of the paper bag to enjoy a hope.

Of course it didn't last until we reached our destination and left the car as far above the gorge as it would go and climbed. I had insisted on eating first so as to prolong the final sorrow and the wine had turned into headache in the sun. When we finally reached the castle's foundations the shadows were stretching to the east from every stone: like all these days it would be a dark and disagreeable negotiation of a bad road on the irritable return.

'Come on. We're not going to spend the night here.'

I took the falcon out of his crumpled bag that said 'Jones' Grocery. Daily deliveries of mussels and double cream from France and Belgium.' I hadn't bothered to slip his jess on today and for the first time since he had lain trussed in my lap as a chick he had been travelling free. I placed him on my arm, unhooded, but he didn't nip me. We stood there waiting. Not one of us moved. Then I undulated my forearm and said, 'Go.' The bird sidled further up its uncertain perch and gripped a little tighter, for once not drawing blood. I did it again and it did it again, this time holding on just this side of broken skin. It watched me intently. In all the uneasy months of our non-adapting it had never done such a thing.

'*Bloody hell!*' said Nicholas with real dislike, 'are you going to set it free or are you just showing off?'

I shook my arm harder and the hawk flapped its wings, lost its balance and rose into the air. It circled over my head and resettled on the wrist, still held away from the body. This time it did draw blood, just a little.

Nicholas threw his car keys, attached to a solid clinking ring bearing some emblem, hard on the ground. Their noise made the hawk flap his wings again but he didn't rise this time. He still kept one intense eye on my face. 'I'm going. I've put up with this nonsense for too long. You can stay with your bird if you want.'

He started, deliberately crashing, down the slope, slipped, fell, and as he fell twisted his body backwards towards us, falling with arms stretched towards my feet. A rattle of stones under his feet's slithering crashed down towards the gorge. The hawk rose in one movement, one visible flap of its pinions – the only time I never thought of them as wings – and before Nicholas had set himself on his feet again was a dot in the sky above us, as we were a dot above the sea. He stayed there, directly above, circling. There was a shot and he fell. A

man came out of the ruined castle, grinning. He wore a
Tattersall's check shirt under a suede jacket and those curious
khaki trousers Frenchmen insist on buying just before the
hunting season opens, full of buttoned pockets in unexpected
places like over the rear ankle and under the right buttock. He
undid one of the flaps and offered, with a good instinct, a
hipflask to Nicholas. I had begun to weep.

'Never got one before.'

'Congratulations. Thanks.' And the two men toasted each
other.

Glossary

amir prince; noble; governor

'araq anise-flavoured alcoholic drink

'ashawiss a Jaffa boatman, skilled in steering through the reefs; not used for boatmen of other, easier harbours

baladi (lit.) of the country: local. During the French and British occupations of the Middle East it acquired a strongly pejorative connotation which is gradually evaporating

bassara a woman, usually a gipsy, who tells fortunes and sells love philtres, etc.

bey Western pronunciation of *beq*, the second-ranking title accorded by the Ottoman Court. Abolished at the instauration of the Turkish Republic but still widely used as a term of respect for men of power and/or wealth

biyyara local variation of *bir/biyyar*: wells; used for the irrigation system of the Jaffa orange-groves and by extension for the area in which they lay

bulbul the favourite songbird in Arab literature and life, often translated as nightingale, though its song is more liquid and melodious

dar the large central sitting room from which bedrooms, studies, etc, give off; by extension the house

dunom a land measure approximately 1000 square yards

effendi lowest-ranking title accorded by the Ottoman Court; came to be used for any educated and/or professional man and consequently became a pejorative term to the British in Palestine and Egypt

'eid religious feast; a festivity

franj Franks; Westerners

freek (culin), green, uncured usually applied to a dish of green wheat and pigeons

galla-galla conjuring, by extension shady tricks

ghaffir watchman; village policeman (= gendarme)

hakawati professional story-teller. Their recitals of epics and legends could last four or five hours or even longer and they were in great demand at feasts and a special attraction at city cafés. Radio and television have virtually wiped them out, but anyone lucky enough to track one down learns what the *Iliad* and the *Odyssey* originally sounded like

hantur horse-drawn covered carriage; a stage-coach

haramlik Turkish variation of *haram* – the holy or taboo; the women's quarters.

hijab a prayer or incantation or charm; by extension the metal or silver or gold that either enclosed the scrap of paper or on whose surface the invocation was inscribed

iradé wish (of the sultan); a Court decree

jihad crusade; war for ostensibly religious reasons

jinn genie, a spirit, good or evil according to its whim and the amount of respect accorded it

jurn large stone or marble mortar used for pounding meat

keffiya the cotton headscarf (variation *hatta*) worn by men in several Middle Eastern countries. In Palestine it was either plain white or a thin black check on white and was worn only by peasants and labourers. However, townsmen adopted it when the British banned it as a symbol of nationalist resistance and it was resuscitated over thirty years later as the badge of the second wave. Second time around, the women wore it too

laban yoghurt

labni a cream cheese rather like *fromage blanc*, made from *laban*

lahhaf a thin cotton quilt used as mattress and coverings. House-holds have enough to supply guests with a quick bed. In the daytime they are rolled up and stored in a *youk* or cupboard

majidiya (*der.* sultan Abd al-Majid) a coin, the late Ottoman equivalent of a gold sovereign

Mandoub (*abbr* al-Mandoub as-Sami) the High Commissioner

manqal rectangular tin receptacle for charcoal used for grilling; a barbecue. Or an elaborately decorated and worked round brass brasier with a high conical lid, standing on a large round brass tray, used to heat rooms

masbaha a string of beads like a rosary but used to keep one's fingers busy, not for religious purposes. The beads are made of anything from plain or carved wood to pearls and amethysts. They are only carried by men, women's fingers being fully occupied anyway

mashriq the eastern half of the Arab world (i.e. West Asia), as opposed to the *maghreb*, the western half (i.e. North Africa); commonly used to denote what Westerners call the 'Middle' East

mastaba a bench made of stone or marble (nowadays cement) built out from the external wall by the front door. In cities, mosques and rich families provide them as a sort of municipal kindness; in villages they keep strange men out of the women's domain. Any traveller may rest on any *mastaba* for as long as he likes, though he will usually be directed to the public guesthouse if he wants to spend the night

mouni the stores; by extension the winter provisions all homes laid in during the centuries of hardship. Refrigerators and supermarkets have begun to allay this nervous habit, but even in peaceable cities a certain frenzy of insurance springs up every October and in Beirut the civil war restored tradition with a bang – sacks of flour, rice, sugar and lentils, twenty-gallon tins of olive oil, are now part of the luxurious furnishings of the once air-conditioned penthouses, and hundredweights of onions lie sunning by the seventeenth-floor swimming pools

mughrabiya a dish

mukhtar a man appointed by the government but paid by his fellow villagers to do the state's work – registering births and deaths, informing the parish of new decrees, etc. An ungrateful post, but it gives prestige, power and, if the man is corrupt, relative wealth. If he is honest he finds himself caught in the crossfire

narguileh construction of glass, water, charcoal and long flexible pipe to filter tobacco

nebi prophet

pasha the first rank of Ottoman titles, roughly equivalent to a duke. It became debased during the last years of the Egyptian monarchy and is often used ironically nowadays as a term of address to a wilful man or a spoilt little boy

qaimaqam governor; district commissioner

qumbaz Palestinian/Syrian men's robe, the *mashriq*'s equivalent of a *gallabiya* or *qaftan*

rutl nearly obsolete measure of weight from the days when people took their *mouni* seriously. Varies: about three kilos, but was less in north Palestine.

sayyidna our lord. Arab terms of address are more formal than English and this is quite ordinary

serai palace; seat of govt. Seraglio derives from it but in the original it has nothing to do with women

shammuti a prized variety of orange, originally grown in Jaffa but since 1948 cultivated in other Arab countries

sidi my lord (see *sayyidna*). Root of both is *sayyid*. *Sidi* is a very common form of address, equivalent to *monsieur*

simsar go-between; agent; usually for the sale of land or buildings or flats. In Palestine it came to have a pejorative connotation of quisling, because certain agents acted as screens for the Jewish Agency

sini Chinese; the china or porcelain produced by China for the Arab world from the thirteenth to nineteenth centuries and part of many dowries. Some of the best Ming blue-and-white sold at Sotheby's in recent years has come out of these *sini* cupboards

sittna our lady (see *sayyid*, etc.)

suq market

tarbush conical maroon felt head-covering introduced by Ottomans and rejected in direct correlation to rise of local nationalism and, oddly enough, Westernisation. It lasted longest in Egypt, but after the 1952 revolution it lost its connotation of upper-class education and is only seen now on very venerable heads. The King of Morocco still wears one but he calls it a fez

tariq road; way; *tareq* means the traveller on a way (by night)

tisht a large shallow basin, once made only of copper but now of aluminium, used either for serving food in immense quantities or for standing in while servers pour water and scrub one

tughra the beautiful calligraphic signature designed for each new sultan as his seal to be drawn on official documents, stamped on the silver made during his reign, enamelled on the tiles and lamps of the mosques he built, embroidered on the covering he sent to the Ka'aba, hung behind civil servants' desks in the way Westerners hang a portrait of their reigning sovereign, etc.

youk large niche, usually arched, carved out of the thickness of the wall for storage space and generally screened by matting or kelims or bokhara embroidered hangings according to one's means

zir unglazed earthernware jar used for storing water. They were large enough to hold about fifty to sixty litres; in Egypt they are much smaller and have conical bases, so they are suspended on a wooden rack which allows the water to cool from every angle. The climate in Palestine is cool enough to leave the *zir* on the stone flags of the courtyard